A second blast of thunder ripped through the night

Dean slammed into Mildred, and the woman managed to hang on to his shirttail, keeping him upright. Doc reached out desperately, latching on to a metal lip that was attached to the bulkhead.

But Krysty had been thrown off her feet and onto her upper back and neck. The suddenness of the explosion smashed her down with terrific force, knocking her unconscious as she slid toward the gaping hole in the hull.

Jak twisted his lithe body as he fell, managing not to break his neck as he slipped through the hole and hit the churning water. Gasping for breath, he struggled to maintain some proper sense of which way was up.

Seeing Krysty's limp body already being sucked into the undertow beneath the vessel, he pushed himself deeper into the chilling ocean and grasped a fistful of long red hair.

Then they both vanished from sight.

**Other titles in the
Deathlands saga:**

JAMES AXLER

DEATH LANDS®

Watersleep

A GOLD EAGLE BOOK FROM

WORLDWIDE®

TORONTO • NEW YORK • LONDON
AMSTERDAM • PARIS • SYDNEY • HAMBURG
STOCKHOLM • ATHENS • TOKYO • MILAN
MADRID • WARSAW • BUDAPEST • AUCKLAND

First edition November 1997

ISBN 0-373-62539-1

WATERSLEEP

Full fathom five thy father lies:
Of his bones are coral made;
Those are pearls that were his eyes;
Nothing of him that doth fade,
But doth suffer a sea-change
Into something rich and strange.
—*The Tempest*, Act I, scene 2
William Shakespeare

THE DEATHLANDS SAGA

This world is their legacy, a world born in the violent nuclear spasm of 2001 that was the bitter outcome of a struggle for global dominance.

There is no real escape from this shockscape where life always hangs in the balance, vulnerable to newly demonic nature, barbarism, lawlessness.

But they are the warrior survivalists, and they endure—in the way of the lion, the hawk and the tiger, true to nature's heart despite its ruination.

Ryan Cawdor: The privileged son of an East Coast baron. Acquainted with betrayal from a tender age, he is a master of the hard realities.

Krysty Wroth: Harmony ville's own Titian-haired beauty, a woman with the strength of tempered steel. Her premonitions and Gaia powers have been fostered by her Mother Sonja.

J. B. Dix, the Armorer: Weapons master and Ryan's close ally, he, too, honed his skills traversing the Deathlands with the legendary Trader.

Doctor Theophilus Tanner: Torn from his family and a gentler life in 1896, Doc has been thrown into a future he couldn't have imagined.

Dr. Mildred Wyeth: Her father was killed by the Ku Klux Klan, but her fate is not much lighter. Restored from predark cryogenic suspension, she brings twentieth-century healing skills to a nightmare.

Jak Lauren: A true child of the wastelands, reared on adversity, loss and danger, the albino teenager is a fierce fighter and loyal friend.

Dean Cawdor: Ryan's young son by Sharona accepts the only world he knows, and yet he is the seedling bearing the promise of tomorrow.

In a world where all was lost, they are humanity's last hope....

Prologue

Ryan Cawdor was drowning.

His chest echoed heavily with the dull thud of a waterlogged pump, each heartbeat growing slower and groggier. He tried to speak, and a precious dollop of his last few seconds of oxygen bubbled out of his open mouth. He watched the air bubbles float upward, following their path with his good right eye, and tried to focus on what might lie beyond them.

At first he thought his vision was blurred, but then Ryan realized there was no sky overhead, no clouds, no stars, nothing but water. He squinted and took in a sight his brain logically told him had to be the murky green fluid of the ocean. No lake or man-made pool had ever offered up such a color of green—a green duskier than the blackest of any moonless night, and just as dark and infinite.

The green was everywhere, surrounding his entire body and being.

Ryan had always imaged the ocean depths as being cold as ice, but he was strangely warm instead. He could almost taste sweat on his lips, but knew the salt on his tongue had to be coming from the seawater. Could a man sweat underwater if the temperature got hot enough, cook like a fish in a pot over an open fire? Ryan thought it was possible, but he'd have to try to remember to ask Mildred when…

Ask Mildred when they ended the jump.

And then he remembered—not where he was, but where he had been.

So many crumbling cities and villes, so many different areas of Deathlands, all of them ultimately left behind as he pressed on, looking for a safe harbor.

Ryan's mind raced, trying to sort out a confusing jumble of images. The last concrete event his memory recalled was in the military redoubt. As he'd done so many times before, he'd hurriedly slammed shut the heavy metal door that activated the mat-trans unit. The sec lock had clicked reassuringly, letting him know all was ready. This locking sound was followed in turn by the spectral appearance of the sinister pale mist that signaled the beginning of a jump.

The light fog continued to gather, thickening around the unearthly shimmering disks in the floor and ceiling, and an almost inaudible hum from within the bowels of the chamber began to make itself heard deep inside the group's heads.

Ryan sat on the floor with Krysty Wroth's hip next to his own. He could see the radiant fire of her long red hair out of the corner of his eye. On his other side, sharing his dark complexion and black, curly hair, was his son, Dean. Until recently the youngster had been a student at the Nicholas Brody School in Colorado, obtaining a much needed education.

A formal education of the sort Ryan had paid for didn't come cheap in the hellish world of Deathlands, but he knew the boy would need some book schooling before returning to the harsh realities of daily survival. Knowledge was just as useful a tool as a good blaster or a working war wag.

Across from Ryan was a young albino with features distinctive enough to bring more than a glancing notice, even among the more unusual appearances in Deathlands. Jak Lauren's pallid complexion was paler than usual, throwing the crisscrossed scars on his face into sharp relief. His ruby eyes were at half-mast, and his mouth was drawn tight in anticipation of the jump to come.

A heavy Colt Python was safely fastened down on one leg. There was no need to have the weapon cocked and ready. The mental and physical condition of everyone after a jump prevented the use of any weapons. Even if they were to jump into the midst of a blaster battle—which was doubtful, since as a rule the gateway chambers were always hidden away— they couldn't lift a finger to fight back until they'd recovered from the physical toll the mat-trans experience extracted.

As usual before a mat-trans jump, Jak had nothing to say—unlike the thin man beside him, who kept up an ongoing discussion with either anyone who would listen or, when that option was out, with himself.

Next to Jak's eerie whiteness was the ancient, weathered face of Dr. Theophilus Algernon Tanner. Doc appeared calm, his lips whistling a silent tune only he could hear, but Ryan noted how tightly he was gripping his ebony swordstick. The silver lion's-head handle of the stick seemed to wink at Ryan in the shifting light of the chamber, as if in acknowledgment of the hidden blade inside as Doc worked it nervously through his hands.

Ryan took note of the unusual handblaster holstered at the man's hip. It was an ornate Le Mat, a weapon dating back to the early days of the Civil War. The weapon was almost as much of an antique as Doc himself, but as Mildred Wyeth had once gleefully pointed out in a particularly ribald bout of teasing, an antique in much better condition and able to fire at will when the trigger was pulled.

Engraved and decorated with twenty-four-carat gold as a commemorative tribute to the great Confederate soldier James Ewell Brown Stuart—or Jeb Stuart, as his friends and folks in Virginia referred to him—the massive hand cannon weighed in at over three and half pounds. The gun had two barrels and an adjustable hammer, firing a single .63-caliber round like a shotgun, and nine .44-caliber rounds in revolver mode.

"'Once more unto the breach, dear friends...'" Doc muttered, more to himself than to his companions. His comment invited a retort, but received no response. Everyone knew what Doc meant.

The circle of companions was completed by John Barrymore Dix, Ryan's longtime friend, known also as the Armorer, and Dr. Mildred Wyeth. The title of Armorer was one of respect for Dix's encyclopedic knowledge of all forms of weaponry and how they were used. From hand blasters to tank blasters,

J. B. Dix had studied and learned the secrets of any kind of offensive weapon.

Although they kept their relationship restrained and private, Ryan couldn't help but notice the comforting arm J.B. had placed around Mildred's shoulders. She leaned back into his side gratefully. Out of all the companions, Mildred came closest to actually understanding the hellish process they were about to endure—but that didn't mean she particularly enjoyed it.

J.B. was ready. Ryan saw that his friend had already removed his spectacles and tucked them safely away inside the front pocket of his worn leather jacket. J.B.'s other hand tightly gripped his Smith & Wesson M-4000 scattergun, reminding the one-eyed man to check his own weaponry. He caught the Armorer's eye, and the man nodded, tilting his fedora at an angle over his eyes.

Ryan did a quick inventory of his own arsenal. The 9 mm SIG-Sauer P-226 blaster was at his side like an old friend, the baffle silencer digging reassuringly into his hip. Looped over one shoulder was his walnut-stocked Steyr SSG-70 bolt-action rifle.

Then the mist of the chamber crept into his brain, interrupting his mental checklist. The tendrils of pale smoke worked their scientific magic, and the jump began. The band of travelers had traversed most of what remained of the United States and even visited other continents during travels via the gateways.

But no matter where they eventually ended up, the one constant in traveling via the mat-trans units was the headlong rush into the unknown. Their destination was always yet another gateway chamber with thick armaglass walls. Despite cosmetic changes of color and size, the gateways were always the same. The mystery was in surviving what lay outside the gateway chamber.

Usually Ryan and his group were oblivious to where they might be until they left the walls of the military redoubts that held the mat-trans units—oblivious until J.B. confidently took his minisextant from one of the many pockets that lined his worn jacket. He would place the sextant to one eye and use it to look at the sky, and after a few moments of mental computations on maps and charts long ago memorized, he would reveal their new location.

They had jumped into hell and into paradise, always appearing in the familiar gray setting of an abandoned underground military base, dusty with disuse and littered with the empty boxes and remnants of the dead. The computers inside still functioned, drawing on a hidden atomic power supply that continued to provide energy long after their masters had departed in the chaos before the nukes started to fall, and the period of skydark fell across the world.

But there was no sky here, dark or otherwise.

Only water. Only death.

Ryan's brain shifted gears. How had he ended up down here?

He was no engineer, but he knew from hard-earned experience that the gateways didn't work like this. He couldn't have been transported into the nothingness of the sea without a mat-trans unit, and there was no unit here. Also, even if there had been some sort of freak accident, Ryan knew some of the others should have accompanied him.

And why wouldn't his arms work? They floated aimlessly above his head, not responding to his frantic thoughts of escape. His clothing billowed around him like a parachute, but without providing any resistance. His legs also hung limply, the toes of his boots pointed down like twin anchors, pulling him steadily to the bottom, past the blind eyes of the elongated eellike creatures that were swimming past, their mouths yawning open as they sifted through the brine for microscopic bits of plankton.

Ryan willed his legs to kick, his arms to push down to check his descent, but it was as if he were an old wooden puppet dropped overboard, and his strings had been cut.

At the rate he was sinking, Ryan knew he'd run out of air long before feeling solid earth beneath his feet. Already a red haze was starting to settle over his field of vision from lack of oxygen. A coppery, bitter taste filled his mouth, mixing with the traces of salt water. So this is how it ended —not in a hailstorm of blasterfire or in a hand-to-hand knife battle, but underwater and alone.

Even as a young boy, Ryan Cawdor had always known he wasn't the kind of man who would die quietly in his sleep, but he expected to go down more valiantly than this.

"A man always has a choice," Trader had always said. "He can either live...or he can die."

But Trader was wrong. There was no choice to be made when it came to living or dying.

The only choice was in how.

As his lungs began to ache and his heartbeat grew louder in his ears, Krysty's face shone like a beacon in Ryan's mind's eye.

He clung to the image, struggled again to make his body work, willing his muscles to pull taut and arrest his descent. Suddenly, in a burst of movement, he was rewarded with his legs kicking out and his arms pushing down.

Even though the adrenaline surge was far too late to save himself now, Ryan fought back as he continued to plummet into the darkness, lost and alone.

Chapter One

Ryan Cawdor opened his eye. Above him was the face of a crimson-haired angel.

"Welcome back, lover," Krysty Wroth said, her flushed cheeks and anxious green eyes belying her light tone. "Decide to go for a swim without me?"

"Uh-huh. Come on in," he rasped back. "The water's fine."

Ryan tried to pull himself to his feet, but gave up when he realized one of his legs wasn't functioning. A pins-and-needles sensation was tingling from his left knee to his foot. His leg was asleep, and it felt like he'd been resting on it for a long time. He was having trouble breathing, too.

He gratefully gulped a deep breath as he slid back into a seated position. "What happened? And what's wrong with the air in here? It's as hot as a triple-stoked blast furnace."

"You ended up facedown when we jumped in, Dad," Dean said, a faint smear of blood under one nostril the only evidence of any discomfort the boy had endured during the jump. "This gateway was half-full of water. You were almost gone when Krysty came out of it and rolled you over."

Listening while Dean spoke, Ryan had observed he

was sitting upright in the familiar surroundings of a mat-trans chamber, his back against one of the armaglass walls. He was also sitting in approximately six inches of filthy water littered with brackish slime and a thin film of green algae. The next thing he realized was how awful the chamber smelled, and the hellish temperature that surrounded him like a soggy blanket.

The very air felt wet. Bile welled up involuntarily from his churning stomach, and he turned and vomited what appeared to be a quart of the murky water.

"Ryan, dear fellow. It warms my heart that once again you are with us!" Ryan knew he had been out of it for a while if Doc Tanner was up and about.

Usually Doc suffered the worst after a jump, lapsing into inane babble, as well as experiencing physical ailments such as the nosebleed Dean had suffered, or self-induced bruises and cuts from thrashing about in the chamber after the jump was completed.

Doc could take the punishment to his body. What hurt him more was the psychic damage to his mind. Visions of his long-dead wife, Emily, and his two young children, Rachel and Jolyon, always haunted him after a jump, and it was during the sluggish period as everyone came back to consciousness inside the gateway chamber that Doc looked truly old, his entire gaunt frame always sunken down inside his faded black academic frock coat.

The man was beyond age, a reluctant time traveler plucked from the year 1896 by scientists and drawn forward to the end of the twentieth century as part of a secret government project known as Operation Chronos. Chronos was only one of the many projects under the banner of the Totality Concept, which utilized the secret matter-trans technology now being used by Ryan and his friends.

Doc proved to be such a difficult subject that the whitecoats thrust the old man one hundred years into the dark future of the postholocaust United States—a world that had become bitterly known as Deathlands.

Ironically enough, they had shuttled him away right before the entire world blew out in a final conflict of nuclear fire.

Between the juxtaposition of past, present and future, Doc had managed to hang on to his sanity, but only by his jagged fingernails. However, Ryan thought he looked good for a change, spry, almost.

Ryan coughed and spit out another mouthful of the vile-tasting water. "Thanks, Doc. Only I'd feel a damned sight better if I could stop puking my guts out."

"A joyous noise is a joyous noise," Doc said, "regardless of where the sound comes from."

"Only Doc could find joy in vomiting," Dean said, grinning in spite of his earlier worry about his father's welfare. "I'd hate to see how happy he got if you took a shit."

"That's probably next, and watch your language," Ryan muttered, feeling his stomach gurgle ominously. Still, he was already feeling better after ridding his guts of what he had swallowed. His left knee still felt like a strand of wet string, but sensation was quickly returning to the limb. "I had one vicious nightmare while I was out. Head feels like someone was playing a rowdy game of Blood Stomper with it."

"I must say I've never played that sport," Doc noted. "Sounds painful."

Ryan eyeballed Doc's lean frame. "Yeah, you don't have the build for it, although you'd probably last longer than I would right now. How come you're looking so good, Doc?"

"No visions of demon fate, my friend. Other than awakening with my trousers sodden from the water on the chamber floor, my journey was unencumbered by dreams."

"None of us experienced the usual nightmares," Krysty said. "I'd say our bodies must be getting used to the mat-trans process—except from the look on your face, I'd say you weren't so lucky."

"Guess my mind game was enough for all of us," Ryan answered, and quickly sketched a verbal portrait of his unreal underwater experience for his friends.

"Gaia, but that's a harsh way to die," Krysty said in sympathy when Ryan had finished. "Perhaps your subconscious was trying to tell you something."

"Yeah, roll over," a new voice said with a snort. "Figure we'd all come through okay for a change, except for you," J.B. noted dryly as he elbowed past Doc. "This was a smooth and easy jump. Hell of a way to die, though, drowning facedown in a gateway."

"Wasn't my choice. Dying's dying," Ryan rasped back, the memory of his underwater vision fresh in his mind. "Once you're chilled, doesn't matter how or why."

"Still a bastard way for a man to cash in."

"I have to admit, I can think of better ways to go," Ryan agreed.

"Indeed," Doc stated. "A most ignoble end for such a brave sort as yourself, my dear fellow."

"I wonder…" Krysty began, then let her voice trail off.

"What?" Ryan asked.

"Well, last time we all came through a mat-trans jump without feeling real sick or having the nightmares was back in the Amazonian basin," Krysty said. "You know, where the natives thought Jak was a god?"

"So? What's your point?" Ryan prodded.

"So, I wonder if heat has anything to do with easing the effects of the jump. There was no air-conditioning working there, either, and it was as hot as Hades inside the chamber. However, we all felt fine. Maybe heat at the destination site makes the mist less invasive.

"Oh, listen to me. I'm starting to sound like Mildred." Krysty laughed, suddenly feeling like she was the center of everyone's intent scrutiny. Her fair skin blushed as she turned her attention to the chiseled silver points on the toes of her dark blue Western boots. "I don't know anything about these mat-trans units."

"You know just as much as the rest of us," Ryan said, "it's a good theory. Even if it doesn't help us out now, it might prove handy sometime down the trail.

"I wonder where we ended up this time?" Ryan said to no one in particular. He knew the Armorer wouldn't have ventured outside the underground redoubt as of yet.

J.B. lifted a hand and swiped at the speckled mold that covered the armaglass walls of the chamber, revealing the surface color underneath to Ryan. The leader of the group stared at the wall for a second, trying to place the color as J.B. said, "I won't need my sextant this time. We're in Florida swamp country. Greenglades, if memory serves."

"Yeah, I remember these blue-green walls from the last time, too. Give me a hand—I'm tired of sitting in this bastard water," Ryan grumbled, and J.B. and Krysty helped him to his feet. His leg was still tingling as feeling returned. The one-eyed man was silent for a moment as he checked his weapons. The pistol seemed to be none the worse for wear and he had noticed earlier that Dean was holding the Steyr SSG bolt-action rifle.

"Here, Dad," the youth said, extending the long-range blaster. "Didn't want it to get wet."

"Thanks," Ryan replied, and smiled back at Dean as he carefully opened the gateway door and stepped out into the small anteroom beyond the chamber. The room appeared to have been untouched since last time except for the increase in mold and dampness. A baseball cap with a torn fastener that Ryan remembered from his previous visit was in one corner, half floating, half submerged in the brackish water on the floor.

"The colors of the armaglass in these gateways has always been different shades of the rainbow, no matter where we've ended up," Doc said thoughtfully. "There has been no duplication as of yet, for reasons lost to me. Our benefactors were indeed lovers of a wide variety when it came to gateway decoration."

The same didn't apply to the actual layout and furnishing of the redoubts themselves.

Like most of the other redoubts they had visited, this one offered row upon row of gun-metal gray desks holding a vast array of computers. However, this time there was a major difference.

All but a handful of the monitor screens in the control area were dark.

"Comps down. Wonder we got here," observed Jak Lauren.

"I couldn't agree with you more," Ryan said, and entered the large control room under his own power, grateful the tingling sensation in his leg was gone He glanced up and noticed the strip lights overhead were almost all dark. The ceiling was cracked, as well, and showed an array of damage from where water had seeped in from above.

"If this is the redoubt in Greenglades, this entire complex has been flooded," Mildred stated, idly running a finger over a dirty comp keyboard. The gritty coating smeared under her touch, revealing the functions of the top row of keys. "I'd say most everything was underwater for hours. Maybe even days. And even if some of the hardware is still up, I'd have to question the software.''

Ryan took a deep breath. The air in the comp room was damp and humid, but infinitely more breathable than what passed for oxygen in the mat-trans unit. "This hole smells like Florida, at any rate.''

"So where did the water go?'' Dean asked.

"We know from past experience these redoubts are equipped with emergency drains, Dean,'' Krysty replied. "The redoubt apparently got rid of the water. Unfortunately for your dad, the gateway chamber didn't.''

"From the looks of this control room, I wouldn't want to make an attempt at jumping out of this redoubt. I think we should take pains to completely disable the unit. We might not be so lucky on a return visit,'' Mildred said.

"In other words, we could end up back here on another go-round with our eyes where our asshole is supposed to be,'' Ryan noted with a glimmer of grim humor.

"Right. Or with our atoms scattered to the four winds,'' Mildred responded.

For a second, Ryan's mind went back to the green sea he'd experienced during his dream. Undoubtedly there were worse places to end up than inside one of the mat-trans units, atoms scattered or not.

"Not that we'd be alive long enough to enjoy the sight,'' the black woman continued. "Molecular dissipation and regeneration isn't the most pleasant thing to endure when the mat-trans works properly. I'd hate to think about what could go wrong if the receiving unit was malfunctioning. Since we have no control over where we jump, I say let's take this stop off the tour—permanently.''

''You forgetting the fail-safes, Millie?'' J.B. asked, referring to the past theory the group held that if a mat-trans unit was malfunctioning or incapable of receiving, the computers automatically rerouted the incoming transport to a second location. All of the friends had agreed the nightmares brought on by the jumps were at their worst if this occurred, due to the longer time spent in-phase.

''No. But we don't have any proof the theory is right, and this dump barely brought us in safe this time,'' Mildred said, idly watching the coded messages dance across the dirty and streaked computer monitor screen as Dean stepped up beside her.

''We had a comp back at the school,'' the boy said casually, peering over Mildred's shoulder.

''Learn anything? Programming? Word processing?'' the woman asked, gratified to hear that Drody had been savvy enough to include basic computer training and usage at his school.

''Not much. On. Off. Diff between a disk drive and a CD-ROM drawer. One of my buds, Rodney, showed me a game or two. Hot pipe!''

Dean reached out and punched the Escape key on one of the working computer keyboards, despite Mildred's telling him such an action was a vain one since the programs were locked out to prevent tampering from unauthorized personnel. All of the group of travelers remembered previous jumps where Mildred had taken the time to prod and examine the redoubt computers in a futile attempt to gain some kind of control over their destinations.

"Let's see, let's try pushing Control, Alt, Delete," Dean said, using three fingers to press the keys simultaneously.

And for once, despite the odds against it, the pushing of a button in a mat-trans control room had an effect.

Before the pair's shocked eyes, the digital display began to change faster than the eye could catch. The monitor and base comp flickered into frenetic life, colored lights glowing and dancing, internal disk drives whirring, and a series of coded messages and graphics began to pop up on the screen. The other operating computer stations also fired into new life, each of them linked.

Directly behind Mildred and Dean, at the same time the boy's hand had pressed down the three keys at once, one of the massive-information storage units suddenly erupted into a white shower of sparks. A sizzling sound instantly followed, as the flickering lights on the master comp unit went out. An acrid-smelling haze of smoke hung in the air as a second, then a third comp unit followed suit within the span of a second.

Mildred swung back while Dean dived for the ground, pulling her Czech-made target revolver—a ZKR 551—from her hip holster. She leveled the pistol at where the sounds had erupted from, ready to

take out whatever had caused the commotion with a
.38-caliber Smith & Wesson round.

Until she saw what it was, and who had caused it.
Dean looked sick in the wrath of her glare, slouching
in his hiding place from beneath one of the mildewed
steel desks. Mildred opened her mouth to speak, then
turned on her booted heel and faced the gathered
party, all of whom had drawn their own various weapons when the fireworks started.

"What the hell did you do, Mildred?" Ryan
barked.

"It wasn't me!" the stocky woman protested.
"Look closer to home, Ryan!"

She pointed to the ashen-faced Dean. The comp
terminal where he had pressed the keys had stopped
functioning. The screen was no longer blinking, and
the tiny green light at the bottom of the console had
winked out. All of the ambient noise in the room had
also stopped with the deaths of the last few operating
systems.

"If that had happened when we were reassembling
in the mat-trans chamber, no safety would have saved
our asses—thirty-minute automatic reset be damned,"
Mildred added as Ryan stepped around the desk to
face his son.

"It was an accident—" Dean began, but was cut
off when Ryan picked him up by the upper arms and
slammed him on his butt on the dirty desktop.

"Is this the way it's going to be?" Ryan bellowed,
his normal raspy tone going up in pitch as he stood,
glaring at the shaken boy. "You lose most of your

survival skills during your stay at Brody's? If you have, you're going to get all of us chilled real fast.''

''Sorry, Dad.'' Dean started to cut his eyes away from his father's piercing glare until the one-eyed man grabbed the boy by the chin and pulled his face back up. Ryan sighed, a long, extended exhalation from deep within his belly, and brought his anger back in check as Krysty's words whispered through his mind, the advice she had given to him back in Vegas when Dean had rejoined them only to fall back into unsafe habits that could get them all shot.

He's still a child, Ryan, no matter how quickly you want to mold him into a man.

Ryan didn't agree. Dean was becoming as seasoned as any of the rest of them. He was just being slack. After nearly a year of being locked away at the Brody school, the boy's survival mechanisms were rusty. Hopefully they'd get a proper oiling before the boy got himself—or one of the group—chilled.

''I know I screwed up, Dad.''

''Fine. Don't do it again.''

''Actually,'' Mildred mused, ''Dean might have solved the question of whether this redoubt's gateway was safe for future use.''

''Mildred's right,'' J.B. agreed. ''The kid did us a favor. We've pushed our luck and then some with this redoubt. If I had any doubts before, this made the decision for me. I'm for walking.''

Ryan turned from Dean to look at Mildred and J.B. ''All right, then. Mildred, you make sure all the mat-trans control comps are really dead. We can leave the sec door open for extra safety in case something else happens. Close the door when you're through and come out after us. While you're checking the comps, we'll fan out to the stairwell and see about making our way up to the top of the redoubt."

"I take it we're here to stay for a while in sunny Florida?" Krysty said sarcastically.

"Not much choice about being here now, but I'm not planning on staying," Ryan replied. "Too damned hot. We'll see what we can find in the quarters above, then head up the coastline and see what we find there. Mebbe grab a boat and sail up to the Carolinas."

"What about Greenglades ville, Dad?" Dean asked. "You think any of those crazies are still around? Mebbe they're the ones who flooded the place."

Ryan paused for a moment and rubbed his chin before answering. "Doubt it," he said flatly. "After all, I chilled most of the sons of bitches myself."

Chapter Two

Greenglades.

A wellspring of bad memories came back to Ryan. Memories of fat Boss Larry Zapp atop his padded throne overlooking his over-the-top concept ville of brightly colored rides and attractions. What had Mildred called the place then? A theme park. A place of lights and sounds where families went for fun and excitement, with sugary sweets to eat and trinkets for prizes for children. A land of make-believe. A land of amusement.

Only things hadn't been too amusing when they had passed through.

Not that it was Larry Zapp's fault. He could have taken them out when they arrived in the ville if he'd wanted, and the overweight baron did have reason enough to want to see Ryan Cawdor dead. A younger Ryan and J. B. Dix had crossed paths with Larry in his prebaron days during their time riding shotgun for the Trader on War Wag One. Ryan knew their encounter had been unforgettable for Larry, who was the owner of a large and successful traveling gaudy and the half dozen or so sluts inside.

Cold Beer And Hot Women was Larry's motto, and he was doing fine with his touring group until he got greedy and tried to bribe one of the war wag's crew-men with a one-eared whore named Bernice. The Trader's stockpiles of guns, ammo and fuel were leg-endary, and the pimp had sought a direct source to the goods. Sex and beer were profitable, but fuel and weapons were shining gold.

When the Trader found out about Larry's scheme, his response was predictable. He sent his two most trusted henchmen to teach Larry a lesson in manners.

After Ryan and J.B.'s not so friendly visit, the wags Larry had used for the gaudy were burned-out wrecks of twisted metal, the casks of golden-tinged beer were poured out on the dirt and the gaily painted girls had been threatened and fled as fast as their high-heeled feet would carry them into the nearby hills for their very lives.

All this while Larry had gotten extraspecial care. As his employees ran, Larry had received a beating that left him broken and bleeding in the mud with both elbows bent backward in the most painful po-sition possible, but at least he was alive.

Barely.

Luckily enough, nearly a dozen years had passed since his youthful indiscretion, and Larry didn't hold a grudge. Ryan wasn't proud of what he'd done to a tub of guts like Larry way back when, but the man had brought it on himself. The baron had gestured with one flabby arm and granted them safe harbor; telling his sec man to give the group back their blast-ers and full access to the park and attractions.

Larry invited them to stay and enjoy what the ville

had to offer, which unfortunately included a sick bastard named Adam Traven, a self-styled cult leader who had arrived in Greenglades three months prior to Ryan and his group. Traven had his own nubile young group of followers who shared his perverted murderous fantasies—fantasies Doc found out about the hard way when a young lady named Sky had tried to strangle him during a bout of lovemaking.

Traven had also arrived with a large supply of the highly addictive—and very rare—form of jolt known as dreem, and wasted no time in hooking the hedonistic Boss Larry on the fine pink powder. To further cement Larry's dependency, Traven had also unleashed on the fat man all the sexual excess his teenage followers could provide.

A sec man named Kelly had told Ryan that Greenglades ville had once been a paradise, with working television and air-conditioning and some of the best food a man could ever hope to see before him on a plate. The restored attractions were a hobby, something to show off to visitors. Boss Larry was a regular techno brain, a genius with electronics who loved wine, women and song.

Until the drugs ate away at his brain.

That was none of Ryan's business. In one day, two tops, his party would be on their way, and Larry Zapp, baron of Greenglades ville, could snort until his fat head exploded.

But nothing was ever that simple in Deathlands, and Ryan was forced to become actively involved when Traven expressed a more than passing interest in Dean. Larry himself had warned Ryan to keep the boy away from Traven.

"Adam likes him, Ryan. Oh, yes. Precious. His precious, Ryan. Boy that young. Pretty. What he wants most," Larry had said in a dreem-induced haze.

It was at that moment that Ryan Cawdor had made the conscious decision that Adam Traven was going to have to die. Not because the sick twist was a control freak and a master manipulator into dominance and submission with a taste for young boys. No, a man's vices were his own.

Where Adam Traven had gone wrong was bringing Dean's name into it.

After earlier skirmishes, the final battle had come inside the tall observation tower that overlooked Boss Larry's domain.

Larry had proved true blue in the end, when he had willed his 450-pound body to topple forward and crush the slender, effeminate Traven beneath his magnificent bulk in a violent showdown. By the time Ryan dragged Traven out, the self-styled cult leader was nearly smothered to death. His skinny body was slick with blood from the eight rounds he'd pumped into Larry from underneath, but the huge boss hadn't budged.

After pulling Traven free, Ryan helped the self proclaimed "master" along to judgment day with some well-placed bullets from his blaster.

Larry Zapp had been the genius behind Greenglades ville. With his passing, Ryan expected Green-

glades Theme Park to have fallen into complete dis-
repair.

"What kind of name is 'Larry' for a baron, anyway?" Ryan mused aloud.

"Could've been worse. He could've been Boss
Moe. Or Boss Curly," Mildred said with a wide
smile. Then she laughed aloud. "Or God help us all,
Boss Shemp."

Everyone in the room looked at her blankly.

"I must admit, madam, that your reference is arcane even to one as learned as I," Doc said. "Who
is this Boss Shemp?"

"Forget it," Mildred said, wiping a tear of laughter
from one eye. "Too silly to try and explain. Seeing
is believing when it comes to the Stooges. Mama
never could understand why I thought they were so
funny—of course, most women didn't care for their
unique brand of comedic talent. Maybe we'll find one
of their old comedy vids some day and I can show
you."

"They were...clowns?" J.B. asked blankly, looking at Mildred for confirmation.

"No, they were stooges," Mildred replied, and
lightly rapped J.B. on the top of the head with the
palm of her right hand. "Now spread out, you mugs!
I'll be right behind you when I'm done in here."

"Sometimes, Millie, I don't understand you at all,"
J.B. muttered, walking past the still-giggling woman
until he faced the steel sec doors at the end of the
control room. The small man raised his weapon in a

combat-ready stance and turned back at Ryan for the nod.

"You up for this?" J.B. asked.

"Feeling better all the time," Ryan replied as he unholstered his own blaster. "Everybody stay alert. I doubt there's anything out there, but this is no time to get sloppy."

"Dad?"

Ryan turned to Dean. "What?"

"I used to always open the sec doors, remember?"

Ryan looked at J.B. "Fine by me."

"Okay, son. Go ahead."

The green lever that was present in almost all of the gateways was in the down position, showing the doors were locked shut. Dean grabbed the lever and slowly began to lift it upward. A sharp intake of hydraulics hissed obligingly, and the door began to open smoothly. When the door was two feet off the ground, Dean dropped to his knees and carefully peered out.

"Nothing. Corridor's clear," he reported as he got back on his feet and activated the lever to bring the doorway open to full access.

Ryan took the lead, and the others joined him in stepping outside the doorway, finding themselves in a wide, curving passage with an arched roof. It was about twenty feet wide, and the ceiling was roughly fifteen feet at the highest point. Concealed strip lighting flickered, casting gray shadows across the expanse of the corridor. When they had last traveled along this passageway, things were deserted, but still in order.

The same mold and signs of water damage that had

been inside the mat-trans control room were also evident here. Ryan glanced back over his shoulder. A familiar sign to all of the gateway travelers announced: Entry Absolutely Forbidden To All But B12-Cleared Personnel. The warning hung lopsidedly in a broken frame next to the door.

"I'll take the point. Krysty, you're behind me. Then Dean, Doc and Jak," Ryan said.

"I'll bring up the rear," J.B. stated, acknowledging the order of their usual skirmish line, with the addition of Mildred, who had come out after checking the computers.

"Hot," Jak said, taking off his outer jacket and tying the sleeves around his waist. The albino's one word summed up the situation for all of them, and the youth was used to living in areas washed with humidity. The interior of the redoubt was much warmer than before, and Ryan knew it wasn't going to get any cooler as they approached the way outside.

"Some fresh air would be nice, lover," Krysty murmured to Ryan. "I'm about to roast in my boots."

Less than two minutes later, the party faced a huge pair of sec doors that stretched from floor to ceiling. The decorator's choice of color for the doors was a shade of green that reminded Ryan for a moment of the dream he'd experienced while jumping. Sea green. Before seeing the ocean for the first time, Ryan had been under the fallacy that the waters were blue.

"Nothing's ever what it seems in Deathlands," Ryan said aloud.

He stared at the small control panel of letters and

numbers for the vanadium-steel sec doors, then punched in the usual code of 3-5-2 and waited for the door to respond.

"Dad, you want me to—?"

"Quiet, son. I think you've done enough for one day, don't you?" Ryan said, peering down at Dean's excited, then rueful, young face. "Everyone stay ready—triple red. We still don't know what's behind this door."

Everyone watched the doors and waited.

Nothing.

Then, after long, sweaty seconds of anticipation, the hydraulics for the doors hissed to life. Like a great gaping mouth in the middle of a yawn, the doors slid ponderously upward into their ceiling slot, revealing the interior of a gaping maw. Ryan had half expected to see trapped water pour in, but was relieved to see Mildred's hypothesized flood had passed on.

Beyond the doors was an identical passage, except this one was damaged even more. The floor was littered with cracks ranging in size from hairline to three feet across. Evidence of a past onslaught of water was visible, but so was structural damage and chunks of debris. The room was nightmarish in the flickering light of the damaged tubes, making movement seem slower in the steady strobe.

The concrete walls, normally cool and dry to the touch, felt warm and damp. Either something had happened above in Greenglades—something drastic enough to affect even the highly protected redoubt—

or the redoubt had been discovered by parties unknown who had blasted their way inside.

Neither scenario was one Ryan found comforting.

Above them along the arched roof were sec vids, but the rectangular cameras were dead. Before, the little gadgets had been quite active, tracking their every step with tiny red electronic eyes.

"Automatics are down," J.B. said. "Last time, we triggered them when we stepped out into the corridor."

"Explains the heat," Ryan agreed. "What juice left in this redoubt must be on bare life support. Emergency lights and oxygen, and that's about it. No extra power for air-conditioning." He turned and looked at Mildred, who had just rejoined the group. "Farther along we get, the more I have to agree with you. This place has completely shot its wad. Atomics must be down to nil."

After closing the sec doors, the companions made their way slowly down the dirty corridor to a slight bend, which would then lead around to where the stairs and elevator would normally be in the standard redoubt layout.

"Bad smell," Jak commented.

"Right on. This goes beyond mildew and moisture," Mildred agreed. "Smells like rotting meat."

"Not much longer now," Ryan said. "As I recall, around this corner is—"

There was a popping sound from underfoot, which stopped him short.

On the floor in front of him was a human arm,

curled back at a broken angle around the corner. Ryan held up a warning hand for the others to wait and glanced around the side, darting his head out, then back to safety like the tongue of a snake. In the brief look he'd gotten, he'd seen that the arm was attached to a corpse, facedown on the dirty floor. He had stepped on one of the dead man's pasty, brittle hands with his right boot.

"Lock and load, people," Ryan said softly. "There's more of them chilled around the bend."

"Dark night," J.B. muttered over the sounds of everyone preparing their weapons for potential battle.

Ryan swung the SIG-Sauer around the corner, peering intently along the line of sight. The wide room on the line to the elevators looked pretty much as he remembered, except for the new addition of a mass of rubble that had fallen down from above, twisting the staircase into an unclimbable mass of metal and totally blocking the ruin of a stairwell. The flat landing area at the top, which contained the doorway to the second stairwell, was also wrecked and jammed with broken concrete.

"All clear," Ryan said, recognizing the irony of the phrase. While there were no live sec men or hostiles to challenge them, the absence of the stairs was going to prove a daunting obstacle.

As they came around the corner one by one, Mildred took note of three more bodies, all in twisted postures with small entry and large exit wounds. "Well, we know this wasn't due to rad poisoning, like we've seen take down stiffs in other redoubts,'' Mildred said in her best clinical voice.

She bent at the waist for a closer look. "They're not in military uniforms, and they all died from gunshot wounds. From the condition of the bodies, the feel of the skin and the heavenly aroma, I'd guess these boys have been getting ripe for at least a month or more.''

"This just keeps getting better and better," J.B. muttered. "How did these guys get down here in the first place?''

"And who chilled them?" Ryan added.

"Chilled each other," Jak responded. "Trapped, had argument. Way bodies fall and positions, they got in fight and everybody lost.''

"Give me a hand, here, John," Mildred said. She was kneeling, attempting to turn over one of the corpses.

The Armorer complied, and together they flipped the body onto its back.

The sight would have been sickening to most, but it was a familiar one to all of the group. They'd looked down on many a dead man during the time they'd traveled together. The corpse's features were nothing special: flat nose, thin lips, hair that appeared to have been dyed blond, but now had a greenish tinge. He looked like a hundred other dead men Ryan had seen over the years. He wore a black leather jacket with lots of tarnished buckles, a red T-shirt, jeans and brown boots.

The only unusual thing was a patch sewn on the

front breast pocket of the jacket. It was round and about two inches in circumference. The entire circle was black, with a white patch in the center.

"Looks like a skull wearing a cycle helmet," J.B. said.

"Yeah, but check the eyes," Mildred replied. "There are little red dots in the eye sockets."

"Looks like Jak wearing a cycle helmet, then," J.B. amended.

"Screw cycles. Two wheels good way to get shot," the albino snorted. Jak was correct. While a cycle gave one speed and more mobility than a wag, a rider was pretty much a deaf and dumb target, since the engine noise shut out any sounds, and one's eyes were naturally on the road.

Jak eyed the patch. "Don't look like me."

"Sure, it does. Just picture yourself with your hair all tucked up under the helmet," J.B. said.

"Wonder what it means?" Ryan mused. "I checked out the others. All four of these stupes have that same patch. Two on a jacket, one on the back pocket of a pair of jeans and another on a neckerchief. They must've been together at one time until somebody drew down on somebody else."

"Hot pipe, Dad! We're in luck," Dean yelled from across the room. Ryan squelched a quick flash of annoyance over the fact the boy had gone off alone, and turned to look at what he was talking about.

Dean was standing at the elevator, but the boy wasn't alone. Next to the youth Doc was focused on the black elevator call button.

"Young Dean is right, my dear fellow," Doc said to Ryan, who had quickly joined them. "The elevator appears to be operating, and I do believe it is currently on this floor of the redoubt."

The rest of the group approached for a closer look. The recessed button was indeed lit and glowing.

"Shall I put my best finger forward?" Doc asked.

After getting the nod from Ryan, Doc pressed the call button for the elevator. The doors obligingly slid open, revealing the empty, coffinlike cabin inside.

"I guess no one wants off on this floor," Mildred said quietly. "Last stop to oblivion."

None of the group ever relished stepping into a redoubt's elevator. Too many things could go wrong. Too many things *had* gone wrong. Still, it was the most direct way up and out. The dull gray walls offered scant comfort, but they also promised access to the surface, a promise that was enticing despite the danger.

"After you, ladies," Doc said, bowing deeply at the waist and gesturing grandiosely toward the elevator's interior.

"Thanks, I think," Krysty replied, her red prehensile hair curling slightly at her nape as she walked inside. No one but Ryan noticed the shift in her almost sentient tresses. Krysty's hair was about the only outward manifestation of her latent mutant abilities, and responded to her moods. The way the strands were tightening, Ryan knew she was nervous about entering.

They all were.

Mildred and J.B. entered, followed by Jak and Dean. Ryan gestured to Doc, and the old man stepped in, accidentally stepping on Dean's booted foot. "Pardon me, young Cawdor. I fear it is getting a bit crowded in here."

"Don't worry, Doc. Think of it as being cozy," Krysty said.

Ryan glanced a final time over his shoulder and placed himself in the last clear spot at the front of the elevator car.

"Going up?" Doc asked.

"Why not?" Ryan replied. "But when we reach the top, I want everyone on a triple red." He unholstered the SIG-Sauer pistol to back up his words. The rest of the group followed suit with their own weapons.

Doc, by nature of his position in front of the controls, had taken on the unofficial role of elevator operator for this trip. He pressed the Up button. The doors slid smoothly shut, and after an almost unnoticeable lurch, the elevator begin to rise.

"Wonder what took out the stairs, Dad?" Dean asked.

"Good question. I was wondering that myself."

"High explosives, mebbe," Krysty offered. "Or I guess there could've been a quake around here. Even swamplands aren't safe from earthquakes. Not anymore."

Overhead the fluorescent tubes flickered once, twice, then exploded in a series of sharp pops, like the echoes of a small-caliber pistol being fired in rapid succession. Sparks filtered down from above as the elevator car shuddered. Hidden machinery gave off a terrific squawk, and all was still.

As the last spark fell brightly to the floor and died, the confined room went dark.

"Fireblast," Ryan hissed. "The elevator's out."

Chapter Three

"Everybody stay still," Ryan ordered. "Give your eyes time to adjust."

"No place to go but up," J.B. said, peering at the ceiling.

"I know. We're going to have to climb out of the car."

"Sweatbox in here," Jak said. "Go out. Climb quick."

"Dean?"

"Yeah, Dad?"

"Come over here. Let me give you a boost. I want you to feel along the upper panels of the ceiling. There should be some kind of an access hatch."

Ryan squinted with his single eye. Vague shapes were beginning to become apparent in the gloom as they moved and shifted in the blackness. His son shifted position with Krysty and Jak and ended up standing next to him. Ryan knelt and cupped his hands, offering a step onto his back for the boy.

Dean placed one foot in his father's hands and used his hands to brace himself on the knotted muscles of Ryan's shoulders. The youth's weight wasn't much, and Ryan was able to lift as the boy carefully balanced himself. He reached up and gripped Dean's upper thighs with both hands, further stabilizing him.

Ryan waited as Dean felt around the roof. No one spoke. The only sound was everyone's breathing, which was starting to become more labored in the stifling heat of the elevator car. Then there was a distinct clack, followed by a slight raking sound.

"Got it," the boy said.

"Good. Now come down."

Dean did so. "J.B?" Ryan asked.

There was another shifting of the mass of bodies, then J.B. was next to Ryan. "You going up?" the Armorer asked.

"Not much of a choice. Dean opened the door, now I've got to take a look outside."

Ryan removed a tight pair of black gloves from one of his long coat's pockets, then shrugged out of the garment, accidentally slapping J.B. across the face and knocking his spectacles off as he struggled to free his left arm.

"Dark night, Ryan, be careful!"

"No space to move," Ryan muttered. "You should've kept back."

"How the hell was I supposed to do that? Just nobody move until I find them," J.B. replied.

"I've got them, John," Mildred said. "They flew back and hit me on the hand. They didn't have room to fall to the floor."

Carefully, Ryan also took off his long white scarf with the weighted ends and bundled it up into a tight

ball. The extra clothing would just get in the way of
what he was about to do.

"Here, Krysty," Ryan said, handing her the still
slightly soggy bundle and his rifle. His callused fingers brushed against her warm skin. "I'll be back for
these in a minute."

J.B. leaned down and interlocked his fingers together as a stepping-stone, unconsciously duplicating
Ryan from before. The one-eyed man took a deep
breath as he pushed his hands into the gloves, then
stepped up into his friend's offered hands. The Armorer lifted as Ryan extended his arms above his
head and gripped the edge of the hatch Dean had
opened, pulling himself up and out of the car.

Half of Ryan still dangled down into the cabin, but
from the waist up he was exposed to the four walls
of the elevator shaft. As inside the car, the lighting
out there was also nonexistent, but he was surprised
to see glowing fluorescence extending vertically up
the far back wall. As he gazed at the glow, Ryan
realized he was looking at a pattern.

With a grunt, he pulled himself completely through
the hatch and managed to brace himself along one of
the sturdy upper beams of the elevator, not wanting
to test the strength of the ceiling with his weight. He
reached up and gripped the steel frame of the car as
he swung one leg to the opposite side of the roof,
then the other and squatted on the beam.

He looked at the glow-in-the-dark shapes stretching
up along the wall of the shaft.

What he was seeing were the rungs of an emergency ladder, no doubt designed for just this kind of happenstance. The rungs were evenly spaced about two feet apart, one after the other, and bolted into place. They snaked up as far as Ryan could see.

"What's the situation?" J.B. called.

"There's an emergency ladder in place along the front wall of the shaft," Ryan said. "We'll go up in two groups. You, me and Krysty will recce upstairs. After we've cleared the area, then Mildred, Doc, Dean and Jak can come up. We'll have to do this one at a time. I don't want to put too much weight on the top of the car or have anybody accidentally fall off. Go in order of how we usually approach a triple-red situation."

From within the elevator, J.B. assisted Krysty up. Once the red-haired beauty was safe, Ryan took to the ladder, giving enough room on the elevator roof for the Armorer to scramble up safely.

The climb was smooth and easy. At a few points, the rungs were slippery with old grease and grime, but it was nothing Ryan couldn't handle. When he reached the end of the ladder and realized he was staring at a hairline crack where the top-floor elevator-shaft doors opened, he was almost surprised.

"We're here," he said in a whisper.

"Good," Krysty whispered back.

"I'll have to force the shaft doors. Hold on until I signal you."

After carefully removing the panga from the sheath at his side, Ryan used it to help open the doors, sliding the finely honed blade into the thin slit, then twisting his wrist back and forth, executing as much pressure as he could on the handle while trying to stay balanced on the rung of the ladder. He had crooked one arm through the rung for extra support, but that limited the amount of pressure he could put on the knife.

Krysty, seeing Ryan's predicament, made her way up next to him. She pressed her firm body against his own to help hold him firmly in place, with her chest against his back as she reached out on either side and gripped the rungs of the ladder tightly.

"Looked like you needed an assist, lover," Krysty whispered. "Be careful up there. Something doesn't feel right."

"What? Squatters living in the redoubt, like those bastard twins back in Old Colorado?"

"Could be that, or friends of the four men we found below."

Ryan nodded. With Krysty's support, he was now free to use his full upper body strength against the closed doors. Sweat dripped down his face and arms as he exerted pressure.

Finally, with a sluggish squawk of protest, the elevator doors slid apart a few inches. Replacing his panga in its sheath, Ryan now had enough room to wedge his fingers in the newly created gap. He felt a fingernail on his right hand peel back as he strained to pull the doors open wide enough to squeeze his body through.

Inch by inch, the doors pulled apart, finally creating a space just wide enough for a man to slip through.

Balancing his feet on the top rung of the emergency ladder, Ryan used the upper part of the now open door for a handhold. He took a deep breath and stepped through to what he hoped was safety.

The area outside the elevator was as dim as the darkness in the shaft. The electricity was apparently out up here, as well. Ryan paused, straining his eye and scanning for any signs of movement.

Nothing. He took one step forward, and a piece of stray plastic snapped underfoot, the cracking sound leaping forward as swiftly and surely as a broken twig in a silent forest.

In immediate response, the wall next to the elevator doors erupted in an answering barrage of sound, small indentations rattling down from floor to ceiling in a sloping pattern of gunfire.

Ryan dived away from the doors for cover, hoping the noise would keep Krysty and J.B. in place on the ladder and not drive them into doing anything heroic. An empty plastiform-and-steel cargo container was lying open on one side. Ryan took cover behind it, knowing from past experience any military redoubt's storage pods were made of sturdy stuff.

Since he was still alive, Ryan figured the shooter didn't have infrared. His guess was that the assailant had been forced to aim by sound, using noises to track as Ryan slipped out the doors from the elevator shaft. He crouched on his hands and knees behind the container and waited, but the shooter kept firing random bursts. That was reassuring. Ryan now knew for a fact he could safely discount a night scope by the way the bullets kept ineptly chewing up the scenery.

The sniper was firing blind.

Ryan kept his head low, listening, attempting to pinpoint the exact location of the gunman over the rapid drumming of what sounded to him like an M-16 assault rifle. Obviously the shooter was firing from a vantage point located around a corner of the walkway—across from the elevator. While this was a safe place to hide for an ambush, it also meant the sniper's aim was compromised.

In one practiced move, Ryan unleathered the SIG-Sauer and waited until the M-16 stopped stuttering. The way his hidden assailant had been spraying ammo, Ryan deduced the shooter had to be reloading.

He reached down and as before, carefully, quietly picked up a handful of the scattered bits of discarded rock and metal on the floor; gracefully overhanding them toward a mass of empty storage pods to his right. The thrown debris hit the plastic, clattering a warning to the person with the assault rifle.

The hidden M-16 responded by spreading an uneven skittering pattern of destruction away from Ryan's hiding place and in the direction of where the new noise had come from.

Sloppy, but Ryan was used to stupes who let weapons do their thinking in a combat situation.

In fact, he counted on it. Such foolishness had kept him alive many times during his long career, if one wanted to call riding back and forth in war wags and traveling by mat-trans across Deathlands a career. Not that Ryan relied on luck. Going into any situation, anytime, anywhere, he was ready for the unexpected, for that was the only kind of luck Deathlands ever seemed to offer.

Surviving was what Ryan and his friends did best, and if their opponents were sloppy, so much the better for them.

There was a pause in the barrage of steel-jacketed death. Ryan had easily placed the shooter by ear, now all he wanted was a final visual confirmation, which came soon enough as the M-16 spit a fresh hail of bullets. This time Ryan clearly saw the white flash from the barrel of the weapon.

Ryan brought his own weapon to bear. Aiming by instinct, he squeezed off three bullets, one of which wormed high into the front of the sniper's left collarbone and out his back. A second bullet punched into the already critically wounded man's cranium and through in a mass of grue. The final slug punched through what remained of the man's forehead. As the sniper's body grew slack, the M-16 fell silent. The next thing Ryan heard was the clatter of the assault rifle hitting the floor, followed by a series of gargling sounds from the dying man as he followed the weapon.

The interior of the hall outside the elevator shaft became loud with silence.

"Ryan?" came a subtle whisper from Krysty.

"Shh! Not yet." Ryan stood and walked warily to the fallen body. As he had hoped, the sniper had been alone. He looked down impassively on the slain killer, striking a self-light while kneeling for a close inspection. The tight circle of light revealed a thin man of about thirty, with dirty long blond hair and a ratty goatee. The upper left of his forehead was missing where the slugs from the SIG-Sauer had struck.

The dead man wore a powder blue dress shirt that had already turned dark with blood from his wounds. A pair of combat boots had the cuffs of baggy, dirty trousers stuffed into their high tops. On the pocket of the shirt was a black-and-white skull patch identical to the ones on the sleeves and pockets of the corpses on the lower floor of the redoubt.

Ryan was getting ready to tell Krysty to come through the elevator access hatch when the interior of the redoubt lit up. For the second time since his arrival in the humid hellhole, Ryan found himself lunging down flat on his stomach, every nerve in his body screaming with alertness. He squinted, his vision colored with tiny explosions of color from his single overloaded cornea.

The pupil of his blue eye had been stretched open to maximum in the dimness, and it now involuntarily misted over in shock from the light as Ryan struggled to recover from the unexpected illumination.

As he blinked, Ryan grimly realized he was temporarily in the earlier blind position of the sniper. He reached out and retrieved the man's rifle, adding the stripped-down M-16 to his own portable arsenal of the SIG-Sauer. Hearing approaching voices, he crawled in the opposite direction back toward the oversize cargo container. Temporarily safe for a second time behind the makeshift cover, he listened, waiting for his best opportunity, depending on who or what came around the corner.

"Geez, this joint makes me nervous," a youthful voice said.

"Everything makes you nervous, Breaux," came a sarcastic response from about twenty feet away. "Gambling makes you nervous. Gaudy sluts make you nervous. I say, take advantage of anything you can and go for the moment. Use your nerves, man."

"Whatever you say, Dunlop. I just wish I'd get assigned to do something more exciting than hiding out and guarding an empty shithole. Aw, Christ! Look at this!" the voice identified as Breaux wailed. "What a bastard mess."

Ryan, his vision now back to normal, peered out from behind his haven and took in the scene. The man with the slight Cajun accent had to be Dunlop. He came running up warily into Ryan's rapidly improving view. He was a tall black man, with a mass of thick dreadlocks sticking out in all directions atop his sweaty face. He was dressed in baggy, ill-fitting pants and a patched tie-dyed T-shirt that read All-Nite Funk Machine in silver iron-on letters. A white headband stretched across his forehead. In its center was the skull patch.

"Makes a convenient target," Ryan muttered.

The black man also carried an M-16 identical to the one the slain man had been using.

The other man—or rather, the other boy—Breaux, was white, and wore a red flannel shirt open in the front, black jeans and a threadbare pair of white canvas tennis shoes that were now splattered with crimson from where he'd stepped into the growing pool of blood leaking from the slain sniper's shattered cranium.

Sunglasses with darkened lenses were perched high on the forehead of his moon-pie face. He looked every bit of fifteen years old. His hair was cut close and stood up on his scalp like freshly shorn wheat. The shirt and jeans were too short, and his youngster's wrists and sockless ankles were showing. Ryan guessed the boy hadn't had a change of clothing in some time, and was rapidly growing out of what attire he owned. An H&K .32 automatic blaster was gripped tightly in his right hand.

"He's dead, then, is he?" Dunlop asked, gazing past his companion and scanning the dead end of the hallway.

"What do you think? Half of his damned head's gone!" Breaux said nervously, eyeballing the thick red pool he'd stepped into. Already the blood was starting to congeal around the ruin of the corpse's head and left shoulder.

"Poor Mikey, he dead. Scared of a little blood?" Dunlop chucked, using the toe of one foot to nudge the dead man. "Got to grow up sometime, little one. Learn to laugh at red."

"Fuck, no—I ain't scared," Breaux protested. "Not of a dead body or some blood. I'm scared of who did this to him. Smells horrible."

"Here's some free advice—try not to step in it.

Shit will stick to your shoes like hot glue. Lucky for your delicate nose Mikey here is done deader 'n dick,'' Dunlop said, keeping his rifle level as he peered down with a clinical eye. "And not long dead. Otherwise he'd be stinking a whole lot worse than usual in this heat."

"Who do you think did him?" the younger man asked, cutting his eyes warily back and forth.

"Don't know. Guess the boss knew someone might be coming back here sooner or later—otherwise he wouldn't have bothered posting guards. Lucky break for you, man."

"Lucky break how?"

"Could be you chilled there on the floor. I walked out here with you from camp as a favor. What if you found such a terrible sight alone, eh?" Dunlop's voice was sarcastic. "Wet your pants and come back crying for help. Too bad Mikey couldn't handle it better than this, though, the stupid son of a bitch."

"Mike was cool, man. Ease up," Breaux said softly, feeling guilty about being so flip over a friend's death.

"Sure, sure. Look, he's been made, too," Dunlop said, pointing down at the corpse.

"How do you know that?"

"His gun's gone, stupe. Unless the man's weapon decided to run for cover, somebody beat us to turning him over."

"You're right," Ryan said flatly as he stood up from hiding with the SIG-Sauer leveled at the men.

Chapter Four

Ryan knew his sudden appearance would result in one of two possible reactions from the pair.

The expected one wasn't long in coming.

Dunlop gasped out a curse, swung his M-16 around and prepared to fire. Ryan didn't hesitate, and the SIG-Sauer thrummed a second payload of death, two rounds drilling into his adversary's upper chest and neck. The man gurgled as his body fell backward, his arms pinwheeling wildly as a wet spray of crimson flew in the wake of the exit wounds. His feet stumbled over the body of his former acquaintance, and he fell flat on his back across the chest of his dead associate.

Breaux merely stood there, not making a sound. His right cheek and head were spotted with red, but he made no move to wipe the gore from his face. The only noticeable change in his composure was how pale his head suddenly looked sticking out of the open collar of the flannel shirt. A slight sheen of sweat covered his ears. He kept his hands low and at waist level.

"So much for the Funk Machine," Ryan said dryly as he stepped out from behind the table, the SIG-Sauer leveled at the standing Breaux. "I'm hoping you're smarter."

"Compared to those two, I already am," Breaux said in a wobbly tone. "I'm still alive."

"For the time being. Drop the blaster now, before I chill you, too."

Breaux followed the order, opening his hand and letting the weapon fall to the ground with a clatter. Ryan stepped forward to kick the pistol away when the nervous Breaux decided to make a move. With surprising speed for someone so young, he lunged forward in an attempt to grab the SIG-Sauer from Ryan with his free right hand.

Ryan had seen the plan of attack coming. To his practiced combat eye, the boy was moving in slow motion, the grab for the blaster an obvious distraction to cover the small but lethal stiletto that had slid down Breaux's checkered shirt sleeve and into his waiting left hand. An old dodge, but a good one in a bar fight over a drunken slut or an unpaid beer tab.

Only this was no bar, and Ryan was no drunk.

"I was really hoping you were smarter than those two wonderful examples. Guess not," Ryan snarled, and lashed out fiercely, catching his surprised attacker flush in the teeth with the barrel of the SIG-Sauer. Blood and drool mixed with bits of white enamel poured from the young man's ruined mouth as he dropped to his knees with a whimper.

The stiletto fell to the floor, forgotten in the haze of pain the youth was suffering. Ryan used the toe of his boot to flick the fallen blade out of range.

"Listen close," Ryan grated as he reached down and pulled up the weeping boy by his collar. "I don't like liars and I like liars with knives even less. I've been on the defensive since walking into this scum-soaked hole, and I don't even know who you losers are or why you're lurking around here. So spill it.''

Breaux stared dully at Ryan. All of the white heat of the attack had been doused with the taste of cold steel against his now bleeding gums. "Who are you?" he asked painfully through his broken mouth.

"Who I am doesn't matter. Talk to me, boy. And make the story interesting.''

"We're part of Northern Panhandle. Sec squad of three. We were sent here to keep an eye on this place." He spit out a gob of pink-tinged saliva.

"Sec squad? That explains the twin M-16s and ut-ter lack of training to use them, I suppose. Who trained you?''

The boy's defiant look from earlier returned in force. "Rollins. Rollins trained me personally back at the barracks in Mobile.''

"Alabama?" Ryan recalled there was a ruin of a military base there.

"Yeah. Trained me good. I'm a professional,'' Breaux said indignantly.

"So tell me, professional, what's up with the skull patches?" Ryan pointed the muzzle of the SIG-Sauer at the round black spot sewn to the pocket of the boy's shirt.

"All of Rollins's men wear them.''

"Who is this Rollins?''

The boy clammed up. Ryan gestured with the pistol. "Do I have to shoot you in the leg to help your memory?"

"Rollins is the boss of all bosses," the boy recited in a chant. "Gonna take over all of Deathlands someday."

"Oh," Ryan said sarcastically. "King of the Deathlands. Now there's a title for you." The one-eyed man shifted his weight from one foot to the other. "How'd you get in here, anyway?"

"Through the door, you old fart."

Ryan's free hand lashed out, cuffing the boy's head.

"Watch your smart mouth, stupe."

"Th-this place was open. Been open for months. Doors were broken up in a quake. You should know! You had to have—"

Then Breaux's gaze fell on the partially opened elevator, and a look of understanding fell across his face. His eyes narrowed suspiciously.

"You came from down below!" It was an accusation, not a question.

"Good eyes. Wrong assumption. There's no elevator there. Just an empty shaft. I was in here already—came through Greenglades park. Got lost in the swamps. After I nearly had one of my feet gnawed off by a mutie frog, I decided to look in here for some shelter," Ryan lied, making up the story as he went along. Not that he cared one way or another if the boy believed he'd come up from the bottom of the redoubt, but why give the scoop to a child who'd previously tried to stab him in the gut with a hidden shiv?

"How old are you?" Ryan asked.

"Fifteen."

"Got any folks?"

"Got an older sister."

"Any message you want sent after I've chilled your flannel-wearing ass?"

"Fuck you," the boy snarled.

"I can spell that. She can chisel it on your tombstone." Ryan raised the muzzle of the SIG-Sauer and pointed it directly between the boy's eyes.

Damnation! Fifteen-year-old murderers with pistols and knives. This might have been Dean's future if Ryan hadn't come along when he did, or if Sharona's plan to see to the boy's welfare had fallen by the wayside. Ryan tried to smother the flicker of guilt that raced up the back of his spine, a flicker that whispered aloud his doubts about letting this boy rejoin his caravan and report to his boss, the elusive Mr. Rollins.

Ryan sighed audibly. "I guess I have no choice," he said aloud. "Turn around and start running, and don't stop until you're long out of Florida."

Breaux, already considering himself dead and buried, blinked in shock. "You'll shoot me in the back!" he squeaked.

"If I was going to chill you, I would have done it already. Now scram."

"But my blaster—"

"Wrong. My blaster. And I'll have your balls as a keepsake, too, if you don't pack up and roll out of here. Now go on, get out of my sight." Ryan took a step forward and gestured with the blaster.

Breaux glared back at Ryan for a few seconds, his

face a mix of fear and distrust, then he was around the corner and out of the redoubt in a matter of seconds.

Ryan stepped softly around the bend of the hallway, listening as the boy's footsteps retreated. He holstered his blaster and stepped back to the elevator.

Krysty was already up and out. Ryan extended a helping hand, which she took to pull herself to her feet. She looked around the corridor at the bodies among the debris.

"And I thought this redoubt couldn't get any sorrier," she commented.

"We need to move. That kid may be back with buddies soon."

"You let him go," she said curiously.

"That's right. So?"

"Why?"

"Why not? Only a scared boy running with the big dogs. Been enough chilling for one day. Besides, by the time he gets back to wherever he's headed to tell about discovering us inside, we'll be long gone," Ryan said.

"You saw Dean, didn't you?"

Ryan didn't answer.

"You took a long look and saw your own son perched at the receiving end of a blaster, and you couldn't blow him away," Krysty said flatly.

Ryan kept silent and turned away, walking over to the elevator. He peered down in the darkness of the shaft and waved at a shadowy J.B., who had continued to cling patiently to the ladder in wait for a signal.

"About freakin' time," the Armorer griped.

ON THE OTHER SIDE of the forced-open elevator doors were the remains of the ransacked redoubt. During the group's first pass through this complex many months earlier, the rooms on the upper floor had offered a safe haven with food, clothing, weaponry and ammunition. This time there was nothing for the travelers but utter devastation. The walls of the compact redoubt were cracked and blackened with soot and bullet holes from random firings or disagreements such as the one glimpsed between the four dead men below. Evidence of cooking fires could be seen on the floor; ashes mixed with dirty water that stood on the floor in shallow puddles.

In the sleeping areas, the dormitories were ransacked. All bedding had been stolen or ruined. Only a few skeletal bed frames remained. The dining area and kitchens were in the same condition, and all of the supply larders were empty, their steel shelves barren of any cans or boxes. The freezers were also clean, each of them offering nothing but a few inches of foul-smelling water in the bottom catch pans and long-emptied steel cans and paper boxes.

Although the failing power supply would probably have ruined any unused frozen edibles, everyone's stomachs still ached for the loss. No tinned ham or recon eggs or cans of beans and self-heat blueberry muffins this time around. Nor would there be fresh clothing or new weapons and ammunition. This redoubt's treasures had been plundered, removed, squandered.

No dry clothing or toiletry supplies was one thing. An absence of a decent haven to lie down and rest one's weary head and body was another. But the absence of food was the most disappointing of all.

"No grub," Jak said. He added as an afterthought, "Shit."

"Well said, my friend, well said," Doc whispered bitterly.

"Damn. I'm starved, Dad," Dean piped up.

"We all are, son."

"This place was swept clean," J.B. said, walking back from the empty redoubt armory and shooting range. "There isn't anything left worth taking. Which leads to the obvious question..."

"Why were there guards posted in an empty redoubt?" Krysty finished as she slammed closed one of the large steel freezer doors. "Who knows? Pride? An overinflated sense of security?"

"Or maybe this Rollins boss the kid told me about expected visitors from down below, and that's why the elevator was sabotaged," Ryan said. "Blow out the steps, and there isn't any other way into the lower levels of the redoubt except for where they had a guard at the top of the shaft, and in through the back door by using the mat-trans unit."

"You think Rollins knew about the mat-trans chamber?" J.B. asked.

"Hell, J.B., these gateways aren't the great secret they used to be," Ryan answered. "Even back when we first hooked up with Trader, he knew about the redoubts, and there were always rumors floating around about some kind of magic superscientific transportation devices hidden inside."

"However, there was no way they could have entered the mat-trans control room without the access codes," Mildred said. "But all the warning signs and other sec bullshit stationed around the door would have been a tip-off that there was something big in there."

It was a sobering thought.

"Maybe word about the redoubts is starting to spread among the general population, lover," Krysty said. "Once a secret like this starts to travel..." She let her voice trail off.

"Right. Next thing you know, we're walking out of gateway chambers and into the waiting ambushes of scavengers," Ryan finished.

"There's nothing here worth taking, so let's get out," J.B. declared, wiping sweat from his brow. The heat was becoming stifling.

The walk to the main access door of the redoubt took only seconds. Ryan and the others saw that the blond youth had spoken the truth. A big hole replaced the vanadium-steel-reinforced sec door, which had been capable of withstanding a direct hit from a nuke.

"Dark night," J.B. whispered. He ran a hand along the jagged edges of the remains of the reinforced door frame.

"I'd say whoever came through here last didn't bother to knock," Mildred said.

Chapter Five

The friends stood together in front of the remains of the sec door and stared out through the gaping hole into the green of the world. Waves of warm, damp air wafted out over them. Even with his long jacket and weighted white scarf off, Ryan felt a new patch of sweat start to spread across his lower back. They'd all be smelling ripe soon enough in this climate.

Greenglades was just as he remembered it: lush and beautiful, and as humid as hell.

And this time there was an added bonus.

"Raining," Jak said.

"Gaia, but it's hot," Krysty commented, reaching her arms behind her neck and grasping fistfuls of her long red hair in her hands. She began to twist the hair into a makeshift bun to keep it off her neck.

Dean slapped at an insect. "Little shit." He scratched at a fresh pink bite on the back of his neck.

"Get used to it," Ryan said sharply. "We're going to be slogging through this mess for a while. And watch your language—you've been cussing more than I do! Didn't Brody teach you manners in that school of his?"

"Yes, sir," Dean said. "Taught me plenty. But he didn't teach me not to cuss."

"Funny, I thought manners were on the agenda," Ryan said. "Leastways, they were when I dropped you off there at the school."

"A lack of vocabulary is nothing to take pride in, young Cawdor," Doc interjected.

"Words is words, Doc," the boy said. "Why use big ones when the little ones will do?"

Ryan had to grin in spite of himself at that bit of logic. Even Doc was speechless.

"Out of the mouths of babes, Doc," Krysty teased. "But I'd appreciate your taking more care, Dean. For my sake."

"Okay, Krysty," Dean replied, scratching again at the bite.

J.B. examined one of the broken sides of the doorway where the vanadium-steel sec door would normally have been entrenched and whistled appreciatively. "Somebody wanted in here bad."

"What do you think they used?" Ryan asked.

"Hmm. A TOW mebbe. It's portable enough to bring into the swamps and has enough kick. I'd say it would have to be some type of heavy antitank gear." J.B.'s words were hurried as they tumbled out of his mouth in a torrent. The only time the taciturn Armorer ever showed any excitement was when discussing weapons and their destructive capabilities. "Or a mortar. Might have taken a dozen or so hits to do the job, but apparently they weren't too worried about shaking up the interior since this redoubt was already quake damaged."

"That's how they were able to get in without a

code," Mildred said. "They huffed and they puffed and they blew the house in."

"Yeah. We know these redoubts were built tough enough to withstand a lot of punishment, but even they can't hold up long against an earthshaker. After the quake did the structural damage, whoever wanted in kept hammering at the door. You hammer long enough, knowing the walls were already cracked..." J.B. let his voice trail off.

"They brought down the walls of Jericho," Doc finished.

"If you have the force of nature on your side, you can force your way into anything," Krysty murmured. "I should know."

Krysty's comment wasn't lost on the group. In addition to her empathetic abilities, the tall woman had been trained since childhood to be in tune with the electromagnetic energies of the great Earth Mother, Gaia. By tapping into these hidden pools of energy, Krysty called upon the strength of a sheer force of nature—but for a limited time, and the transformation took a terrific physical and mental toll.

She rarely forced herself to go that far, for when she was in the throes of the Earth Mother, she couldn't be held accountable for her actions. Her private fear was that she might injure a friend instead of a foe during a transformation, or even inadvertently kill one of them.

"As you were telling young Dean earlier, nobody has any manners these days," Doc said. "Still, these redoubts were built with the taxpayers' money. I suppose all have the God-given right to use them as they please.''

Doc was right. The group of travelers had grown to become somewhat possessive of the hidden redoubts, and they were far from masters of the technology inside. Mildred had once said the places were like a sick version of their home away from home. Like the old-fashioned motel chains of her youth, all of the redoubts tended to be alike, from city to city and state to state.

Since Ryan's group was in many ways nomadic, traveling from point to point with no real destination, perhaps the doctor was right. Perhaps the redoubts were indeed becoming home.

Not that any of the group of friends was ever going to become a homebody.

The mass of green outside smelled of damp, and the rain was pouring down. Outside, there was the unknown, and each and every one of them would rather venture out there than remain inside even the plushest and safest of the redoubts.

"Looks like home," Jak said about the swamplands, referring to his time spent back in Cajun country in Louisiana. "Pretty."

"That's right, Jak," Krysty said. "You weren't with us last time we set foot out here."

"No. Was back in New Mexico then. With Christina."

Krysty immediately sensed a shift in the albino's entire mental aura. The mention of his late wife had caused her memory to leap back into his mind and drop him into an even deeper funk than the glum albino normally wore as a shield against the world. It was almost like a purple shroud had suddenly enveloped his entire body, a shroud only Jak could feel, and only Krysty, by virtue of her mutant abilities, could see.

"Oh, Jak, I—" Krysty began.

"No. Not forget her. Never forget," the albino replied. "Not your fault, Krysty."

Krysty smiled gratefully at Jak, but still mentally cursed herself. She knew that Jak cherished the memories of his time spent at peace at the New Mexico ranch. Until their untimely deaths, the young man had experienced the kind of love with his wife and child that only a family can bring. For a short time, Jak Lauren had known the peace of having a place of his own away from the constant death and violence, and Krysty envied him for it.

"Where to, leader man?" Mildred asked Ryan.

"Straight ahead, to the farthest star, and take a left to morning," Doc interjected before Ryan could reply. "Or not," he added, seeing the flash of annoyance in Ryan's eye.

"J.B., what do you think?"

"Not much point in going west—that's where the Cajuns were camping out last. If we stay on the path we took before, we'll end up inside the park."

"At least we're familiar with the layout there," Ryan said. "We'll go that way until we see or hear something to convince me otherwise."

THEY PASSED by the shredded remains of an animated Zulu warrior and his rhino companion outside the redoubt's doorway. On their previous visits, when they had first ventured outside, Ryan had stepped on a trigger switch that brought the pair to life. In retaliation, his companions had laid down a hail of bullets so fast Ryan had barely enough time to hit the grass.

Androids. Part of the attraction at Greenglades Theme Park.

What was left of the pair had now fallen prey to the growth of the swamp, the heavy rains and the earthquakes. Both warrior and rhino were completely enveloped by tendrillike green vines. If Ryan hadn't known where to look, he never would have spotted the pair a second time.

"You know, now that we're not out here with our guns blazing away at those droids, something just occurred to me."

"What's that, Mildred?" Ryan asked.

"I wonder why this redoubt was located in the middle of a swamp that served as a public site for family amusement? I doubt mat-trans units were listed on the official see-and-do itinerary."

"Perhaps it was a way of getting the top political bosses and their families into the park unseen," Doc mused. "Security for government leaders has always been a problem whenever the power elite took a notion to mingle with the common folk."

"True. The First Family could step into a chamber in Washington, and in less than a minute, appear here. Want to suck up to a senator? Bring him down south.

Got a major conglomerate head you want to grease? Impress him with a magic visit to Florida. The same could apply to visiting foreign dignitaries and heads of state. I mean, what better way to impress a Russian or Chinese leader than to transport them into the fantasy kingdom of Greenglades Park for a night of fun and games?" Mildred asked rhetorically.

"That's all well and good, but you're forgetting that the redoubts and the mat-trans units were supposed to be top secret," Ryan said. "I doubt any leaders were shuttling in the wife and kids for a day's entertainment at government expense, unless he was the big boss or something."

"Ryan, you'd be surprised," Mildred replied, thinking of the endless parade of political scandals over the abuse of perks and privileges she'd witnessed on the six-o'clock news. Once, the leaders of the United States were on the front pages of newspapers day in and day out over using too many stamps for personal gain or playing footsie with underage assistants or commandeering public-funded transportation for their own personal use.

A man who didn't hesitate to climb aboard an emergency federal aircraft for a weekend on the golf course with his buddies wouldn't think twice over hopping into a mat-trans unit to get somewhere scenic and entertaining.

But that was a part of Mildred Wyeth's previous life, a life that seemed more like a dream or a story she'd read in a book as time passed on.

"This redoubt was stuck in here because Greenglades offered the perfect cover. They probably included the redoubt blueprints in with the ones for the park, then built them at the same time," J.B. said flatly. "Never been any logic to where the Totality Concept placed their mat-trans units."

"Got a point," Ryan said, thinking of the surreal journey he and Mildred had taken a few months back, secured in icy coffins that were raised up by crane through Abraham Lincoln's stone nose into the hidden fortress known as the Anthill. There, inside the cavernous interior of the remains of Mount Rushmore, were cargo and human mat-trans units, sec droids and mad cyborgs.

"One day, I'd like to meet the stupe bastard who came up with all the stuff the Totality Concept had their fingers in," J.B. mused.

Ryan was surprised. His friend rarely expressed much of an interest in anything beyond weapons.

"Why?"

"It would be my greatest honor to personally chill him or her."

THE RAIN WAS THE WORST possible kind to have to endure. J.B. had given up on trying to keep his glasses clear, and now walked resolutely at the back of the group, depending more on sound and his own combat-honed senses than his vision. He'd thought about just taking his glasses off, but his poor eyesight had quickly changed his mind. Better to be half-blind than completely in a blurry haze.

The grass beneath their feet was thick and long,

curling up around their ankles as they slogged through the marshland. The earth was moist and spongy, sucking at everyone's feet with each tedious step. The entire group was miserable. Some, like Ryan, had taken off a layer of their outer clothing, while others, such as Doc, kept fully dressed. Neither method offered true relief since bare skin offered up a banquet to the small, darting mosquitoes that had bitten Dean back at the redoubt, while keeping covered was like having to march in a blast furnace while wrapped in a mass of sodden quilts.

"Hard to believe anyone would want to come to this hellhole for a vacation," Mildred said, wiping at her forehead with an already soaked sleeve.

"As I recall, madam, the young and the old flocked to Florida for the scenic beaches and tanning rays of the sun, not the steady drizzle or the state's varied swamplands," Doc said, his long white hair drooping around his head like the strands of a dirty mop.

"Give me the mountains any day of the week," Mildred responded.

"Hold up," Ryan said from the front of the line. He'd been following the slowly moving river, looking for some kind of a landmark they might remember from before. Nothing as obvious as a sign or a chained-off area presented itself, but ahead of them was a huge fallen tree made of fiberglass and plastic, part of the park's once carefully cultivated veneer. The path Ryan had been following vanished beneath the fake redwood, and an even denser growth of bushes lay beyond.

"Used to be a bridge here," J.B. said confidently, his remarkably sharp memory coming into play. "Stretched out clean across the water."

"And boats," Dean added. "All kinds of plastic boats with ripped-up roofs and funny names."

"*Queen of the South*," Doc said. "I recall that was one of the poor stranded hulks. But where the sad *Queen* and all of her familiars have vanished, I cannot say."

"Bridge probably fell in the quake," Krysty suggested. "And those boats weren't exactly secure."

"Doesn't matter," Ryan said. "I recognize the tree."

"Alas, even the mighty redwoods cannot withstand the power of the land," Doc said.

"Sure, Doc. Whatever," Ryan said absently, trying to get some relief from the rain by standing beneath a second, unfelled mock redwood.

"All right, this spot here is close to where the sec man Kelly got the drop on us first time we came through. This visit, I think we'll try and be a little more subtle until we see what the situation is."

"Think folk still here?" Jak asked.

"Could be. One thing we do know is that many of the people living in the ville were chilled in the fight with Traven, and my guess is with Larry dead, there wouldn't be reason to hang around this place for long once the rides went down and the electricity messed up."

"Debate as you will, friends. I'm going to fetch a

drink," Doc said, heading for the shallow edge of the riverbank. "I am frightfully parched."

"Mildred, any chance of this water being drinkable?" Ryan asked.

"No reason it shouldn't be," the doctor replied. She turned after the departing Doc, unable to resist adding, "My advice is to be more worried about what's *in* the water."

Ryan agreed. "Got a point, Mildred. J.B., go with Doc. Keep an eye out for snakes. If the water's okay, we can refill our ration canteens."

The Armorer nodded and followed Doc to the edge of the slowly moving water.

Standing near his father, Dean looked a little uncomfortable at the mention of snakes, since he had nearly had the life squeezed out of him by a multi-hued mutated boa constrictor in his previous visit to this section of Greenglades.

"You thirsty, Dean?" Ryan asked.

"No. No, I think I'll stay right where I am, Dad."

"Be nice to go skinny-dipping in there, lover. Take the edge of this wet heat." Krysty said, crooking an arm through one of Ryan's elbows. "After sweating for so long in the redoubt, then stomping around all afternoon in this fetid mess, I'm sure all of us could use a dunking."

"I hear you, but I think I'd rather go for a swim when the rain stop—"

Their conversation was interrupted by a high-pitched shriek from Doc.

Chapter Six

Less than five minutes before Ryan and Krysty would be interrupted by his panicked cry, Doc knelt carefully at the muddy edge of the murky waters and cupped his hands to drink.

"How's it taste?" J.B. asked, stepping up behind the kneeling Doc. The Armorer was scanning the surface of the water, looking for signs of movement. He took off his glasses for the hundredth time since venturing into Greenglades, and tried to wipe them clear on his shirt. Even with the scene in front of him being blurry, J.B. could tell the river's flow could be tracked in centimeters, like slow, sticky molasses. Where the water began and ended was open for debate.

Doc took a tentative sip of the liquid, then another. He smiled and lowered his face into the remainder of the water in his hands, washing his face and eyes. He leaned back and gave out a lengthy exhalation of relief.

"Cool and wet, my friend, cool and wet." Doc took out his swallow's-eye kerchief and dipped it into the water, soaking the fabric and then wringing out the excess moisture.

"Real or fake?" J.B. asked Doc.

"What? This water? Real as it gets!" Doc replied.

"No, the river. Natural or man-made?"

Doc pondered the query for a second. "I am perplexed, John Barrymore. In the scheme of all things great and small, does it really matter?"

"Guess not," J.B. replied. "Just wondering."

"I question my sanity at moments such as these," Doc said, placing the damp rag on his neck beneath the collar of his frock coat. "In the midst of a steady, warm rain, I am trying to ease my discomfort with the touch of more water. Such is the logic of Deathlands."

J.B. removed his canteen from his belt and extended the small metal canister to Doc, who ignored it. Doc was busy shifting his body, leaning back on his haunches and getting out of his kneeling position. For a brief time, his body froze in an awkward pose before flopping backward and allowing him to end up sitting on his butt on one of the larger rocks jutting up from the river's edge.

"While you're down there playing in the water, fill this up, would you?" J.B. said, waving the battered canteen for a second time.

"In a moment, John Barrymore," Doc replied, reaching down to pull off one of his high black boots. "I have personal duties to attend to first. If you cannot wait, please avail yourself personally of the facilities. I am afraid we have no running hot water, but at least it is safe."

J.B. snorted, watching as Doc removed one boot and one grayish white sock. A long bony foot whiter than the pallor of Jak's skin appeared as Doc peeled away the unwashed hosiery.

Once he realized what Doc was preparing to do, J.B.'s inclination to tend to his own canteen was spurred into frantic action. He bolted forward and knelt on one knee, dunking his open canteen into the river and filling the portable container.

"Help me with my second boot, friend Dix," Doc asked, struggling to remove his other boot. "I fear it has become a permanent part of my left leg."

His canteen refilled, J.B. stood and clamped it back securely to his belt. Next to him, Doc impatiently waggled his still-booted foot. "You pull one way and I shall pull the other, and together we shall free my appendage of its leathery imprisonment," Doc said. "Allowing me to wave all ten toes in a gesture of gratitude."

"Need my hands free to draw in case some mutie bastard crawls out of the water."

Doc used his bare foot as a brace on the booted heel and pushed. At the same time, he utilized both his hands to shove down on the upper part of his boot. The result from his efforts took both Doc and J.B. by surprise.

The footwear exploded off his leg and went sailing away, wobbling as the empty boot came down with a splash nearly midpoint in the river.

J.B. almost fell over in the shallows of the river, his entire body shaking with laughter. Doc got to his feet, one leg bare up to his calf, the other covered with a white sock, and marched out into the water with as much dignity as he could muster to retrieve his boot.

"Hold up, Doc," J.B. called. "We don't know how deep that river is. You might need some help finding your flying footwear."

"Thank you for your words of caution, John Barrymore, but I think I can find my way to where my boot landed without your holding my hand."

"Suit yourself." J.B. grinned. "But if a croc takes a bite out of your scrawny ass, don't come crying to me."

Still, J.B. kept a careful watch. Doc waded out easily enough, and the water never went beyond his waist as he reached his half-submerged boot. He grabbed the boot and held it high like a trophy as he began to return to the riverbank, never dreaming his movements had indeed triggered the attention of a silent parasite, but a parasite unlike any he'd ever been exposed to before.

Even in Doc's day, a few quack practitioners could still be found in back rooms and barber shops extolling the curative powers of the common leech. As a young lad in the 1870s, he had an aunt who swore by the slimy creatures. Doc's primary memory of her appearance was that the old woman was missing many of her teeth.

The aunt came to visit on holidays with a jar of her favorite leeches. She'd laugh at the boy's discomfort as she plopped an assortment of the pulpy beasts on her fleshy arms.

"Suck the poison right outta there," she would say,

laughing, and always end by extending one of the remaining leeches out under the young Tanner's nose. "Make you feel twenty years younger! Sure you don't want to try one?"

Doc would flee the guest room in tears.

Now, with the horror of the mutated leech directly under his bare feet, Doc would gladly have take a baker's dozen of the small leeches his aunt Mary had carried around in her glass jar.

The leech was on Doc before the old man ever knew what had happened. Stirred up from slumber by his walking along the river's sediment-covered floor, the creature was nearly eight feet in length. The wormy mutation was vibrantly colored in shades of red and turquoise against black.

Already one posterior sucker had softly attached itself from below to Doc's unprotected foot, and now, using the anchor his flesh provided, the other end of the leech elongated up out of the river from behind. The pseudopod stretched around and above Doc's shoulder, a tentacle intent on finding another haven of flesh to attach to.

Unfortunately for Doc, the widest possible area was his unprotected face.

The first attaching from the disklike sucker below the river's surface was as gentle as a baby's kiss as it clung to the upper part of Doc's bare foot and calf. The many jagged teeth centered inside the other, front sucker came into play as they oozed over and down upon his unsuspecting face.

Watching from the shore, J.B. didn't comprehend

what was occurring since his vision was still less than reliable from the mist covering his glasses. It took Doc's sudden shout of horror—and the abrupt ending of his cry—to alert J.B. that something had gone terribly wrong.

Hearing the scream, the others on shore raced toward the river. Ryan's keen eye spotted the problem immediately as the old man stumbled back and forth. He hadn't fallen down in the water yet, but it was only a matter of time before he lost his footing.

"Bloodsuckers," Ryan murmured. "Fireblast, but that's the biggest one I've ever seen."

"Christ, Ryan, what kind of leech is that?" Mildred asked in disbelief.

"Mutie. Drain a man dry in minutes."

Dean raised his Browning to fire, but Krysty slapped it down.

"No, Dean. The bullets will tear right through that horror. You might hit Doc!"

Ryan had already dropped his blasters. He'd drawn his panga and run toward the river as soon as he heard Doc's panicked voice ring out. But J.B. was closer. The Armorer had cast aside his Uzi and the Smith & Wesson M-4000 scattergun and was preparing to dive into the water when Mildred cried out a warning.

"John, don't go in. There's bound to be more of them!"

J.B. hesitated, but only for the span of a second, only until Ryan kept moving past him and went under, choosing to swim. As the one-eyed man took the lead, J.B. jumped in after him. However, J.B. chose to keep his body above water, wading out toward the struggling Doc as his old friend swam below. The Armorer had also pulled his own blade, a keenly honed Tekna knife.

In the dirty haze of the river, Ryan was soon able to spot Doc's legs, and pushed his body closer while trying to keep alert to the presence of any more of the huge mutated leeches. Or worse yet, any other kind of mutations that might approach, attracted by the commotion.

Behind Ryan, J.B. kicked up dirt and silt from the river bottom and was rewarded with a bloodsucker of his own. The orange-and-yellow creature had been lying in wait, disturbed at first by the other leech's efforts to ensnare Doc, and now by the vibrations and the stirring up of the muddy floor of the river.

The beast slithered toward J.B.—eyeless, blind— drawn to him as the other had been drawn to Doc by the vibrations in the water. The freakish creature came up, undulating around and behind the Armorer, slithering its anterior end up under his leather jacket.

J.B. felt the movement and tried to crane his neck around to see what was on his back. As he turned his head one way and then the other, he spied the lower part of the vibrantly colored leech extending down from under his coat. Each ringlike segment was quivering obscenely as it slid farther and farther into his clothing.

"Dark night!" he muttered in disgust as he hurriedly pulled off the jacket as well as he could, first freeing one arm and then the other. He began to twist the sleeves tighter and tighter, finally managing to crush part of the bloodsucker inside the coat. A brackish red fluid started to pour from under the leather, and a horrific smell of decay flooded J.B.'s nostrils, making him gag even as he continued to crush the mutated leech with his bare hands.

When Ryan reached Doc, the old man had fallen over in the water, his legs kicking up as he struggled to breathe. The panga bit deep into the pulpy surface of the leech, releasing a pulsing stream of red blood. More and more of the thick fluid came rushing out as Ryan pulled the blade downward in a vertical slash along the leech's body.

Ryan pulled Doc upright, trying to get him to stand on his own two feet, while J.B. staggered over and wrapped an arm around Doc's waist. The old man's body continued to thrash and contort as he struggled for survival. "He hasn't gone limp yet, and that's a good sign," Ryan said as he gripped the edges of the dying bloodsucker's anterior end that still clung to Doc's face.

He hesitated, not knowing just how tightly the leech had attached itself. The creature had dozens upon dozens of tiny, needle-sharp teeth, and all of them were buried in Doc's flesh. Ripping the leech away might save Doc's life but disfigure him permanently.

"Do it," J.B. said, sharing Ryan's thoughts. "Better alive and ugly than dead and pretty."

Ryan begin to tug, hoping he wasn't going to pull away most of the old man's face. Unfortunately the leech proved to be annoyingly true to its name. Even after the beast's death throes, the now slack creature refused to let go.

"No good. I'm going to pull his eyes right out of his head like this," Ryan said. "I'll have to cut it off."

He peered intently at the join where the bloodsucker's skin met Doc's and gave himself a quarter-inch margin for error. The tip of the honed blade of the panga slid into the bloodsucker, and Ryan pulled the blade down. More of the creature's red life's fluid poured out, coating his hands and upper arms. The coppery smell of fresh blood hung in the air like a sodden blanket. Ryan knew the new color was Doc's blood, sucked out by the parasitic beast.

He had cut away half of the leech's head when it finally let go, the evil teeth releasing their hold. The one-eyed man peeled the rest of the sagging mess of grue back from Doc's pale white face like a gory death mask.

"Thank you!" Doc gasped, sucking in a chestful of air. The dead-fish pallor of his skin was offset by an almost perfect red ring from chin to forehead where the attaching teeth of the bloodsucker had bit. He coughed in between gulps of air.

"Can you walk?" Ryan asked, glancing at the river water. "We've got to get out of here before more of these bastard leeches show up."

Doc didn't say anything, but his body did the talking for him as he stepped forward and headed for shore. J.B. spied the lost boot half floating, half submerged behind Doc. He snatched it up, pouring out the water that had collected inside as he and Ryan followed the old man as quickly as they dared.

"THERE IS NO SAFE HAVEN," Doc whispered, all of the fight sucked out of him along with what Mildred guessed to be over two pints of blood.

"Not true. Safe haven was at the riverbank. You're the one who left it to go splashing around the water, and look what it got you," Mildred replied as she cleaned the deep wound on the upper part of his left foot. "This will take a little longer to heal than your average abrasion, and this rain isn't going to help. Bloodsucking leeches produce a chemical called hirudin. It prevents the blood from thickening and makes it easier for the leech to—"

"I get the picture, Dr. Wyeth," Doc said weakly. "Your words and terminology paint a most disturbing portrait."

"How soon before he can walk?" Ryan asked.

"Now—if he wants to. He may look like hell, but there's no real damage to keep him off his feet. I wouldn't recommend a long march until he's had some sleep and a chance to build back his blood supply, but he's good for a while. I had some antiseptic to clean out where the leech attached to his foot and face. Luckily the teeth on his face didn't go deep. Those marks should fade soon without any scarring."

Looking at Doc's bandaged foot, Dean held a mental picture of the wound beneath the gauze and suppressed the urge to vomit. If he had any say-so in his lifetime again, the boy knew he would never venture into another swamp. They were triple-bad luck.

Mildred pulled a dry sock onto Doc's injured foot and over the bandages—the extra pair had been squirreled away by Dean in a pocket. Although too small for Doc's long feet, the donated hosiery had the advantage of not being sodden.

J.B. assisted Mildred with pulling on Doc's long boots. Using their shoulders as a brace, the older man pulled himself to his feet. Krysty handed Doc the silver lion's-head swordstick, and he began to hobble around.

"Funny seeing Doc use stick for walking 'stead of sticking," Jak commented.

"Good as new?" Krysty asked hopefully.

"Not hardly, but I am not ready for the scrap heap of the broken-down bodies and minds of the elder folks' home as of yet, madam," Doc replied, balancing himself carefully and holding up his injured ankle. "The good Dr. Wyeth has managed to patch my hide yet again, and for that, I am grateful."

J.B. was peering around the grassy jungle. He turned and waved Ryan over to where he was standing.

"See something?" Ryan asked, holding his blaster in a defensive position.

"Through this murk?" J.B. replied sourly, taking off his glasses and glaring down at the rain-streaked lenses. "Not much. Glad we're not under attack by some marauders right now. Chopping up mutie leeches under my nose is one thing, but I'd hate to have to try and aim my blaster at something smaller than a barnyard door.''

''So, what did you want?'' Ryan said. ''You're facing in the wrong direction. I don't feel like backtracking.''

''Glance over there to the right, back a little from where we came,'' the Armorer replied. ''I can't be sure without my glasses, but I believe there's a break in a wire sec fence over there. That's a fake backdrop on top. Must've been to fool folks out here. If we can squeeze through, should bring us right out in the park.''

Ryan peered at the spot. ''You're right, J.B. I'll tell the others.''

ONE QUICK EXPLANATION later, and the party collected at the torn fencing.

''Once was trail here. Short cut,'' Jak said, kneeling. He stood and halfheartedly brushed the mud off of his knees. ''Not used in long time.''

''I'll go through,'' Ryan said, pulling aside the rusted mesh and stepping through.

On the other side, he extracted himself from the fencing as carefully as possible, enjoying the feel of hard asphalt under his feet. He saw some machinery and a lone open control panel; deep, dark grease and oil stains that time and the rain still hadn't managed to clear away; faded white and yellow lines on the ground. Ryan decided he was behind one of the mechanical attractions of Boss Larry Zapp's amusement park.

Ryan made his way around to the front, seeing a fallen mass of painted metal. Some cables were still attached, spiderlike, to a scaffolding above. The ride looked small, like a thrill-cart adventure that spun in a tight circle for the thrill junkie.

He gave a tuneless whistle, and the rest of the group joined him.

"I'd say the baron's place is closed for the season," Mildred said.

Ryan was about to agree with her assessment when a new complication presented itself. He inwardly cursed himself for not being more thorough in his initial check of the area.

"I remember you," an unfamiliar leathery voice said from behind Ryan's left ear. "I remember you all."

Chapter Seven

Ryan spun in the direction of where the words had come from, dropping to one knee and pulling out his blaster with practiced ease. Other members of the group followed suit, taking out their own assortment of weapons and aiming in the same direction as Ryan.

The sudden appearance of firepower was more than overkill for the sad sight they discovered they were confronting.

A lean man dressed in a yellow shortsleeved sport shirt and threadbare plaid shorts was standing next to the entranceway of the ride formerly known as The Whirling Upchuck. He wore a pair of well-used tan leather sandals, and the top of his bald head was beaded with raindrops as he looked at the plethora of weapons aimed at his face, neck and groin. He raised a liver-spotted hand in a universal sign of greeting.

"You can put away the cannons, young fella. I'm not packing any heat today. Left it inside where I was watching you. Too wet out."

"That's a good way to get chilled fast, old man," Ryan said.

"So what? I'm one foot in the flippin' graveyard anyway. You'd be doing me a favor," the man snorted. "What happened out in the swamps? I thought I heard gunfire, but it was too muffled for me to be sure. Course, you hear all kinds of things from out in the swamps these days.''

"We made some new friends," Ryan said cryptically. "But they weren't too friendly."

"What, the man-eatin' frogs? Killer snakes? Mutie cranes? I've seen 'em all."

Ryan chuckled mirthlessly. "You make all that sound almost funny."

"Well, it is, unless you're the one with your balls caught in their teeth."

Dean piped up, "Naw, all we had to contend with was a couple of giant leeches. Almost sucked Doc but good and dry."

The old man blinked. "Goddamn, that's a new one on me," he said. "Giant leeches. Hell's bells."

"So, you think you know us?" Ryan stated.

The old man nodded.

"Well, I don't remember you," Ryan replied. "You must be losing it—happens with age."

"Nope. Uh-uh. I may look like a decrepit old rip to you people, and I'll be the first to admit I'm nowhere near as fast as I used to be, but my eyes are still sharp and the mind's clear. I used to work in the now nearly extinct art of creating illegal identification cards and access passes, and I was always good with faces.

"Let's see now," he muttered, nodding to each member of the group as he spoke. "A black woman beside a white man with spectacles, a tall drink of water with long white hair, a beautiful woman with flame red hair, and a boy on the shirttail of a grim man wearing an eye patch. Don't recognize the pink-eye—he's new, and the boy's grown a bit, but still…yeah, you were the outlanders who passed through here when that son of a bitch fairy was trying to take the place out from under Boss Larry."

Ryan's keen warrior senses, developed over the long years of survival in Deathlands, had gone into triple red from the time the man appeared. There were plenty of spots for a sniper's nest in this part of the park, along with ample cover if one wanted to plan an ambush. The wrinkled man in the ugly summer clothes could be a diversion.

Still, none of the danger signs had come creeping across his skin.

"Krysty…?" Ryan didn't need to verbalize the rest of his request. He knew the woman would already be using her "seeing" abilities to check for any kind of hidden presence or threat.

"Not feeling a thing, lover," she replied. "I'd say the old coot is exactly what he appears to be."

"No need to be insulting, young lady," the man said. "The name's William B. Chapman. You can call me Wild Bill, if you can say it with a straight face."

Actually to say the man was an "old coot" was about as accurate as referring to the nuke war that had brought about skydark as a "friendly pillow fight." William B. Chapman looked like a walking frame-work of bones and sinew, topped off with a sunburned raisin for a head. He made even the skeletal Doc Tanner look as young and rosy as Dean.

"I'm Ryan Cawdor. This is my boy, Dean," Ryan said as a greeting, then introduced the rest of the travelers in turn.

"Glad to meet you, Mr. Cawdor. All of you. We don't get many visitors these days," Bill said.

"You're one of the wrinklies from outside the park," Dean said, referring to the condo development located between Greenglades ville and the swamps. In his more coherent days before the dreem rotted his intellect, Larry Zapp had set up the place as a walled safe haven for the old and infirm, as long as they had enough jack to afford his protection.

Never one to pass up the means to make a profit, Larry had taken a former minimum-security prison equipped with separate bungalows and modified it for his own use. After first learning of the setup, Mildred hadn't been able to resist commenting that Larry had managed to make retiring to Florida take on a whole new meaning.

Getting old in Deathlands had to really be a bitch, Ryan reflected. He'd never really thought about getting older—watching Doc deal with the weariness of body and soul on a daily basis was enough to push the image of a seventy-year-old Ryan Cawdor hobbling around the rad-strewed byways far from his mind. In his younger days of riding at the Trader's side on War Wag One, Ryan had always assumed that he'd never live long enough to worry about advancing age.

Now he had a son to care for, and a group of friends who depended on him.

He also had, for all intents and purposes, a wife.

Ryan knew that located in a guarded corner of Krysty's well-protected mind was the hope they would all be able to return someday to a safe haven and spend the last years of their lives together content and safe. A noble dream, and Ryan shared the sentiment.

He only hoped he lived long enough to see the day.

"I am indeed a former resident of Zapp's Rainbow's End Retirement Complex," Bill confirmed.

"Former?" Doc asked.

"Boss Larry's passing meant an end to our security, young fella," Bill said. His choice of term for Doc caused everyone to grin. Doc hadn't been addressed as young in a long, long time. "Although, truth be known, even with all of Larry's alarms and motion detectors and armed security men, we were still trapped on the inside like chickens in the henhouse when the fox came calling."

Ryan knew firsthand how the security of the retirement complex was a blessing and a curse. The elderly compound inhabitants had been one of the lures for Adam Traven, who in addition to his pimping and drug selling, also had a sick blood fetish. Soon after his arrival in Greenglades, Traven had started leading his youthful followers over the wall in the retirement area on a regular basis for long bloody nights of "dark snaking," a term Traven had invented for the murder sprees he'd conducted.

Those who owned the tidy homes inside the complex had paid a bundle in order to sleep at night with the impression that nothing could get in to harm them. They were wrong.

Once past the guards into the backyards, it took little effort to break a window, slip a latch, then enter and creep around the interior of the chosen home as the elderly inhabitants slept, blissfully unaware of the horrors that had invaded their lives.

Unaware until Traven woke them up and the gutting began.

An unarmed Ryan had been forced to accompany Traven and seven of his followers on one of the killing sprees. By the time Ryan had gained the advantage, only two of the killers had escaped his own murderous wrath, and it was the last time Traven would ever harm an innocent.

"I remember seeing your group when the late Mrs. Owen accosted the park's head sec man about wanting Boss Larry to add more protection," Bill said. "Guess Larry had his own problems at the time, huh?"

"Yeah, you might say that," Ryan agreed.

"I came out here to offer you folks some supper and a dry roof," Bill said, gesturing at the gray, stormy sky. "This joint ain't what it once was, but I've managed to keep my own patch of heaven functioning. Come on, you can check out Central Avenue. It's the main spoke toward the Centerpoint tower and restaurant and the best and quickest way to cut through the park."

A STATUE OF GUSSY GOOSE held up a broken wing in a sad greeting as they went through the twisted iron gates that led to the incredible Greenglades replica of a turn-of-the-century small-town American street. Central Avenue was a collection of shops and eating establishments, with a city hall, a fire station, an old-time cinema and even a post office all located shoulder to shoulder. An appropriately seedy penny arcade promised thrills and excitement for a mere cent. A ladies' boutique advertised the latest in spring hats from Paris.

Near the end of the street, a large granite railroad station was tucked away in a far corner. A twin extension of elevated spaghettilike tracks for silver monorail cars to glide to and fro, carrying passengers to other parts of Greenglades, stretched out from the second floor. The monorail tracks had fallen in several places near the exits of the station, eliminating the possibility of any future journeys.

More evidence of transportation could be seen on the avenue proper, as well—horse-drawn trolleys minus the steeds to pull them along, double-decker touring buses with stripped engines and flattened tires, pitted yet somehow still red fire engines and ancient replicas of horseless carriages once gave visitors the option of riding instead of walking, but now all the vehicles were frozen and silent.

Some of the little buildings along Central Avenue were in better repair than others. Boss Larry hadn't allowed Ryan and the others to tour this section of the park during their earlier stay, probably because of its ill repair. The fat baron's ego wouldn't and couldn't have allowed guests to view any part of his domain that was less than perfect.

The memories and thoughts the quaint street triggered in each member of Ryan's party were different—for Doc and Mildred, a vision of what America once was during their individual lifetimes came rushing back, more so for Doc, who had literally lived in such a turn-of-the-century setting with his family, but even the younger Mildred had seen this type of homey ambience on a daily basis during her small-town Southern childhood.

For J.B. and Dean, such period architecture had only been glimpsed in books and vids, yet at the same time, there was a sense of place and community here, even in the exaggerated form the theme park provided. And for Ryan and Krysty, the cracked sidewalks and overgrown flower beds, the broken shop windows and elegantly sculpted rooftops, the nonfunctioning fountain at the center of the hub at the end of the street—all of it was a whispered kiss of what a man's and a woman's life could be, and once was, before the darkness fell across the world.

Only Jak seemed unmoved.

"What happened after we left?" Mildred asked as they walked down colorful Central Avenue and approached the central hub of the theme park.

"All hell broke loose, missy, that's what happened," Bill replied. "Most of us still in the retirement complex didn't know much about blasters or fighting. That's what we were paying Boss Larry's boys for. A few of us had blasters and at least had the presence of mind to take up the guard stations, but after a week or two, we decided we were guarding ourselves against nothing but a case of boredom. The murders in the complex had stopped. We found out later Traven was sneaking in with his band of crazies and killing off families for kicks.''

The group strolled past the mock streets of Central Avenue and entered a new section, easily identified by the new color of the curbs, trash cans and other markers.

''Here we go—Magicland. The most popular part of Greenglades Theme Park.'' Although the old man tried to sound jovial in his mock introduction, there was no mistaking the hint of bitterness that lurked in the back of his throat.

This section of the amusement park was a shock to everybody. Even though some of the rides had started to exhibit signs of age or lack of adequate repair during Larry's reign, now the once carefully cultivated grounds were overgrown and tangled with vines. The paved walkways were chipped and cracked from the earthquakes, and many of the larger colorful rides had fallen over in a massive heap of metal, creating a rusted shambles.

''What happened to this place?'' Ryan asked as he stepped over a flattened weather-beaten sign of a cartoon seal in a striped vest and straw hat that instructed Younger Magicland Visitors Shorter Than Me Need To Wait Until They've Grown Another Few Inches!

''Cajuns is what happened,'' Bill replied, his lined

face wrinkling even further at the mention of the name. His brown eyes had almost disappeared into cavernous pits under his long forehead. "Crazy sons of bitches. Once word got around about Boss Larry going down for the count, Greenglades became open season."

"Cajuns long way from home," Jak stated.

"Yeah, I guess they were at that," Bill replied, rubbing his white-stubbled chin. "Even back in the days of Boss Larry, bands of 'em had crossed over from Louisiana into the upper panhandle. Time passed, it just got worse. The Cajuns were always causing Boss Larry to have fits, but none of his sec men were willing to wade out and try and take 'em on in their own environment, no matter how much jack Boss Larry put up. I heard it was nuke trouble— some kind of rad leak cooked the bastards right out of their swampy hellhole."

"You heard right," came J.B.'s voice from the back of the group. "We've been there. Nothing left of that part of Louisiana but a sunbaked desert."

Ryan nodded in agreement with his old friend's words, remembering everyone's shock when they had first stepped out of the Louisiana redoubt. They knew from a previous journey the dark blue colors of the gateway armaglass walls were located in a redoubt in the Louisiana swamplands, close to where they had first encountered Jak Lauren.

They'd gone up to the sec door of the redoubt and opened it, expecting a picture similar to the one when they arrived in Greenglades: majestic pecan trees and groves of ancient cypresses covered in a shroud of Spanish moss, all growing up from the dank waters of the bayous. Instead, their eyes had almost been fried in their sockets by the glare of white light. Outside was nothing but glassy sand and scrub brush, topped off with a coating of shimmering heat so thick you could almost touch it.

Ryan remembered stepping out into the yellowish haze and immediately wanting a drink of water, due to the heat and how parched the area looked. Just to make extracertain they hadn't gotten their redoubts confused, J.B. had risked a quick glance at the sweltering sun to take a reading from his sextant. His reading concurred with the color of the armaglass, and Doc's memory of the single, heartbreaking word of graffiti "Goodbye" scrawled in pen at the redoubt's exit.

This was indeed the swamplands of Louisiana, and in the time between their jumps, the entire area had become a wasteland. Sudden change never came as a true shock in Deathlands, but there seemed to be no logical explanation for what had caused such a radical transformation.

Still, there was no time to investigate, even if Ryan had possessed the inclination. Their button rad counters had also immediately gone into overdrive, the warning arrows shifting from a safe green to orange, and finally into a full state of crimson before Ryan and J.B. hurriedly stepped back inside and sealed the door.

For once, no one had minded a second jump.

"Ace on the line there, J.B. It makes sense now. I couldn't figure out for the life of me why Cajuns had come all this way," Ryan said. "Now we know."

"We think they saw the rad poisoning coming, so they decided to find another home with the same climate. Probably got some boats to make the trip along the gulf," Bill said. "I hear they've set themselves up along the coastline of Mississippi and Alabama, long about where Biloxi and Mobile used to be. There's all kinds of tales about a Cajun boss by the name of Rollins. Guy takes being a midget a little too close to heart, and fancies himself to be the next Napoleon."

"I know about him, Dad!" Dean interjected excitedly. "Learned his game back at the school. He was a shrimpy man with a thirst for conquering way back. Saw himself as the biggest baron in the whole world! Took over every ville he could find."

"Ah, but did you also learn that Napoleon had his Waterloo—and his Elba?" Doc asked. "The ultimate fate of any and all who become crazed with power."

"Well, he had a triple-good time while it lasted, Doc," Dean retorted.

"Napoleon, Boss Larry and now Rollins—sounds to me like another tin-plated, swaggering asshole with delusions of grandeur," Ryan commented.

Bill laughed heartily at that comment and slapped his bony thighs in delight. "Aren't they all?"

IRONICALLY ENOUGH, after passing the varied amusements, then hanging a left at Centerpoint, Bill took

the group to the Gator Motel, the very same place
they had stayed during their last visit.

The building had once been cruciform in shape,
with a central lobby at the midpoint of the four arms.
A fire from long ago had destroyed three of the arms
of the cross, therefore effectively leveling three-
fourths of the motel.

The surviving section was known as the Gator
Wing. The motif was pure jungle, with once bright
hues of shocking purple and pink and blue. The carpet
had been nearly trod through, but enough remained
in places to hint at the sea green color the floors of
the hotel had once been.

Still, despite the run-down appearance, the place
was dry.

"I would love to grab a shower," Mildred said. "I
haven't felt so sticky in I don't know when."

"You're in luck, my good woman," Bill said.
"Place still has running water, but don't overdo it
with the hot. The heater's been moaning and groaning
something fierce. The emergency generator's still up
and sparking, so there's electricity for lights as long
as we don't overdo it."

"A bath! Man, that'll be a hot pipe!" Dean said.
"Maybe they've still got some of that Prince Maya-
kovsky Splash On smelly stuff!"

Remembering the rancid odor of the long gone bad
after-shave, Krysty wrinkled her nose. "Gaia, but I
hope not," she said with a laugh.

"How many rooms do you need?" Bill asked.

"Four, if you can spare them," Ryan said, glancing

over the faces of his companions. That would provide
a double for J.B. and Mildred, Jak and Dean and him
and Krysty. A single would suffice for the compan-
ionless Doc, who deserved a reprieve from putting up
with the younger and more rambunctious Dean and
Jak. "But I guess three'll do in a pinch."

Bill laughed softly. "Four shouldn't be a problem.
Plenty of space in the Gator Wing here at the finely
appointed Gator Motel. I'm here all alone."

THE HOT WATER of the shower felt good on Ryan's
skin. After waking up soaked in the gateway chamber
that morning, and then being sodden for hours during
the rainy trek into Greenglades, with the added bonus
of the dunking courtesy of those giant leeches, he'd
debated subjecting himself to yet more water by bathing, but was now glad Krysty had insisted.

First he shaved with good hot water in the salmon
pink sink—shaving cream courtesy of the medicine
chest in the room's bath—then he discovered actual
toothpaste in the same chest, as well as a pristine cake
of soap, still shrink-wrapped in the original wrapper.
A worn but clean Gator Motel washcloth from the
storage closet outside the room would help top off the
experience.

As he turned his back to the showerhead and allowed the soothing warmth to massage his shoulders,
Ryan decided he could get used to staying in motels
when traveling. Large red welts left from the leech
along his right side from under his armpit to his buttocks were already starting to fade. He'd been lucky.

The battle could've gone much worse if he hadn't been quicker with the panga, and he might be carrying oblong scars permanently or have been sucked dry by the freakish creatures.

What had caused something like leeches to mutate into eight-foot-long monsters like that? Exposure to radiation?

Ryan sighed and decided he didn't know or really care. He pushed the memory from his mind and blanked his senses, enjoying the warm water beating down.

"Room for one more?" a feminine voice said from the other side of the thick shower curtain.

"Depends."

"On what?"

"On who that is behind the curtain. I don't want any old dried-up wrinklie in here with me."

"Sometimes you have to take a chance. Go with your gut instinct."

"It's not my gut advising me right now," Ryan admitted, feeling another kind of warmth, this time from the inside of his body, starting to spread along his groin.

"Good." Krysty pushed aside the edge of the curtain, stepping into the shower stall with him. Her fair white skin was in sharp contrast to Ryan's darker body as she turned to face him. He could see a light dusting of freckles on her shoulders and he fought the urge to reach out and cover them with caresses.

"Need some help scrubbing your back?" she

asked, reaching down and doing delicious things with her fingers.

"That's not my back," Ryan said distractedly.

"You want me to stop?"

"Not on your life."

Krysty laughed, a sensual, throaty sound that aroused Ryan even more. The tone of her laugh revealed a hint of the earthy lust he knew took over her mind and body during these interludes.

Ryan reached out a hand of his own, sliding the washcloth from her neck down to her breasts.

"You wash my back and I'll wash yours," he murmured, rubbing the cloth gently in ever tightening circles over her left breast, then her right, then back to her left. Both nipples were now erect as Krysty sighed deeply. Ryan kept rubbing, varying the pressure from hard to soft, sometimes focusing directly on the nipple, sometimes on the soft underside of the breast.

"Been too long since we've had—" she began, then Ryan covered her mouth with his own.

"No talking," he whispered. "All I hear, day in, day out, is talk. Not now."

At first the kisses were soft, teasing, but quickly escalated into a flurry of rapid tongue movements and quick inhalations. Krysty's soft breath exploded from her nostrils as Ryan lifted her up and pushed himself fully into her inviting soft warmth. They met at the waist, joined, and he had to freeze, lengthening the pleasure before sliding himself back and almost out before thrusting back in.

Once again, as he gazed down at her beauty, Ryan

silently thanked whatever fates had thrown him and Krysty together. The rare moments such as these, when they were truly alone and away from the eternal vigilance of traveling into new and dangerous territory, were a taste of true freedom and independence.

They made slow love, Ryan standing, Krysty in his arms and her legs wrapped around the small of his back, the dull pink tile of the shower stall serving as a backdrop to their impassioned coupling.

She came, once quickly and the second time much slower, willing herself to allow the pleasure and the pressure to build. The first orgasm had been sharp and fast, brought about by her body's demands, but the second was for her, and she selfishly held back until the sensual demand for release couldn't be denied. Ryan, knowing her physical arousal responses and patterns as well as his own, quickened the pace, timing his own explosive passion to match hers.

He closed his eyes, burying his face in her shoulder, beneath her heavy, wet hair, savoring the moment.

They held each other in the gentle spray of the shower, and for some reason he couldn't quite yet fathom, Ryan clung to her tight, like a drowning man to a life preserver. Again the sensation of being trapped underwater flooded across his mind, but this time he went down willingly. With Krysty at his side, he would gladly fall all the way to the bottom and beyond.

Chapter Eight

Long days had passed since Ryan and the others left the walls and attractions of Greenglades ville. Wild Bill had pointed them in the direction of what he said were the broken remains of Highway 10 from the edge of the theme park's parking lot. Surprisingly enough, numerous stripped, burned and corroded cars still dotted the asphalt lot, each one parked in its lonely slot, waiting vainly for its owner to return.

"Greenglades was located right off the highway for easy access. At least, that's what the old park brochures say. A lot of the structure was damaged in the last quake, but it's still passable. Go up this ramp here," Bill said, pointing to a broken but climbable concrete-and-steel overpass that could be seen towering above the tree line edging the park area. "And then turn left. Stay on the old road, and it'll carry you clean across the state to Jacksonville. It's pretty much a straight line to the East Coast. There should be some small villes set up along the way—nothing much, but enough to trade with and get the latest info on any marauders or other road hazards you might be walking toward."

"You're welcome to come with us, Bill," Ryan said. "Nothing left for you here, and when those Cajuns back in the swamp don't report in, I imagine there'll be others out looking for who chilled them.''

"Thanks, but no. I'm staying put. I'm too old to change my ways now, and I know where everything is. Don't want to have to go and relearn. Those Cajun bastards won't bother me. Besides, my wife's buried here, and I'd just as soon stay close to her until my time comes." The older man's voice dropped. "Don't know if a man like you can understand that, Mr. Cawdor, but that's how I feel."

A younger Ryan Cawdor wouldn't have understood Bill's logic of wanting to remain behind, tending to his dead wife's memory. A more experienced and wiser Ryan Cawdor knew exactly what their new comrade meant.

"I never question a man's feelings," Ryan said, and extended his hand. The old man took it and gave Ryan a firm handshake back. "Watch your rear flank."

"And you, yours."

The old man stood in the rain and watched the group depart. He stood there for a very long time before he turned and went home.

As a BENEFACTOR, Bill was second to none. He had insisted on sending them out with a small smattering of foodstuffs from his own kitchen, and some fresh underclothes taken from one of the plastic-wrapped supply rooms that once fed the numerous Greenglades Theme Park souvenir stands.

"You'd look great in mouse ears, Doc," Mildred had said.

"Wrong theme park, madam!" Doc snorted. "No mouse ears or ears of any sort other than my own shall adorn my noble brow, and I am not about to wear a hat decorated with the bill of that cursed goose mascot that adorns so much of the decoration here. However, you would do well to wear such attire."

"Why's that, Doc?" J.B. asked, playing along.

"All the better to tell the world firsthand she's a quack."

"Ow," J.B. cried out as Mildred slapped his upper arm. "He's the one who said it!"

"Yeah, but you were the one encouraging him, John."

However, despite Doc's reluctance to serve as a corporate shill, Dean and Jak had both eagerly accepted standard-issue baseball caps with the official Greenglades logo embroidered on the front. The rest had decided to stay with their own familiar fedoras and hats for protection.

"A little keepsake of your stay," Bill had said wistfully as he pulled the hat down on Dean's head.

Considering the rain had only let up for intermittent periods during their journey, the hats had been a wise choice. Day upon day and night upon night had been dank, dark and wet.

Roughly at the midpoint of their journey across the state, the small procession slouching through the pummeling rain for yet most of another long day's walk discovered a sign.

The sign, in red letters on white, read Good Fod Fast.

"I fear proper spelling is following close on the heels of the eradication of the King's English in modern society," Doc commented, tapping the misspelled word with the end of his swordstick as the group stood in a half circle and looked at the badly painted enticement.

"Doesn't matter, long as the food's good," J.B. said.

"You mean 'fod's good,' John," Mildred said with a smile. "You're right, though. Illiteracy never stopped a good cook unless he mixed up the sugar and the salt."

"They must've painted over an old highway road sign," Ryan said, using the edge of his panga to scratch away at the outer coating. He was rewarded with a flash of silver-and-bright-green metal beneath the badly applied cream-colored layer.

"I'll bet this was the exit sign for drivers," Mildred agreed. "Not much use for it now."

"We talk or we eat?" Jak asked impatiently.

"Might as well," Ryan said, taking the point and leading the group down the exit to the restaurant below. "Get us out of this rad-blasted rain for a while, anyway."

"Who's Tuckey, dad?" Dean asked, looking at a ruined but still legible mass of plastic that rose imposingly on twin steel legs above the sloped roof of the restaurant. One corner of the towering edifice was missing, but the name of the eatery was still readable. "Think he owns this place?"

"No," Ryan replied. "That sign's beforetime. Tuckey went down along with everybody else after the nukecaust."

Mildred was about to attempt an explanation, then thought better of it. At times, it was better to keep silent and let some of the less memorable customs and institutions from her past remain buried in the refuse and rubble of time.

"Tuckey's. Sounds like stickies," Krysty said, turning up her nose in distaste.

"Now, there's a meal I want to eat," Ryan said sarcastically, grinning back at her. "Give me a heaping helping of stickie meat."

"Gross," Mildred added.

As they approached the building proper, another sign near the thick glass-and-wood door proclaimed Visit Our Pettin Zoo. Beneath the pronouncement, in small letters, was added, Real Live Mutants!

"Wonder what's in the zoo, Dad?" Dean asked after reading the sign aloud in a careful voice. "You think they really got muties?"

"Probably, but a mutie is nothing I'd want to pet, son, and I'd sure as hell not want to put up any jack for the experience. Best leave the poor bastards alone."

Ryan held open the glass door into the restaurant and allowed the others to enter. When he pushed the door's handle, a small bell tied to the wall over their heads gave a jaunty jingle to signal their arrival.

"Well, I guess it's nice to know some things never change," Mildred said softly, her dark eyes drinking in the room's furnishings and decoration. Tuckey's was almost a perfectly preserved relic from the pre-dark days of 1974.

The interior of the eatery held everyone's eye. The dominant color was a faded reddish orange. The tables, the chairs, even the walls were covered in the vibrantly toned yet well-worn Formica. Overhead, nonworking electric lights came with plastic orange shades. The scuffed floor tiles underfoot were a mix of off-white and a light yellowish orange, arranged in a checkerboard pattern. Each of the tiles came with a small letter *T* embossed in gold in the center.

"This Tuckey guy must've loved orange," J.B. muttered.

Ryan, once he'd had his fill of the orange, took in the rest of the dining room. One older man sat at the bar, sipping at a mug of what looked like coffee-sub. A small saucer in front of him held a few blackened pieces of bread. Across from the man in a booth sat another traveler who appeared to be in his midthirties. He was eating from a bowl with a spoon and stared back at Ryan as the one-eyed man gave him the once over.

Deciding the eatery was apparently what it appeared to be, Ryan strode across the floor to a windowless wall and chose a large round table located in a corner of the dining room. Two thick orange candles were in brown bottles at the middle of the table, serving the dual function as a centerpiece and as light to eat by. He took the seat nearest the wall and leaned back. From this vantage point, he could see anyone who came in or out of the entrance, and had a good view of the dual kitchen doors to the back.

J.B. sat on his left and Dean on his right. Krysty took the chair next to Dean. Jak, Doc and Mildred completed the circle.

Summoned by the ring of the chime over the door, a waitress came from the kitchen. Attired in a dirty uniform in two shades of orange, she looked to be in her late forties. Her dark brown hair was tied back in a severe bun and tucked under an orange paper hat. A name tag above her left breast read Hi, My Name Is Sandy. The "Sandy" had been added in black marker. She carried a well-chewed yellow number-two pencil that was almost a nub in her right hand and a small notepad in the left.

"Afternoon," she drawled. "You folks passin' through, are you?"

"Right about that," Ryan said.

"I knew. I know all the locals," the waitress noted with a nod.

"Saw your sign out on the interstate and thought we'd come in and eat before it got dark," Krysty added.

She seemed pleased they had read the sign. "My husband and me, we painted that advertisement up all by ourselves. You made a good choice stoppin'. Nowhere else to eat for another forty miles, and not a better place until you hit the East Coast."

Doc rubbed his hands in anticipation of warm food.

"Pray tell, Madam Sandy, what is on the famed Tuckey's menu for a hungry traveler?"

"Same as what was on it last night. Stew."

"What kind of stew?" Doc queried.

"Stew...stew, I guess. Hell, I don't cook it, I just serve it. There's some meat, not much, but enough. Some vegetables. Pepper. You know. Stew."

"Looks like we're having stew, then," Ryan said. "You serving up real coffee?"

The waitress snorted. "We both wish, mister. No, we've got Bojar's Blend. It's a sub. Not too bad if you mix it thick."

"Fine. We'll have that, too. Bring the pot."

"How about dessert?"

Ryan was about to decline, but then caught the excited look on Dean's face. "Depends. What is it?"

"We got the special of the house," Sandy drawled.

"Any good?" Ryan asked.

"Well, it's been the special long as I can remember," Sandy replied, sidestepping the question.

Ryan frowned. "I still don't know if that's good or bad. What is it?"

"Ever sink your teeth into the chewy goodness of a pecan-nut log?" the waitress asked. "They're a specialty of the house. Each bar individually wrapped in plastic for your sanitary protection."

"Good Lord, no!" Mildred cried out before anyone else could answer.

"I think we'll pass," Ryan said, exchanging curious looks with a poker-faced J.B., who had taken his rain-splattered glasses from his coat pocket and was using a piece of his shirttail to clean them. Although seated next to Mildred, he paid her outburst no mind. "My doctor told me to lay off nuts."

"Suit yourself. Seven stews and coffee it is." The waitress spun on one orange high-heeled shoe and strode away into the back.

"Mind explaining what that little scene was all about?" Ryan asked once the woman was out of earshot.

"I used to stop in places like this on vacations as a kid," Mildred explained. "Take the word of one who knows. If you've been in one tourist trap in Florida, you've been in them all."

"What kind trap?" Jak asked.

"Not a death trap, Jak," Mildred told him. "A 'tourist trap' is a predark slang term for a spot that suckered in the rubes. Take my word for it. You do *not* want a pecan-nut log."

"Speak for yourself, dear lady. Some of us here like pecans," Doc protested.

"I should let you eat one, you old goat, but we don't have time enough to spare for you to drop your trousers with the squirts every five minutes when we get back on the road. Besides, they're probably left over from over a hundred years ago—all that business about 'individually wrapped.' I'm guessing the damned things had a shelf life of over a thousand years and they taste like it, too. Worse than self-heat meals."

"Really?" Doc said, surprise falling across his face. "I had no idea."

"Take my word for it," Mildred assured him. "Stay away from any candy in the shape of a log."

THE WAITRESS RETURNED first with a tray of seven steaming-hot mugs of coffee-sub that everyone agreed tasted like recycled wag coolant, but at least the fluid was thick and plentiful. Mildred and Dean revised their requests and asked for water instead, but after seeing what color the liquid was in the clear glasses, went back to the coffee, which at least was dark and hid any impurities.

The stew was a step up from the beverages. Chunks of real potato and bits of green parsley and cabbage were mixed in with some finely diced carrots and a kind of mystery meat that nobody could discern exactly.

"I've had worse," Doc said, speaking for all of them.

"Must be why you went for a second helping," Dean said.

"As did you, young Cawdor," Doc responded over the rim of his coffee cup.

"Dean's a growing boy, Doc," Krysty said. "He needs his nourishment. You'd better watch out or you'll be dragging around a potbelly."

"Nonsense," Doc pronounced through bites. "The Tanner clan has always been blessed with a high metabolism. The more we eat, the leaner we get."

"How about some bread for the broth?" J.B. asked the server toward the end of the meal.

"Bread's extra."

"No problem," Ryan said. "We've got the jack. And pack up an extra round to go. Two pieces each."

Sandy left to accommodate the requests.

There was a jingle of the tarnished silver bell mounted above the entrance to the eatery. Four men stepped in through the door, and oddly enough, they stepped in by order of height.

"Damn, something done smells like it up and died in here!" boomed a loud bass voice from the largest of the quartet. "By, God, it had better taste better than what my nose is telling me!"

Chapter Nine

On the edge of his peripheral vision, Ryan saw Krysty's red tresses begin to gently coil and uncoil of their own will. Not a good sign. Especially since his own radar had also kicked into triple overtime from the moment the four men swaggered into the restaurant.

The quartet was dressed in a mix of tech and Western. The short, older man in front seemed to have the carriage of leadership. He also had a receding hairline, making his furrowed brow disappear into the brim of his crisp cowboy hat. Silver gray muttonchops and white wisps of hair at the back of his ears stuck out from under the hat.

In appearance, he was what Doc would term as a "dandy." Only a few drops of rain had fallen on the small man's suit since a second man, who was much taller, held a faded black umbrella above his head.

The small man looked like a well-preserved sixty-year-old, and wore a dark blue pair of trousers, a cream brocade vest with matching puff cravat and white spats. The spats were pulled over a pair of ancient brown lace-up shoes. A single stray speck of red mud dotted one of his feet, but otherwise the outfit was immaculate.

The only nod to the modern world in his accoutrements was in his choice of holster.

It was hand-tooled leather, with a wide sliver-plated buckle that matched the color of his hair. What looked to J.B.'s trained eye like a 6-shot old-style Smith & Wesson rimfire revolver was holstered on his left leg. The blaster was a near antique, but still deadly in the right hands.

The little man also carried a slim walking stick with a silver handle. Ryan caught himself wondering if the man's cane contained a hidden blade like Doc's.

"That guy sort of looks like a sawed-off version of Doc, doesn't he?" Dean whispered, echoing Ryan's thoughts. "Walking stick, funny old clothes, nose high in the air. Like he was better than us."

"Shh!" Ryan hissed. The boy was right, though.

"Afternoon," the small man said, removing his hat and showing off a nearly bald pate. "I'm Benjamin Green. This strapping young lad behind me is my son, Jackson. We're traveling with a second party for protection. This is Mr. Briggs and Mr. Constantinople."

He was speaking to the waitress, Sandy. The man identified as Green's son, Jackson, had been carrying the umbrella. He now pulled the collapsible shade closed and shook off the excess rainwater. Ryan could see the family resemblance behind the unfortunate waxed mustache that Jackson had chosen to wear. The facial hair was coal black, like the man's hair. The black was too much and looked artificial. Ryan suspected the liberal use of a bottle of hair dye. Perhaps the son was prematurely gray, and that was his way of rebelling against the unstoppable onslaught of age and/or resembling his father.

Vanity was usually the first thing to go when traversing Deathlands, but the father-and-son team looked to have an ample supply. In addition to vanity being a deterrent when attempting to move quickly, a vain man was almost always a man with too much jack in his pockets. Ryan suspected the Greens' traveling companions weren't friends. The one they referred to as Constantinople had the look of sec man written all over him. Hired help.

Like his father, Jackson was dressed in the splendor of the old West—with selected nods to modern-day touches—a dark blue high-cut jacket with leather lapels, a white shirt starting to droop from the dampness, a loosely tied lariat necktie held closed by a silver bolo. His trousers were tight and appeared to be made of a mix of shiny black leather, dark gray nylon and canvas. The toes of his once gleaming black cowboy boots were also tipped with silver, sterling tips very similar to the ones Krysty favored and currently wore.

For protection Jackson carried a stripped-down remade Uzi, a simple firehose with a pistol grip, capable of emitting a steady steam of bullets. The weapon hung from a shoulder strap down at his left side for easy access, right below the bottom of the short coat he wore.

"Nice suits," Sandy told them.

"Thank you. Will you seat us?" Green asked the waitress.

"Pick a table. Don't matter which," she replied in a bored voice. "Get yourself situated, and I'll take your orders."

"Are you on the menu?" asked the big man, Constantinople, with a leer.

"No," she said flatly, "I'm not. And if I was, you couldn't afford me."

As the blonde disappeared in the back, Constantinople watched the shallow movement of her hips and snorted. "Not much of a ride back there, but I guess it'd do in a pinch."

"You'd crush her, big man," Jackson replied. "Smash her right into the ground once you got pumping."

"Damned straight," Constantinople replied. He glanced at the older man. "Well, Ben," he said, "you planning on eating before dark or we gonna go out and catch our own? I guess we could continue to stand here with our thumbs up our asses waiting for the lady to bring us our grub, if you want."

Green nodded and gestured for the others to choose a table.

As the group strode past Ryan's table, the one-eyed man noticed that Constantinople was the classic example of a big man gone to seed. The broad shoulders and imposing height and weight had probably once made him an unstoppable opponent in hand-to-hand combat, but an appetite as huge as his frame had added weight to his flabby cheeks, his thick neck and his colossal stomach. A patch of hairy pelt could be seen at the apex of his middle where a shirt button had buckled and fallen under the constant assault of his gut.

Constantinople was no intellectual; that could be seen in his wide face and half-lidded, cruel eyes. Unlike the Greens, he was no fashion lover. He wore a dirty brown duster, red-checked flannel shirt, jeans and boots that were more mud than leather. Perched on his skull was the quintessential ten-gallon hat, a tall hat with a wide brim, much like its owner. A semiautomatic handblaster was tied down to his right leg.

The last man, the one called Briggs, took the initiative and sat down first, picking a table across from Ryan's group in the opposite corner of the dining room. As if to express his own lack of interest in his fellow diners, he sat with his back to them. Briggs was all in shades of brown: brown kerchief, brown gloves, brown hat, brown coat. Even his hair and his bushy eyebrows were brown.

The waitress returned when the men were seated. She held her pad and looked at the new customers impatiently.

"What's good tonight?" Green asked.

"Stew," Sandy replied.

"Stew," Green parroted.

"Got grits on the side if you want them," she added. "All out of bread. Won't be no more up for another hour or so."

"We'll have stew, then. And grits. And four cups of coffee."

"Four stews and subs coming right up," she an-

nounced cheerily, happy to escape the obvious gaze
from Constantinople. She quickly returned with four
chipped mugs and a lime green metal pot. After filling
all four mugs, Sandy had nearly made it away from
their table before silently having to endure a quick
slap on the rump from Jackson.

Ryan couldn't help but notice that Jackson seemed
more interested in impressing Constantinople than actually getting any sort of thrill from smacking the
waitress's buttocks.

The sniggering of the two men ringing in her ears,
she turned her attention to Ryan's table.

"Refills?" she asked stoically.

Doc and J.B. took her up on the offer, but the rest
abstained. They'd had enough of the lackluster brew.

"'Tis poor to the palate, but it does give one fire
in the belly," Doc said after taking a large gulp.

"Fire in the belly, hell, that's gas," J.B. retorted.
"You could run an engine off this stuff."

"Cut the chatter and drink up," Ryan announced
in a low voice. "I've got a bad feeling about the boys
who just joined us. I'd rather avoid any trouble if we
can help it. My stomach's full, and the last thing I
want is to exert any energy dealing with a bunch of
stupes."

Sandy returned from the back of the Tuckey's with
a serving tray bearing four wooden bowls of stew and
a stained brown paper bag. After setting down the
bowls of food, she tucked the tray under one arm and
stepped over to Ryan with the bag.

"Bread's inside," the waitress said. "I've got your

check up at the register. We can settle up whenever you're ready.''

"Let's do it," Ryan said, and pushed back his chair. The legs made a low screeching sound as they were dragged over the floor. However, before any of them could rise, Jackson Green made a comment under his breath.

"What did you say?" J.B. asked.

"Nothing to you. Talking to the waitress."

"I don't care who you were talking to. I want to know why it was you felt a comment was necessary."

"If you must know, Four-eyes," Jackson began, but was stopped by Mildred.

"Four-eyes? Now there's a classic insult that never goes out of style," she said.

"I was wondering why there was bread for you and none for us," Jackson finished, continuing to speak over Mildred's sarcastic interjection.

"They were here first, ordered it before you come in," the waitress said. "Sorry about that. Today's been busier than usual. Plenty of stew left. Should fill your belly."

Ben Green spoke to them next. "There you go! Problem solved. Sit down, Jackson." The son obeyed, staring hard at Ryan and J.B.

"Which way you all coming?" Green asked pleasantly.

"West," Ryan lied, shifting the paper bag with the bread into his left hand and smoothly dropping his right beneath the table and to his holster.

"Smart to travel in a group. I try and do the same."

"I noticed that. Right about the same time you made a point of telling everybody in here," Ryan said in the same even tone.

"Hey, I gotta know something," Jackson said, taking the conversation back from his father and peering over at Dean. "See, I'm not used to seeing men traveling with two such fine pieces of ass. Three if you count the boy—"

Jackson was interrupted by a loud snort from Constantinople, who found this last statement to be utterly hilarious. A double-nostril load of the pale brown coffee sub exploded through the large man's nose and onto his plate of grits and stew.

"And I was wanting to know where I could buy myself some. Traveling leg, coose on the loose, a walking, talking velvet snap-trap—you know what I mean."

"Brother, there isn't enough money in all of Deathlands," Mildred said. "You keep looking, though, hon. You might find yourself a real relationship, instead of the one you've got going on right now with your hand."

Mildred's statement amused Constantinople even more. "Who's the banshee?" he managed to ask between snorts as he tried to catch his breath from laughing so hard and exhaling the coffee sub.

The big man was pointing at Jak. Ryan could see the albino's muscles tense across the table, but the youth kept quiet.

"I'd say he was one of those frigging vampires I heard about down along Louisiana way, but when I last looked, it was still daylight outside. He some kind of fucking mutie or what?'' Constantinople asked.

"Or what," Jak spat, sliding one of his small leaf-shaped throwing knives from the secure hiding place along the underside of his left forearm. "Chill your fat ass quick."

Ryan gave the teenager a warning look. The ruby-eyed albino gave a barely perceptible nod and again fell silent.

So did the obese man, who chose to have another large swallow of his coffee brew.

Jackson did the replying for him: "That's a lot of double-big talk from a scrawny pecker like you, whitey. I think you're some kind of spook. Yeah, some kind of ghost who walks and talks, but ain't real friendly, eh? Freaking horrorshow."

"Ease up, boy," Green said sharply. "Let these folk be."

"Better listen to your daddy. We're not looking for trouble," Ryan said, keeping his tone deceptively easy, like the initial rumbling of a storm in the distance before the first signs of chem clouds began to creep across the skyline. "No muties here, just hungry folks like yourselves. We just want to pay our tab and get back on the road."

"Well, what's your big hurry?" Jackson asked in a snide voice.

Ryan decided he'd had enough mouth. "Trying to get away from pricks like you. To be honest with you, pretty boy, I don't need the aggravation."

"Ryan," Krysty warned from his right. The timbre of the one word said it all.

The one-eyed man had the ability to read a situation, although his own gifts weren't the result of mutation, as was the case with Krysty. In his years of roaming Deathlands, encountering the good and the bad in people from all walks of life, Ryan had become a keen observer of human nature. Not universal nature, although he understood quite a bit about what drove a person to act in a manner to injure his fellow, but more of a face-to-face understanding of what a man would do under the right circumstances.

Mildred would have termed it an ability to read body language. Others might have said Ryan possessed a sixth sense: observation and comprehension; the manner in how a person spoke, whether the tone was tinged with even the slightest hint of menace or friendship; the posture of his back and how he held his body; even the way his eyes cut back and forth—all of this could offer the crucial tip Ryan needed in knowing how to play a situation.

One bad guess or false move could mean a crippling wound, a loss of limb and property and, more often than not, instant death from the barrel of a blaster or the blade of a knife. Ryan Cawdor enjoyed being alive. From time to time, he liked to tell himself he was getting pretty damned good at staying that way.

The Green boy was trouble—handlebar mustache, fancy duds, dyed hair and all. Some burst of testosterone had flooded his brain. Now the conversation had dropped all pretense of being civilized and had gone the way of a pissing contest.

"Mebbe I'll just chill your one-eyed ass and take what I want," Jackson snarled, leaping to his feet and hoisting the Uzi.

In response, Jak's right arm snapped down like a released cobra, spitting out one of the albino's wafer-thin throwing knives. The blade spun at an angle, singing across the standing man's throat in a near invisible blur of movement, ultimately embedding itself in one of the orange seat cushions of an empty booth across the dining area.

Jackson's neck split open in a yawn of crimson, spraying the table, the plates and his three companions in a fine mist of blood.

"One way to shut him up," J.B. muttered philosophically, whipping out his own scattergun to back up Jak's play.

Before his friend hit the floor, Constantinople was moving. While he was as fat as any of the barons Ryan had ever encountered, at the same time he possessed that smooth grace of movement and natural agility that many large men have at their command.

In other words, while he looked lumbering and slow, his moves in a pinch proved otherwise.

His gleaming side arm was out of its side holster and in his hand. He had time for only a single shot, which went wild, before Ryan's group responded in unison.

The companions, well versed in working as a unit when a threat presented itself, split into two groups.

One half went for the shelter of the orange-topped bar that stretched along the back wall of the eatery. The other half stayed with their leader. J.B. assisted with his shoulder when Ryan pushed down on the edge of their dining table with all of his upper-body strength. The move caused the dishes and utensils to flip up, spinning in the air as a temporary distraction, while also giving them the back of the overturned table as badly needed cover.

"Goddammit!" Constantinople bellowed over the roar of his blaster as he pulled the trigger again and again. "There was no cause to cut his throat!"

Jackson, he of the formerly smart mouth, was rolling around on the checkered linoleum, gagging loudly and making unintelligible gasping noises as his hands squeezed together on his own throat, trying to hold his slit neck together. Wet red oozed from his fingers, and drops of spittle mixed with blood were being coughed up by the dying man.

Mildred watched and kept herself detached. She didn't know which would come first, strangulation from lack of air or bleeding to death.

The short man, Jackson's father, took all of this in while firing a steady stream of lead from the dropped Uzi. He was shrieking in a terrible voice over the blasterfire, "My boy, my boy, you've chilled Jackson!"

Constantinople was attempting a more careful aim when he was lifted off his feet at the same time a deafening explosion came from behind the eatery's bar. Doc had triggered the Le Mat, unleashing the

terrific force of the weapon's .63-caliber round. Doc
had only a single shot of such power, but when it
connected, the recipient usually knew he'd been hit.

Doc hadn't gone for anything fancy, and had chosen to aim for a chest shot. He scored clean, wiping
the smirk off the big man's wide face and replacing
it with the slack-jawed gape of the newly dead.

"Catch that thunder, you overweight oaf," Doc
called out, a hint of glee in his voice.

Ryan knew the situation had gone beyond a mere
squabble when Jackson had uttered the first insult. Jak
had responded to the threat without mercy, and now
with Doc's accurate aim, the second of the quartet
had been eliminated. Unless the older leader could
calm the fourth member of his group, and fast, there
would be more killing.

"Drop it! Drop it or you're both chilled," J.B.
called out from behind the table, but the chance at
survival was given too late. For a millisecond, the
quiet sec man, Briggs, looked like he was eternally
sorry to have gotten mixed up in such a sorry state
of affairs. Before he could try to lower his own drawn
weapon to surrender, the old man at his side completely lost all control and started spraying the Uzi
again.

"Fireblast. That tears it," Ryan said.

The crack of Dean's heavy Browning was in unison
with Mildred's target pistol. Both shots found their
mark, Mildred's in the upper left of Green's chest,
and Dean's lower down, in the gut. The old man staggered backward, his finger locked in a death's grip on

the trigger of the compact Uzi. A spray of bullets fanned from waist level up to a ninety-degree angle, skittering like lead insects into the already crumbling ceiling panels. Bits of foam and plaster rained in a sad parody of a snowfall, flakes of white falling and landing in the crimson puddles collecting on the floor.

Briggs whirled to Green, as if he were going to try to catch the older man. Instead, all he caught was some of the lead from the old man's Uzi. The sec man fell forward without a sound, a new red pool of blood rapidly spreading out from beneath his ruined face.

"Damn," Dean said incredulously, breaking the sudden quiet. "He chilled his own man."

"Not on purpose, Dean," Mildred replied, stepping out from behind cover.

"Yeah, accidents tend to happen when you're blasting like this in close quarters," Ryan said. "And apparently the father wasn't much smarter than the son."

The rest of the group came out of their defensive positions, returning their weapons to holsters or other places of concealment.

"Once, just once, I'd like to finish a meal in peace," Krysty said wearily as she surveyed the carnage.

"They started it," Jak said while wiping the blade of his retrieved knife on the bottom of the fat man's jacket.

Krysty glared down at the albino. "Don't 'they' always start it, Jak?"

"Yeah, 'they' always do," Ryan said, speaking for Jak. He caught Krysty's eye and held her gaze in his own, until she turned away. "And we always finish it, one way or another."

"Well, I don't have to like it," Krysty replied.

She retreated out of the eatery and through the front door, walking out alone in the rain. As she exited, the small bell gave a last jingle, then the room was quiet.

"Like tomb in here," Jak commented.

"Don't sweat it, Jak. We're still alive, tomb or not," Ryan said as he calmly ejected the spent clip from the SIG-Sauer and reloaded it with bullets taken from his cartridge belt. The rest of the group followed his lead, checking out their own artillery and reloading any fired bullets. By the time they had finished this necessary chore, Sandy had slunk out of hiding from an alcove between an old cash register and the swing doors under the coffee machine.

"Would you look at this!" she whispered. "All in less than a minute."

"I know those kind of men aren't the sort of clientele you'd normally want to have in such a fine eating establishment as Tuckey's," Ryan said. "Am I right about that?"

"Y-yeah," she said, but didn't sound too certain. "But I'm the one who's stuck having to mop up after these stiffs."

J.B. and Mildred finished a joint examination of the four dead men, the Armorer for any usable ammunition or jack, Mildred to see if any were still alive.

However, she already knew before attempting to find a pulse that she was wasting her time.

So was the Armorer. The blasters were passable, but had little or no ammo. Worthless when compared to the weight they would entail for a weary traveler looking for a place to sell them. He found a little jack and some tiny precious stones and bits of metal, which he stuck in an inner pocket of his leather jacket.

The cook finally made his way from the kitchen, carrying a pump-action scattergun. A pear-shaped black man, he was working bare chested under a dirty apron and work trousers.

"Need any help?" he asked in a voice full of bravado.

"No thanks, chef," Ryan said as he paid the bill. He took an extra octagonal-shaped golden coin from the secure pouch beneath his shirt and dropped it on the counter near the old cash register. "We can handle it from here. Why don't you put away the firepower and get back to your stove? You look like a man more comfortable with a spoon in his hand than a blaster."

"I was busy," the cook said lamely.

"Of course. A chef is always obsessed when at work in the kitchen crafting his culinary delights," Doc said in a knowing voice.

"Sorry about the mess," Ryan said to the waitress. "Once he's got his pots and pans under control, get the big guy to help you dump the stiffs behind back, and mebbe you can have things cleaned up in time for the supper rush. And you might want to think about anteing up for a halfway decent sec man to watch the door of this place. Pay him in food. There's men who'd be glad to do whatever you told them to for less.''

OUTSIDE, KRYSTY HAD TAKEN temporary shelter beneath the overhang of the arched roof. A torrent of water poured down the rusted broken drainpipe near her legs as she leaned against the boarded-up side wall of the eatery. Ryan and the others came out of the building and walked past the flame-haired beauty without any comment.

Ryan hung back, letting Jak take the point as the group began the march back up to the main highway.

''Let's go,'' he said softly, extending a gloved hand.

''I just get tired, Ryan. Tired of killing,'' Krysty said.

''I know. We all do. Each of us just have different ways of dealing with it.''

Krysty reached out and took her man's hand, gripping it tightly and intertwining her fingers with his.

''I love you, Ryan,'' she said. ''Nothing will ever change that.''

He didn't reply, but held her hand even tighter, as if he would never let go. They would have to pry away his cold, dead fingers first.

Chapter Ten

Many days had passed without incident, other than a battle of wits between a hungry Jak and a hungrier J.B. for the last piece of bread from Tuckey's. Mildred had averted any overt displays of bad temper between the pair by declaring *she* was going to eat the final helping, and she did so with a smile that openly dared either of the men to say otherwise.

There had been some small game along the way, and thanks to the endless rainfall, plenty of water to drink. Dean took a bad tumble when a piece of the crumbling old asphalt gave way and he slid down a muddy embankment on his butt, whooping all the way. Luckily the only real injury seemed to have been to his pride and to his clothing. Soon after the mud began to dry, his jeans were extrastiff and able to stand up by themselves.

"Keep you on your feet," Ryan told him.

The rain had finally let up a few days earlier. Ryan reckoned they had walked right through a near permanent monsoon season over the upper stretch of Florida.

Now they had reached a destination of sorts. The marina might at one time have been attractive. All it offered the exhausted group of companions was a

crowded maze of black rotting timbers, both underfoot and overhead. Most of the structure looked to be
in poor condition, but down at the edge of the water
two empty slips gave all of the indications of recent
activity. The wood of the individual piers of both
these slots had been replaced or repaired with fresh
lumber.

More than half of the marina was protected from
prying eyes by a high wooden wall.

A faded red-and-blue sign proclaimed the site as
being Schwartz's Marina. Ryan could tell from the
shape of the sign that Schwartz was either long dead
or completely lacking any pride in the place.

Most of the boathouses that could be seen from
outside were open, while the rest contained partly or
fully submerged wrecks in the brackish water.

The group had arrived at dusk. In the fading light
of the sun, the ruin of a marina looked even more
forlorn and spectral. Still, as far as Ryan could see
from where he was standing behind the mesh-wire
restraining fence, there were no guards or would-be
protectors in place.

"What do you think?" Ryan asked, addressing the
group.

"Place could use a coat of paint," Mildred offered.
"Something festive, in orange."

"Gaia, don't remind me of that place," Krysty
said.

"You volunteering to pick up a paintbrush?" J.B.
asked, winking at Mildred from behind his spectacles.

"Not on your life, John," Mildred replied, sticking

her chin out and tilting her head back in a haughty pose. "I didn't go to medical school to become a painter."

"Know tired of walking," Jak replied. "Boot heels wore off."

"Mine, too," Dean chimed in.

"As are my own. A sea voyage is sounding better and better to my weary bones," Doc said.

"Then it's settled," Ryan said, glancing at his companions for confirmation. All quickly agreed that what little novelty walking across Florida on the old interstate had initially offered had long worn off. Even Ryan had suffered some deep pains in his ankles from the constant days spent treading on the paved highway.

"Joint looks deserted. Probably won't find anything that floats," J.B. said. "My guess is, if the boats were worth a damn they were scavenged long ago."

"Tell me something I don't know, J.B.," Ryan retorted.

"I thought that fellow back on the highway said we could purchase transport or, better yet, a vessel at this docking port?" Doc said, stretching his arms wide and yawning like some kind of tattered, spindly crow.

"He could have been lying. Or wrong. Or mebbe the sellers have gone home for the day or been put out of business. Either way, let's recce and see what's what before all the light is gone," Ryan said. "Split up. Dean, you and me and Krysty will check the boathouses."

Ryan gestured to J.B. "Take Mildred, Doc and Jak and go over the private ports. Look for any supplies we can use or a boat that's still halfway afloat. We'll meet back here at the gate of the sec fence in twenty minutes."

J.B. glanced at his wrist chrono and mentally noted the time. "Twenty. Right. Got it," the small man said. "But don't start the clock until I've opened the door."

The lump of a lock and the rusted links of the chain wrapped around the main gate of the marina entrance were easily navigated by J.B., who had taken a flat black case from a pocket and removed a tiny collection of antique locksmith's tools.

"You'd have made a heck of a thief, John," Mildred commented, watching with an amused eye at her lover's dexterity and expertise with the metal picks.

"Why, thank you, Millie," the Armorer replied, and added a muttered curse at the uncooperative lock. "Son of a bitch!"

"Not as easy as a redoubt sec door, huh, J.B.?" Dean said.

"I'll take pushing buttons and pulling levers over picking a lock any day of the week. This is triple-hard work," J.B. said. "Could use a squirt of oil to grease it. However, it's always good to keep your skills sharp."

And then, as if the Armorer were a magician who had uttered the magic word, the hasp of the heavy lock came open. The mess of rusty chains wound around the gate and held in place by the lock fell to the gravel pathway with a rattling clank.

"See you soon," Ryan said, walking away to the right with his team.

"Not if I see you first," J.B. replied, taking the left.

"GOOD FRIENDS, perhaps our luck is changing," Doc said.

Ten minutes into their search, a well-maintained cabin cruiser had been discovered.

"Something this nice has got to belong to somebody," J.B. said, looking at the hull. "Jak, take the rear point. See if anybody wants to say hello."

"They might be scared, John. I know I'd be concerned if someone came sniffing around my boat," Mildred said. "That gate was locked for a reason."

"Not planning on stealing the thing, Millie, just curious. I want to know where the owner is."

A loud whoop of laughter rang out from behind the boat where Jak had gone to investigate. "Think found our boat!" he called out.

The rest of the friends went around to see what had ignited Jak's interest.

"This has to be Ryan's ride, no question," J.B. said.

Emblazoned on the rear of the boat in tall blue cursive letters was the craft's name. Jak was pointing and grinning.

"The *Patch*," Doc read.

"Dame Fortune seems to have smiled on us at last," Doc intoned.

"Yeah, she's good at that—right before she kicks you in the teeth," a new voice piped up. "Nobody flick an eyelash, and you might get out of this alive."

J.B. cursed himself. The joy of the discovery had distracted them all.

Now they would have to pay whatever price the men who had gotten the drop on them decided to ask for, and he knew from hard-earned experience that nothing came cheap when you were under someone else's blaster.

"You planning on stealing our boat?" the voice asked.

"No," Jak said. "Just looking."

"Who are you people? We were just getting ready to shove off. Did Sommers send you?"

"No," J.B. said. "Don't know him. We're just looking to head up the coast. Man told us boats could be bought here. Way you're acting, don't guess yours is for sale."

"Got that right. Who are you?"

"J. B. Dix. The lady's Mildred. Old guy's Doc Tanner, and the teenager's Jak."

"Name's Gardner Boyd," the lean, unsmiling man said in a monotone. He jerked a thumb toward the behemoth standing to his left and behind. "This here's Frank Bowman."

"Hey," Bowman said dully.

"He don't say much. I do all the talking," Boyd said arrogantly.

"I guessed that," Mildred replied, starting to get annoyed. "You look like the genius of the couple."

"Nobody asked you, bitch," Boyd retorted.

Mildred's face was carved in stone as she glared back at the man.

"You've stepped in it now, friend," J.B. said laconically "You're dead."

"We'll see about that." Boyd replied "I know your black bitch ain't going to be the one chilling me, so she might as well get over it and stop staring at me like that."

Boyd was all angles, sharp and pointy: his chin, his nose, even his ears. He had close-cropped black hair and a three-day growth of bristly beard. His eyes were bloodshot and brown. J.B. put him at just under six feet tall. His arms and legs were gangly, coming off a long torso. He was dressed in a light green wool cap set back on the crown of his head like a skullcap, a navy blue shirt with four rows of buttons stitched up the front, a faded pair of denim pants and canvas sneakers.

The big man, Bowman, was round—round face, round belly and a round, slack-jawed mouth that didn't utter a sound beyond a slight asthmatic wheeze. He was nearly bald, with a smattering of bright orange hair gathered in clumps along the sides of his head.

Boyd was holding a handblaster, Bowman a oddly shaped pump-action shotgun. Both weapons appeared flawless and well maintained.

"Nice guns," J.B. drawled. "Nine millimeter

Heckler & Koch P-7 semiauto, weighs in at right under two pounds. Old-style policemen and the German army were big on the H&K.''

"I like it," Boyd snarled. "Does the job."

"That's an Italian Franchi SPAS-12 shotgun," J.B. continued, pointing at Bowman. "Wicked dark gun. Semiauto, designed for paramilitary use and sec work. The butt of the pistol grip can hook under your arm for single handed firing. Eight-shot magazine. Weighed right between nine and a half and ten pounds according to the old spec manuals.''

Boyd listened to the roboticlike dissertation while peering at J.B. as if the Armorer were some sort of fedora-wearing alien insect.

"Looks like we got us a real know-it-all! Mebbe the Admiral would like to have a chat with such a gushing font of wisdom," Boyd said, looking to Bowman for confirmation. The big man's face spoke for him. He looked as though he couldn't care less one way or the other.

"'Gushing font'?" J.B. said in a mocking tone of voice. "What the hell kind of phrase is that? You some kind of pansy?''

"Wouldn't you like to know?" Boyd replied, his eyes narrowing at the implications of the insult.

"What are you gents doing here, anyway?" Doc asked.

"Why, we're doing the Lord's work—the good Lord Poseidon. You might say we're his loyal disciples." Boyd giggled at his own phrasing. "Yes, sir, we're loyal, steadfast and true, preaching his wisdom up and down the coast, aren't we, Frankie?''

Bowman shrugged his massive shoulders. ''If you say so.''

''You know something? You're no fun at all, you know that?'' Boyd sneered at his companion.

''Get over it,'' Bowman replied.

''Sorry to interrupt your spat, but there's something I need to tell you,'' J.B. interjected.

''Did I ask your opinion, Four-eyes?''

''Again with the 'Four-eyes,''' Mildred said with a sigh. ''We've got to get you some contacts, John.''

''Oh, what is it?'' Boyd asked. ''I can tell you right now the answer is 'Hell no!'''

''Don't have a question, just an observation. There's one other thing you ought to know about those H&K semiauto pistols,'' J.B. said lazily.

''Yeah? And what's that, genius?''

''Their most interesting feature is the long safety lever at the front of the grip. You have to hold it firmly before the gun can fire. And guess what? You're not holding it.''

J.B. said this so matter-of-factly that Boyd actually glanced down at his hand to see if his prisoner was right. Boyd saw that the know-it-all had been in error regarding his grip, and he was about to correct him when the angular man realized he'd been taken. In the mere fragments of a second it took his eyes to focus as he looked back up, Mildred had swiftly drawn her own target revolver.

The change in the situation registered, but by the

time he truly realized what had just happened, Gardner Boyd was a dead man.

"I'm a doctor. I preserve life. But nobody calls me a black bitch," Mildred hissed, and drilled Boyd with a single shot between the eyes.

WHEN RYAN HEARD the distinctive bark of Mildred's ZKR pistol, he, Krysty and Dean immediately started to race toward the source of the sound, which had come from the far end of the marina. Ryan glanced at his chrono. Only fifteen minutes had passed. It hadn't taken J.B. long to wander into a firefight.

"Move," he said, drawing his own blaster as he willed himself to run faster. On his heels, Krysty and Dean struggled to keep up with the pace he had set.

A second shot rang out, this one deeper and unfamiliar. Ryan hit the brakes and flattened his body against one of the damp marina walls that separated the twin docks. Krysty and Dean almost collided, but managed to follow suit.

"Sounded like a shotgun, lover," Krysty said.

"Yeah," Ryan replied. Times like this, he caught himself wishing for some kind of portable comm system. There was no way to know which way the situation had gone without an actual look-see. However, even if J.B.'s party was pinned down, he could still give Ryan their location if they had radios.

The one-eyed man mentally made himself count to twenty before peering around the corner.

Nothing. He walked briskly to the next bend in the wooden frame tunnel, the tar-paper roofs flapping in the strong sea winds. Ryan stopped at the next corner and took up a position, waving Krysty and Dean over.

"Anything?" he asked the redhead.

Krysty frowned, closing her eyes. "No. Feels fine."

"Okay, then." Ryan leaned over and peered down an alley of boat slips.

First he saw the *Patch*, then he saw his friends.

J.B. was looking back at Ryan, knowing the gunshots would bring the one-eyed man running.

"What took you so damned long?" J.B. said impatiently.

"YOU DIDN'T CHILL HIM?" Ryan asked, looking down at the heap where Bowman was sprawled, breathing heavily. The hair hanging over his forehead was plastered down with sweat.

"Nope," Jak said.

"Why not?" Ryan asked.

"I didn't want hear Krysty complain."

"Don't mistake compassion for cowardice, Jak," Ryan said.

"You two are arguing for nothing," Mildred interjected from where she was examining Bowman's wound. "I can't do anything for this man. He'll be dead in minutes."

"If you hadn't chilled Boyd between the eyes, he might've told us something we could use," J.B. said to the physician. "Can't blame you, though. Knew the 'black bitch' crack was his signature on the death certificate."

"Where's Boyd now?" Ryan asked.

"Fell overboard," Jak said innocently.

"Hear that?" Ryan said to the dying man at his feet. "Your last few minutes can go easy or harsh. Answer a few questions about your boat, and we won't toss you in alive."

"I want to know about this 'Poseidon' we heard about earlier," J.B. added. "And Sommers."

"He does not look much like a sailor to me," Doc sniffed. "From his corpulent midsection, all I can think of is Captain Bligh, except that our friend has proved he lacks the proper intelligence required to be a proper despot."

"The brains of the pair is that triple stupe floating facedown next to the boat," J.B. commented, gesturing to the side of the dock where Boyd's corpse was bobbing lifelessly in the water. "I know your charming companion did most of the talking, but I suggest you come up with why you two were here."

"F-f-ferryboat," Bowman wheezed. "Supposed to get supplies from Sommers, then head back home."

"Home? Where's that?" Ryan asked. "Farther south, or on up the coast?"

The dying man didn't say anything.

Jak gave him a sharp kick in the ample waistline. "Asked question," the albino said.

Bowman coughed violently, the sound a rattling rasp. The man turned his head to one side and spit out a mouthful of pink mucus. "Upstate," he finally said, each word an effort. "Was supposed to pick up package, but it was a fixed deal. Sommers was running a scam. No warhead.''

"Warhead?" Krysty mouthed to the rest of the group.

"Where upstate?" Ryan demanded.

Bowman didn't answer; he couldn't, and no amount of prodding from Jak or anyone else was going to be able to pry anything more from him. His eyes were still open, but they had gone from the wide bulge of pain and suffering to a glassy and lifeless stare.

Each of the companions stood on the dock, pondering the meaning of the man's last word.

"Warhead," J.B. said finally. "Wonder what he was planning on carrying around in that tub?"

"Since it's our ride out of here, we might as well take a look," Mildred suggested.

"Warhead," Dean mused. "Sounds triple deadly."

"It is, son," Ryan replied. "It is."

Chapter Eleven

Ryan winced as the darkness surrounding him turned to blinding white light. His right eye strained to focus on the helm controls in front of him as a blast of thunder followed the lightning, a deafening crash so close he could feel the damp air press sharply on his eardrums.

"Fireblast!" he growled between clenched teeth, peering out into the night through the rain-streaked windows of the boat's bridge. Ryan was many things, but a seaman wasn't one of them. He had spent time on boats, but never long enough to learn the intricacies. Unfortunately none of the others on board the spacious one-hundred-foot cruiser were nautically inclined, either.

"I can't see a damned thing," Ryan muttered, glancing over the chrome-plated controls.

"Nothing to see," J.B. replied from beside him.

"I've never liked boats," Ryan admitted, squinting as another flash of lightning lit up the sky. "I'd rather swim to the Carolinas than try and sail around in this mess."

"You first," J.B. told him.

"At least the rain's clean. Glad this isn't a chem

storm. We'd be screwed facedown to the boards with our asses in the air then.''

"Ain't that the truth," J.B. replied. Both men had driven through enough of those hellish nuclear-spawned aberrations of nature to know their dangers.

"Boat not take much this," Jak yelled over the din of the storm. His red eyes were shining eerily in the glow of the flickering electric lamps of the yacht's bridge as he stood in the doorway across from Ryan, his wet mane of white hair hanging limply around his skull like sodden tendrils.

Ryan glanced away from the windows of the craft and over at the teenager. Ryan couldn't help but notice that while he was struggling to keep his footing, Jak was effortlessly standing and compensating for the roll of the deck.

"Boat'll do fine, Jak. We've just got to hang on until this is over. How are things below?" he asked as the deck rose and fell below his booted feet.

Jak's ruby eyes revealed a faint glimmer of amusement. "Fine. Doc's seasick."

"No surprise there. Doc's usually the one who pukes whenever we make a jump," J.B. replied.

"Tell everybody to hang on. There's not much else I can do but try and keep the wheel steady until we ride this thing out," Ryan said.

At the moment, Ryan thought that the nightmares generated by a jump were more appealing than the wild ride the companions were enduring. And then, almost involuntarily, his mind turned back to the peaceful scene of a few hours earlier.

AFTER THEY LEFT the marina, the rest of the night had passed without incident. Morning brought up a deep orange jewel from the horizon, as if the ball of the sun had been plucked from the waters of the ocean. The course had been set by utilizing J.B.'s minisextant, some trigonometric tables left in the crumbling manual for a malfunctioning on-board nav comp and some worn and taped but still intact charts. Ryan was glad for J.B.'s knowledge. They would have been forced to set out blindly in a generally northward direction otherwise.

The cruiser was making way northward, with the destination of North Carolina's Outer Banks as a stopping point.

For all of the talk of a warhead, there were no weapons on board beyond what the group had carried on. A box of ammunition for Boyd's 9 mm Heckler & Koch P-7 semiauto pistol was found on a table, but the blaster had fallen into the water with its owner when Mildred chilled him. Dean had claimed Bowman's Italian Franchi SPAS-12 shotgun and stuck it under one of the boat's bunks for safekeeping.

The galley of the craft was the only amenity lacking on the tidy *Patch*. Empty packages and peelings in a trash can hinted of the previous existence of canned and fresh foodstuffs such as tinned meats, apples and peaches. Now most of the cabinets were bare except for staple rations of stale wheat crackers, a plastic bag of jerky and part of a case of twelve-ounce tins of water. Ryan's long arm had swept the back of the cabinets and come up with a glass container of green beans.

"We can thank that pig Bowman for all of this or the lack of," Mildred said. "He didn't look like he'd been missing any meals."

Doc had pondered doing some fishing, but instead spent most of the trip on his back, exhausted from the trek across Florida and nauseated from the ship. An informal series of watches had been set, with some of the group sleeping during the day and others at nightfall.

The sunset was as strikingly beautiful as the sun had been when rising. As a rule, sunsets were always spectacular in Deathlands due to the pollutants and the chemicals and, to some degree, the radiation still hovering in the upper atmosphere.

Doc had finally ventured out into the evening breeze, his feelings of nausea passing with the coming of night. He was wide-awake and restless, and since Jak and Krysty were below sleeping, their watches over, he really had no choice but to try to socialize.

The sky around the *Patch* was strikingly clear, the night open and beautiful, with a multitude of stars stretching out across the horizon. Ryan hadn't seen such celestial beauty in a long time, not since the long summer nights in the mountains of his boyhood. Back then, he'd spent many an hour outdoors, the dew wet and cold beneath his bare feet, looking at the sky and trying to sort out the stars from the glowing lightning bugs.

Doc, taking strength from being revved up in full

educator mode, had been challenging J.B. and Mildred to a friendly game of naming the constellations. Unlike the knowledge necessary to comprehend his numerous literary aspersions—the spouting of which put Doc in a class all by himself—both the physician and the Armorer knew a bit about the stars and the heavens. With J.B.'s eidetic memory, they were matching Doc constellation for constellation. Usually J.B.'s mental expertise only came into play when he used the minisextant to get a reading on their position, or when he was spouting out a series of specs for a piece of hardware.

Ryan knew they were enjoying giving Doc a run for the old man's money. He hadn't seen his old partner this happy in a long time.

Across from them, flat on his back in a swaying rope hammock with his hands behind his head, was Dean. For once, the boy was staying silent and not asking questions.

"Why aren't you in there with Mildred and J.B. trying to stump Doc?" Ryan asked his son. "You falling asleep in that rigging?"

"Don't know any constellations," the boy said, turning his face skyward.

"Watch and learn, then," Ryan replied. "Pretend you're back in school."

"Those days are over," Dean said. "Triple glad to be back with you, Dad. Glad to have the excitement. Thought I'd go crazy sitting at a desk all day."

"There's more to life than roaming the countryside, and the world can change—never know when things come in handy," the one-eyed man said. "Besides, if you know your stars, you can always get some kind of directional fix no matter where you are. That's how J.B. does it at night when he doesn't have the sun to go by."

"J.B.'s got a sharp memory," Dean grumbled.

"For some things. We can all remember stuff we want to," Ryan said. "You remember Sharona, don't you?"

"Yeah," Dean said defensively. "She was my mom."

"Remember what she looked like? What she liked to wear? What kinds of food she liked to eat, and how she took care of you?" Ryan asked.

"Yeah," Dean said, taking an interest now in where Ryan was going with this line of questioning.

"Think you'll ever forget?"

"No. Not even when I'm chilled and gone."

"There you go," Ryan said, stepping away from the boy. "You hold things in your memory you need, or that mean something to you—or both. The stars might save your life, son. Keep it in mind, and learn."

"Ah, my dear Ryan. Perhaps you would like to join our little competition?" Doc asked. "I am in need of a partner, since I am currently being double teamed by the good Dr. Wyeth and her friend who seems to know all of the answers."

"I'll pass, Doc. You seem to be holding your own, though."

"So much has changed in my life," Doc said to

his companions as they looked heavenward. "But the stars have always remained."

"Yeah, too bad you can't recollect half their names," Mildred retorted, the tiny beads in her plaited hair rattling as she moved her head. Still, the woman understood precisely what Doc was saying, and in many ways shared the same sense of loss.

Mildred was a time traveler of a different sort than Doc. Unlike the violent time trawling that had ripped Doc from the bosom of his family and career, she had undergone her one-way journey to Deathlands in an entirely different fashion.

Mildred was a leading expert in the field of cryogenics by the time she was in her early thirties. A few short years later, she was admitted to the hospital for a routine operation three days before the advent of the year 2001. During the surgery, the anesthetic triggered a near fatal reaction. To save her life, the physicians used Mildred's own experimental techniques to freeze and place the woman into suspended animation, where she had remained until Ryan and the others found and awakened her. Surprisingly the cryonic process had reversed the negative effects of the anesthetic.

The constellation game was interrupted when the first signs of the storm arrived in the slender form of Krysty, who had been unable to continue sleeping below.

"Air's wrong," she said quietly, stepping into Ryan's arms. "There's a storm coming. A bad one."

Ryan was dubious, as the night sky was cloud free.

But he knew from past experience not to dismiss any of Krysty's feelings. Her exterior might reveal nothing more than a tall, strikingly beautiful woman, but what lurked behind her intelligent emerald eyes was more than human.

Nothing was ever what it seemed to be in Deathlands, and Krysty was living proof.

Krysty Wroth was a mutant. One of her powers was the empathic ability to sense danger, whether from man or nature. Her vibrant mane of fiery red hair was the outward manifestation of this power, stirring, curling, moving as if it were a separate, sentient organism as she became entranced with the vision of a premonition.

It was a handy ability that had saved their lives more than once.

"Let me take a look, see what the instruments say," Ryan said to her.

He walked over and checked the old-style brass barometer mounted on the exterior bulkhead, tapped the glass and frowned. The needle was showing 25.5 inches of mercury. Krysty was right. Between the needle's drop and the stillness in the air, even a lander like Ryan knew they were in for a bad spell.

"Oh, dear," came Doc's voice from behind. The old man's curiosity had gotten the best of him when he noticed Ryan checking the barometer. "That does not look good at all, my friend."

"No, it doesn't," Ryan said. "And we don't have time enough to turn back."

THE PARTY BROKE UP quickly after that. Jak was awakened and given the bad news. The good feelings shared quickly dissolved into the tension of worry with the discovery of the upcoming storm.

"I knew this peaceful scene was too good to last," Mildred said, her voice bittersweet. She hugged J.B. tightly before heading down below.

Doc, Jak, Dean and Krysty followed, all staying close to the handrail along the passageway. Already the seas were becoming choppy.

"Why do we have to slink down here?" Dean asked. "Hiding out like a bunch of scared night stalkers at sunrise."

"Don't let your father hear you talking like that," Krysty said, her keen ears picking up on Dean's monologue. "He's doing the right thing."

"Why isn't he coming, then?"

"Ryan knows if we're below, we're safe. He doesn't have to worry about anyone being thrown overboard or hit by lightning or falling down on the deck and breaking a leg. This way, he can fully focus on keeping us on course."

"Yeah, I guess you're right, Krysty," Dean said as he sat down on a wall bunk. "Still sucks, though."

"I must stress even at this early juncture that your slang is most vile, young Cawdor, but I have to agree. This does indeed suck," Doc said weakly.

"Doc, you look even paler than usual," Mildred said. "What's wrong?"

"Nothing, Dr. Wyeth. Put away your medical bag."

"You've been acting funny since we came on board. If I didn't know better, I'd say you were—"

"Seasick," Jak interrupted with a snicker of delight. "Right, Doc?"

"Affirmative." Doc stumbled over and sat down on a folding chair. Both man and chair wobbled as the boat encountered choppier waters.

"Glass stomach's bad," Jak said. "Worse than jumping."

"As you might recall, young Lauren, I am usually not the only one stricken during our mat-trans excursions," Doc said tightly, rubbing his stomach.

"Only one turning green now!" Jak said, grinning.

As LONG MINUTES TURNED into hours, all of the comrades knew the storm wasn't getting any better. Rather than turn back, Ryan and J.B. decided to sail farther inland in an attempt to avoid the demon storm clouds that had been bearing down on them mercilessly.

A good plan, but it didn't make for an easy voyage.

Still, all was as quiet and uneventful inside the long stateroom when Krysty suddenly bolted upright from the bunk she was resting on.

"What?" Jak said, instantly alert.

Krysty didn't answer, her green eyes wide as she took in the room, looking but not comprehending what she was staring at in the real world.

She was somewhere else than the *Patch*.

"Something wrong, Krysty?" Dean asked.

"Mebbe so," she said. "I wonder if everything's okay above."

"Take look. Back soon," Jak replied, and vanished up the stairwell.

"Woe is me, for I shall never take another sea voyage for as long as I shall live," Doc moaned. "I have nothing left to give—my stomach is empty, cursed sickness! Shall I donate a vital organ to your lust for watching me suffer?"

"Quiet, Doc! I've got to concentrate."

There was a new menace, an unnatural threat beyond the storm and the thrashing sea.

This threat was man-made, but of what type she couldn't tell. Her latent mutie senses had been in turmoil since they had left port in Florida. Drawing much of her inner strength from the land itself, Krysty never felt at ease when on water anyway, and she had attributed her feelings to that.

"Something's wrong, something's bad wrong," she murmured to herself like a mantra.

Mildred got up and reached over to feel the redhead's sweaty brow. "God, Krysty, you're on fire," the doctor said.

"Got to warn Ryan. There's danger. I'm seeing red—bloodred."

"What kind of danger? The storm?" Mildred was starting to get caught up in Krysty's mounting hysteria, the buffeting of the boat, the loud crashing of the thunder, all had started to take a toll on the doctor's usual internal calm. And for Krysty to mention seeing red, that meant they were all in even greater danger than they might have earlier expected.

But from what?

Before Mildred could verbalize her own fears, a second loud boom of thunder exploded in the night, but unlike the others, this one came from below the boat. Everyone in the crowded cabin was thrown back, then heaved forward as the yacht yawled from the impact. Doc fell to his knees, not hearing but still feeling his worn bones crack in protest. His lion's-head swordstick flew out from his right hand, skipping like a tossed stone across the soaked carpeted floor.

"Accursed ocean," he said bitterly from clenched teeth, trying to shake off the pain from his aching kneecaps. "If I survive, I shall be a bloody invalid by the end of this sea voyage."

Dean slammed into Mildred, and the woman managed to hang on to the boy's shirttail, keeping him upright. Doc reached out and was able to latch on to a metal lip that was attached to the bulkhead.

The remaining two members of the party weren't as lucky. Krysty had been thrown off her feet and onto her upper back and neck. The suddenness of the explosion smashed her down with terrific force, knocking her instantly unconscious as she slid toward the gaping hole that had just appeared in the hull.

Jak, who had been coming back down the companionway into the lower part of the boat when the blast occurred, didn't have a second to react as he was thrown forward down the narrow passageway and

directly into the newly created hole, almost simultaneously with Krysty's descent.

"Jak!" Mildred screamed, but there was no time
to respond.

The albino twisted his lithe body as he fell, managing not to break his neck when he hit the churning
water. Gasping for breath, his lungs emptied from
both the impact and the sudden cold, Jak struggled to
maintain some kind of proper sense of which way was
up. Seeing Krysty's limp body already being sucked
into the undertow beneath the vessel, he pushed himself down farther, under the chilling ocean, and
grasped a fistful of long red hair.

And both of them vanished in the water from Mildred's sight.

ON THE DECK OF THE CRAFT, Ryan had turned the
controls over to J.B. seconds before the blast. The
one-eyed man was hurled into a console and he
grabbed for purchase, trying to keep erect.

"What the fuck was that?" Ryan bellowed. "You
hit a rock?"

"Out here? No way!" J.B. replied, his voice shrill
and loud against the backdrop of the storm. "That
was an explosion of some kind!"

"Who would try and attack us in the middle of
this?" Ryan yelled, pulling himself up from the slippery deck to his feet.

The Armorer's keen mind raced for an answer.
"No one. We must've hit a mine."

"Then we're going down," Ryan said flatly. "Find

the life rafts. I'm going below to check on the others. Don't worry about the controls. We're triple screwed now anyway. I don't think we're going to crash into another boat out here alone in this mess.''

"On it," J.B. said, heading out behind Ryan onto the unprotected deck and into the full brunt of the storm. Already the yacht was starting to list badly, and the stern was beginning to rise on a incline as the lower hull took on water. Whipping whitecaps were everywhere across the surface of the churning ocean. The increased activity caused heavy seas to spring up and crash down over the *Patch*'s bow, sending shudders down the length of the boat's hull.

As Ryan entered the stairwell that led to the galley and berths, he was met by a weeping Mildred, who was trying to help a pained Doc up the steps. Below Doc, Dean was pushing the old man by the buttocks. A look of sheer panic was pasted on the boy's face. Ryan reached down past the struggling Mildred and snatched Doc by the collar of his frock coat, boldly pulling the older man up with one hand. Coasting on adrenaline, Ryan stared past his son and realized no one else was coming.

"Where's Krysty?" Ryan shouted in Mildred's ear, trying to make himself heard above the din of a loud crack of thunder. "Where's Krysty and Jak?"

"She went under—through the hole," Mildred screamed back over the creaking and groaning of the hull. "She was limp! Had to be unconscious. Jak fell in after her, but at least he was alert and awake. I think he was trying to grab her."

Mildred had known Ryan for some time now, and she'd seen him caught up in the throes of any and all emotions. Usually his face was a mask. The only way to judge any emotional turmoil was to look at the color of the long scar that stretched from his eye to his chin. The more upset Ryan got, the redder the scar would pulse.

This time, even the scar was ghostly white.

Ryan spun back up and away from Mildred. He spotted a dirty coil of rope hanging beside the companionway and snatched it off the hook, unraveling the coil as he stepped as quickly as he could toward the edge of the boat. Once, he fell down in a sprawl as the bow of the vessel rose, then suddenly dropped away. Removing his blaster, he tossed the pistol to Dean with one hand.

"Hold this!" he bellowed, then began to quickly tie the rope around his waist. By now, the boat had a near thirty-degree angle with the nose beginning to rise high in the night air.

J.B. ran over, carrying a tight bundle of plastic. "Only one raft, but it's big," he yelled. "Should hold us all."

The Armorer paused, noting the absence of Krysty and Jak. "Where's—?"

"Overboard," Ryan said. "Get that raft up and everybody in it. I'm going over, but I'll need an anchor so I can find my way back."

J.B. pulled a cord, and the raft began to fill with compressed air. Once Ryan could see the old predark inflating mechanism wasn't going to malfunction, he handed his oldest living friend the end of the rope.

"Tie this to the raft."

"We've lost them, Ryan," the Armorer bellowed, making an effort to be heard over the din of the storm. "You'll never find her in this muck!"

"I've got to try," he replied, then he was gone, over the side.

Below the surface, the water was no calmer. The sea churned all around, and his sense of direction was compromised. A vision from his dream in the mattrans chamber rushed into his mind's eye. In that vision, the water had been much clearer, and had color.

Ryan realized the vision had been wrong.

The ocean was neither green nor blue. The ocean was black.

NOT FAR AWAY from the sinking yacht, down lower on the Georgia coastline, in a tiny, dimly lit room crowded with blinking lights and softly whirring computer equipment, a white blip appeared on a normally blank sonar screen.

The sight was so unusual, the crew-cut man seated in front of the screen rubbed his eyes in disbelief. A blip meant something big was going down, at least, that was what his training had told him. The antiquated gear in the room was prone to hiccups such as this one in their attempts to register phantoms in the deep.

Normally no one would have even been in this chamber, but there was a test in progress, a preliminary run. As such, he felt his duty required him to pass this information along to his commanding officer.

In the days before the nukecaust, this was known as "passing the buck."

"Sir?" he asked a man who was watching over operations from across the room.

"Yes?"

"You might want to check this."

The man approached. He was dressed in the same type of uniform, with tan, pressed slacks and a short-sleeved buttoned-up shirt of the same color. He was also wearing an embossed name tag that read Brosnan.

Brosnan exhaled a burst of air from his lungs as he stepped up next to the seated man at the screen. "What is it now, Regis?" he asked tiredly.

"Something's set off one of the mines," Regis said.

"Second one this month, both times during tests. Wonder what triggered it this time?"

"Don't know, sir. Maybe another one of those weird-ass mutie fish."

"Maybe," Brosnan said, checking another screen. "Maybe not."

"That's what I think," Regis said confidently.

"Weather reports a hell of a storm blasting across the water out there. The mine was hit by lightning, no doubt," Brosnan said. "Or maybe you're actually right, and it was another one of those mutant fish. They seem to be becoming a problem. I think the communication buoys we put out there are drawing them in somehow.''

"Lightning. Sure. No doubt," Regis agreed. "Sounds good." A pause. "So, I guess you'll be the one answering to the Admiral if you're wrong?''

Brosnan considered it for a moment. He was second-in-command to the Admiral, but the title was merely a formality given for his loyalty and seniority. The title also came because Brosnan knew not to make even the slightest move without consulting with his master first.

Brosnan picked up the microphone at the far end of the room and pressed the Send key.

"Mothman One, this is Base. Mothman One, this is Base. Do you copy?''

"Copy that." The comm units provided excellent clarity, even with the nearby storm.

"I need to speak to the Admiral.''

There was a slight burst of static.

"Mr. Brosnan, I requested radio silence," an icy voice said. "You were supposed to track and observe, not talk.''

"Yes, sir, I know, but something's triggered one of the mines across the bay. Thought you might want to have a look, seeing as how you're already out that way.''

"Our own sensors already caught the explosion, and we're almost at the site now," the voice of Admiral Poseidon said briskly. "Is there anything else?''

Regis winced at Brosnan as he replied "No, sir, Brosnan out.''

"Wonder what he thinks set it off?" Regis asked.

Brosnan didn't answer.

They would both hear about this when the Admiral returned to port.

Chapter Twelve

The yellow life raft bobbed in the ocean, a lifesaving cork of inflated plastic and canvas. In the raft, in varying degrees of condition from the ordeal of the night before, were J.B., Dean, Mildred and Doc. Ryan was also seated in the raft, but on the other side, as far away from human contact as he could manage in the limited quarters.

All of them were sodden with seawater, but their clothing was rapidly starting to dry out in the heat of the sun.

Each person in the raft was silent, each one adrift physically, but also mentally in his or her own private thoughts and memories. Ryan could hear the calling of gulls, blown out to sea in the storm, now stuck hovering, far from land.

"Not quite ten o'clock," J.B. said quietly after glancing at his chrono. "Going to be another hot one."

Receiving no answer, he returned to tending his Uzi, taking the weapon apart to clean and dry it as best he could without the right supplies.

"At least it stopped raining," Mildred noted softly, trying to pick up J.B.'s thread of conversation. The lapping of the waves was starting to slowly hypnotize her, so she was glad even for the sound of her own words. Talking to herself was better than returning to the stupor she'd been drifting into before the Armorer spoke.

Doc had finished draining the seawater from his bulky Le Mat and had returned the large pistol to its proper resting place in the holster tied down against his leg.

"How are the knees, Doc?" Dean asked.

"Better. I should be able to walk and skip once more if, or should I say *when*, we reach dry land. Between that horrible bloodsucker back in the swamps and my unfortunate fall last night, I could certainly use the steadying support of my walking stick."

"Here, you babbling old fool," Mildred said, handing Doc a long slender object she'd pulled from beneath her coat. "I was able to get this down the side of my jeans before the shit hit the fan...." Her voice trailed off as she caught a brief, almost unperceptible look of pain cross Ryan's face.

The one-eyed man's countenance quickly returned to its frozen, stoic calm.

Ryan was scared of what might happen once he did show emotion.

Doc didn't notice Ryan's discomfort in his momentary joy of recovering his beloved ebony-and-silver stick. "My walking stick! Woman, you have produced a feat of sleight of hand that even the greatest of stage illusionists could not hope to compete with! Perhaps I will allow you to win the next argument between the two of us."

"Yeah, well, try not to poke yourself. Or the loft," J.B. said as he continued to strip the Uzi.

"John Barrymore, I assure you, this finely hewn blade of Toledo steel will taste nothing but the rich ichor of our foes," Doc replied in his most haughty voice.

"Who'd mine this stretch, J.B.? Doesn't make sense," Ryan said, the first words to come out of his mouth in hours.

"I know it doesn't make any sense," J.B. agreed, relieved to see his friend speaking again. "Naval mines are usually on the ocean floor or anchored to it. You keep the damned things floating around freely; they're completely unpredictable. What hit us had to be a contact mine. Old ordnance."

"Not that old, It still worked."

"Hell, Ryan, it might have been floating out here since predark," J.B. continued. "No telling what might have fallen overboard or been dredged up when the bombs fell. Once everything fell about, predictions went south. We've run into enough unexplained crap to prove that ourselves."

"Shit, J.B. The coast of Georgia wasn't exactly a strategic site. Were they trying to keep it safe for tourism?" Ryan said disgustedly.

"Didn't say it was strategic," the Armorer protested. "Just gave my theory why the fragger might have been out where it was when it detonated."

There was no anger in J.B.'s voice. He'd seen Ryan

in these moods before, and it didn't pay to argue. He knew his friend was hurting over the casualties from the night before. Hell, they all were hurting. Jak and Krysty were family, and the sudden erasing of their presence still hadn't fully sunk in.

Yet, out of everyone, J.B. had known Ryan the longest, and even he couldn't gauge the extent of his grief this time. This loss cut deep. Krysty had been Ryan's lifeline, his shining beacon in the darkness. Now, with that light extinguished, there was no telling what Ryan might do.

If they lived long enough to find out.

Ryan fell silent once more, trying to work the previous night's sequence of events in his own mind into a semblance of logic. If he was going to lose the woman he loved, there had to be a reason beyond blind, stupid luck and a lost contact mine.

"What do we do now?" Mildred wondered aloud.

"No way to paddle. No oars." Dean was sullen. "Guess we could swim back to shore."

"Excuse the hell out of me for not packing oars," J.B. growled. "I was busy finding us a safe way off the boat."

"Too busy to grab some chow?" Dean queried.

"What? More of those shitty crackers? I didn't see you snatching up stuff in the galley, Dean," J.B. retorted. "You were clinging to Doc's ass with both hands last time I looked."

"The lad was merely giving me a push," Doc protested.

"Enough!" Mildred ordered. "Not another peep,

John! That goes for you, too, Dean. Doesn't matter who got what and what was left behind."

"At least everyone did have presence of mind to hang on to their blasters," J.B. said grudgingly.

"Lot of good that does us now," Dean grumbled. "Can't eat bullets."

"Bullets can chill your scrawny hide," J.B. said.

"Bickering isn't going to help a thing," Mildred told them.

"Dean's right. There's no food, except for the emergency jerky rations in our pockets. No water, except what's left in the canteens. Face it, people. We're fucked blue," Ryan said wearily.

The sound of defeat in the one-eyed man's voice was much more upsetting than their current status. If Ryan was giving up, there was no hope for any of them.

"Bullshit, Dad," Dean said. "That's not what I meant."

"What did you say to me?" Ryan asked.

"I said, bullshit. We're not dead yet. You're the one who always told me to not give up until I was six feet under. Well, I'm not, and neither are you," Dean said angrily. "So, I'm not. I'm just griping because I'm hungry, and even some stale crackers would taste good right now."

Ryan pondered that one for a long moment.

"I must be getting old," he said finally. "You're right, son. We're not dead yet."

"I do not want to hear a word about you claiming

to be old, Ryan,'' Doc said. ''You have no earthly idea.''

"What do we do?'' J.B. asked.

"Nothing. For now. What can we do?'' Ryan said. "But I'm not giving up yet.''

RYAN WAS HALF-ASLEEP and wanted to escape by dreaming. His body was drenched in warm sweat. There was no relief from the hellish sun that was now directly overhead and pounding down on the lost and drained group in the raft.

He was still too awake to dream. He wasn't fully immersed in the type of REM sleep that would normally have kept him deep inside the images his mind was replaying, and he stirred restlessly.

Once again he was in the sea near the rapidly sinking *Patch,* attempting to find Krysty and Jak after they had been lost, but all he was surfacing with was handfuls of water. He couldn't see a thing either above or below the waves, not even where the boat had been before he leaped into the churning waters. He knew his lifeline was secure as long as it was being held by J.B., so he went down and came up again and again, diving into the gloom and reaching out with both hands for an arm or a leg, but there was nothing to wrap his fingers around and save.

That was the way the search had ended—with empty hands.

A groggy Ryan opened his eye and half closed it again to escape the sunlight.

There was no way to cheat this one as he had

cheated the odds so many times before, no way to pull a hidden weapon or signal a backup, no way to outthink or outfight a storm. Ryan had no control of nature, no way to smell a hidden bomb while wrestling in the middle of such weather.

She was gone. Krysty was gone, along with Jak. Ryan could feel no sense of loss for the athletic young albino, at least not now. The loss of Jak would be dealt with in time. Ryan had lost other loved ones and could still summon up an ache in his psyche for them when he dwelled in that forlorn section of his soul. Jak would join other companions that had been sacrificed to Deathlands. His bravery, his courage, his always dependable loyalty wouldn't be forgotten.

Still, there was no grief for Jak. He couldn't grieve for his friend until he was able to accept that Krysty was no longer going to be at his side, in his bed, in his mind. She'd been swept away, vanished before he even had a chance to look upon her beauty and hold the image in his brain for a last time.

And even though his conscious mind wouldn't accept her death, the second brain knew. The primordial part of every human psyche that stretched back to the dawn of mankind had taken in the full measure of the facts, digested them and accepted the only logical outcome.

Krysty Wroth was dead.

And as he slumped in his own nook of the raft, his lone eye shining bright with unshed tears, Ryan leaned the blind side of his face against the wet plastic and dealt in his own manner with yet another bad hand dealt to him. Dean was right. He wasn't the kind of man who could just accept defeat without a fight to the death.

Ryan Cawdor dealt with the pain by wanting revenge.

AFTER LONG HOURS of misery, the sun fell and night stepped back into place. There was talk and debate, and ultimately no solution to the problem. In the relative cool of the darkness, everyone fell into restless sleep, and this time, minus the rain and the heat, actually got some needed rest during their second night spent in the raft.

Everyone succumbed except for Ryan, who saw something that made him feel as though he were experiencing a nightmare. The only difference between this one and the numerous others he'd endured while having his molecules scrambled during the transitional phase of matter transfer was that he was wide-awake.

He'd been staring at the water when a series of splashes appeared unexpectedly at the edge of the raft. Fearing the worse, Ryan peered intently at the glassy surface while putting his right hand on the butt of his SIG-Sauer. If some sort of mutated killer shark or radioactive electric eel or giant crab monster he didn't like decided to show itself, he had no problem with blowing it away.

He wanted to kill something. The placid personality he'd been inhabiting since the boat had gone down was smothering him. He had to rid himself of the grief and anguish soon before it fed upon his own soul and swallowed him up, drowning him just as effectively as the sea had fed upon Jak and Krysty.

However, he wasn't expecting a human head to raise itself up from the inky black liquid.

The back of the head was all he saw. Lank hair from the head was long and blond and in a mass of tangled curls that all dripped water. Ryan held his breath and waited for long seconds, until the head turned to a profile view that was human and not human.

The being spotted Ryan, then spun completely around for a face-to-face look. As they met each other's gaze, Ryan sensed no fear in the intent of his aquatic visitor, only curiosity. Ryan felt the same way. He'd never seen anything quite like the humanoid paddling patiently in the water next to him.

The face was primarily a pair of eyes, oval orbs of milky white tinged slightly with a coating of lemon yellow. Blue veins were running like a predark road map through the milk, and the pupils were saucer shaped. Below the twin ovals was a pair of vertical slits in a slight protrusion that might have been a nose, and a half-moon mouth with the corners turned downward. The lips on the mouth were pencil thin and dark purple, and the skin of the face was peeling in several places, as if the creature had been caught outside unprotected and suffered a slight sunburn. The new skin under the peeled-away epidermis looked shiny and wet, not dry.

Ryan decided that he knew what he was looking at—some kind of water mutie.

"Help?" the mutie asked in a slow, dragging voice.

A question? Ryan couldn't be sure. He couldn't be sure of anything anymore.

"Sure," he said. "Help."

Then, without a sound, the face was gone, and Ryan was left gazing at himself in the black mirror of the ocean's surface.

LATE IN THE SECOND DAY, as Ryan drifted in and out of a dehydrated haze, he thought he saw movement on the horizon. Not wanting to raise false hopes in the others, he kept quiet and rubbed his good eye, trying to keep what he thought he saw into focus. Salt from the dried seawater on the back of his hand stung when he wiped it across his line of vision, and his eyesight momentarily clouded up, but Ryan kept his gaze on the dot.

Dean noticed his father staring and decided to see if his young eyes could help identify whatever had captured his father's rapt attention.

The boy saw the dot, too, and realized it was moving toward them.

"Hot pipe, Dad! You see what I see?"

"Yes, son, I believe I do," Ryan murmured.

"Looks like…people," Dean said. "They're swimming over here."

"What's swimming?" J.B. asked, taking a look. All of the group was now staring at the approaching sight. The one absentee was Doc, who snored on, oblivious to the mounting excitement.

"Shit," J.B. said. "More shipwreck victims? No room in the raft."

"Relax, John," Mildred said to him. "As fast as that pair seem to be moving, I doubt they're interested in setting up quarters with us."

The couple stopped, then paddled easily in the salt water, peering at the group from a distance of about thirty feet.

"Now what?" Dean asked

"Up to them," Ryan replied. "Guess we wait."

The manlike creature that Ryan had seen over the side of the life raft had returned with another of his kind. His companion was smaller. Once or twice, she flashed the group in the raft with an impressive set of breasts that were dotted with the fibrous scales that also covered the male creature's chest, so they all felt comfortable terming her as female.

A long hour passed and started to spread into a second, yet the creatures wouldn't go any closer to the raft.

"Muties," J.B. said.

"Eh? What? No, no, Nanette, not the bailing twine," Doc cried out as he awakened from his slumber.

"Shh! Don't go insulting our rescuers, John," Mildred admonished. "Just because they're choosing not to swim over closer and talk doesn't mean they're deaf."

"Rescuers? I think you're giving those two credit

they don't deserve,'' the Armorer replied. ''They don't look like they have half a brain between them.''

''They can communicate,'' Ryan said.

''How do you know?''

''I heard one speak to me, J.B.'' Ryan said. ''I was half out of it at the time, but the big one said 'Help' as plain as day. But that doesn't mean much if they just want to stay where they are and watch us like some kind of free peep show. Hell, they may be waiting for this sun to cook us into big slaps of jerky so they can have a snack.''

''Is that what you make of them, Dad?'' Dean asked. ''Think they're waiting for all of us to die?''

''No. My gut says that's not the case. He came back,'' Ryan mused, rubbing the beard stubble on his chin. ''Came back and brought a friend. No blasters, no blades.''

''No clothes,'' Dean said.

''Could be they do want to help us out. I imagine they're just as nervous about us as we are about them,'' Mildred said.

''Such queer-looking mutations almost make one believe in the existence of mythical Atlantis,'' Doc said, unable to keep himself from joining the conversation, weakened condition or not. ''Perhaps our little raft has crossed over into their realm. Their magical jeweled city could be on the floor of the ocean directly below us.''

Doc reached forward and grabbed Ryan's shirt. ''Imagine, Captain,'' he said, his eyes misted over, no longer seeing Ryan, but another leader entirely as he continued to spin his theory, "imagine an entire populace of water breathers! What better way to escape the hellish holocaust that has spread its poisonous fire across all of the lands of the planet?"

As Doc continued to speak, his voice became pitched higher and higher. All in the raft recognized the symptoms—the older man was entering into the mind-set he sometimes exhibited after a particularly grueling mat-trans jump, or after any other type of strenuous mental and physical activity. Shipwrecked and afloat with no provisions for several days was exhausting to the healthiest of men, and while Doc was as tough as dried leather, even he had his limits.

"Doc might not be that far off the beam about our visitors," Mildred said, squinting and trying to get a better look at the pair.

"What? Atlantis? Sure, Millie," J.B. said. "And those two are going to come spurting up to give us a lift back to shore on their dolphins."

"Not Atlantis We're in the wrong part of the ocean, anyway," Mildred retorted. "No, I mean what he said about there being no better way to escape the disease, the violence and the mental pain of living on the surface than by going down below, beneath the sea."

"Under the sea," Doc sang in an unfamiliar tune, "under the sea, dear, just you and me, dear, under the sea."

"I doubt those two are true amphibians, anyway," Mildred added, ignoring Doc's musical outburst. "They've been keeping their heads above water with no problem. They might be able to stay under a long time, but they seem to live on air just as easily as breathing oxygen through some kind of gills. The mutations appear purposely induced.''

Ryan recalled some of the horrors he'd seen back when taking a stroll through the Anthill's laboratories. They had been generating many of the same sorts of survivalist mutations there.

"Could be right, Mildred," Ryan said.

"Look at their eyes. I'll bet they're covered with a second protective membrane. That's what makes them so damned pop-eyed."

And then, as if they had heard Mildred's theories, both of the muties' heads vanished beneath the water in unison.

Chapter Thirteen

The color of the ceiling was industrial off-white. A bare light bulb, shining hot, hung a few inches from the painted surface. There was a roughness in the paint, a kind of swirling pattern.

Krysty closed her eyes in an attempt to adjust to what she had just seen, then reopened them.

The ceiling and bulb were both still there. She was flat on her back, and looking up.

"Ryan?" she said, almost not recognizing the sound of her own voice. The one-word question came out in a feeble croak. She cleared her throat and coughed hoarsely. Her mouth was as dry as chalk.

Krysty turned her head to the right, then left, taking in her surroundings. She was in a small room, no windows, a single closed door with a twelve-inch square of glass inserted at eye level. The walls were the same industrial off-white as the ceiling. She glanced down to a carpeted floor. The carpet was well worn but clean, its color a neutral dark blue. Very unassuming, very unthreatening.

She tried to sit up, and suddenly the beigeness of the room erupted in a variety of colors, all violent and nauseating. She laid her head back down on the pillow, and the sick sensations disappeared. She began a mental inventory. What had brought her to this place?

Then she remembered the water, the storm and the fall into the abyss.

Krysty lifted herself to a sitting position, this time much slower. The walls stayed bland. She swung her feet over the side of the bed—realizing for the first time she was barefoot—and let them fall onto the carpet. The woman sighed deeply. She was wearing a cotton pair of canary yellow pajamas, a matching set of top and bottom. She was alive, and dry, and wearing a man's nightclothes.

How she'd ended up here remained to be seen.

Krysty staggered on her feet as she stepped over to the door, consciously willing the returning small explosions of color to go away. She tried the doorknob, which was locked. How utterly...predictable.

She craned her neck and tried to see through the door's viewing portal. Outside was a hall, and directly across from her was a door that appeared to be identical to the one she was now housed behind. Printed on the door in stenciled black paint was the word Unit 2. No matter how she turned her head, all she could really see was the single door for Unit 2, along with the walls of the hall, which came complete with a silver handrail.

After looking at Unit 2, Krysty decided she was probably in Unit 1.

She turned back and took in her room. There was an open closet with a pull curtain near the head of the small single bed, and a bare end table stood between the closet door and the bed. She stepped over and pulled aside the curtain to the closet. Empty. She pulled open the drawer of the end table. Empty again.

"Enough of this," Krysty said, willing her voice to sound as menacing as she could make it. She balled up one fist tightly and began to pound on the door.

Time for some answers.

ACROSS THE HALL from Krysty in Unit 2, Jak had been awake for the past two hours, glaring at the locked door that held him prisoner. There were no hinges to lift, no inside locks to pick. The ob glass in the door was unbreakable and thick, offering nothing but a cloudy view of a door labeled Unit 1.

A realist, Jak had determined he wasn't going to be escaping through the door anytime soon. He'd turned his bed over in hopes of finding a bit of metal bedding he could use as a weapon, but the beds were of a single piece, cast in curved metal, with a soft mattress stuffed with foam pellets. The pillow was also self-contained, with no zippers or fasteners. Jak had used his teeth to tear it open, only to find more of the same foam pellets.

The end table was also a single piece of lightweight metal. The tabletop and drawer were empty and useless.

He climbed on the bed and managed to reach the Spartan light bulb gleaming overhead. He took off his pajama top and used it to protect his fingers from the heat, intending to unscrew the bulb...until he realized doing so would plunge him into near darkness. Jak decided that would be a pointless endeavor, and he stepped back down to the floor and shrugged back into his nightclothes.

The pajamas were another reason he was in such a foul mood. Jak hadn't been pleased to find his clothing and weapons taken from him. No Colt Python. No throwing knives. No boots. He was dressed in a pair of deep burgundy pajamas.

Jak was miserable. He despised being closed in.

So he lay on his bed, a few of the stray foam pellets spilling out from where he had torn open the pillow, and sulked.

Until he heard Krysty's pounding.

That caught his interest. He hadn't thought of knocking to announce himself.

Jak got to his feet and pounded on the wall of his room.

As KRYSTY HAD INTENDED, others also heard the strident thumping from Unit 1, which was soon joined by identical sounds from Unit 2. At the end of the hallway, hidden from the line of vision the secluded units allowed their inhabitants, sat a man behind a desk.

The man at the end of the walkway thumbed a comm button and spoke into a walkie-talkie he wore on a belt around his waist.

"Both of the visitors are now awake," he said into the device. "The sedatives kept them under for the forty-eight hours, as you requested."

"I had research to do," a resonant bass voice responded. "I'll be right there."

WITHIN FIVE MINUTES, Krysty's ploy had succeeded in getting her door opened. Two men entered.

One was the same who had first heard her and used the comm unit. The man was now wearing a vest adorned with an array of small gadgets and ammunition. He was carrying an AK-47 in one beefy hand, and Krysty had no doubt the man knew how to use it.

The second person to enter the room was the one the sec man summoned, obviously a leader from the dress and demeanor. The man was well built, large and handsome in a self-assured way.

"Ah, our mermaid has come back to us. How do you feel, my dear?" the lead man asked in a professional tone.

"Thirsty," Krysty rasped.

"I imagine so. You've been unconscious for nearly two days."

"Two days?" Krysty cried.

"You were given a sedative when you arrived. It was decided complete bed rest was the best cure for your ordeal."

A third man came into the room carrying a metal tray. On the tray was a plastic pitcher of water and a matching cup.

"This isn't the finest in wine, but I think water is what you need to get into your system now," the leader said.

For a fleeting second, Krysty wondered if any drugs might have been added to the water, but then discarded the thought. If that was true, so be it. So far, no one had harmed her. In fact, it looked as though they only wanted to help.

The orderly poured a cupful of the water and handed it to the seated Krysty, who quickly drank its contents. A second cup was poured and given to the redhead with the admonishment that she should sip or she'd make herself sick drinking so fast. Sound advice. Krysty sipped as the orderly set down the tray and left the room, closing the door behind him.

Leaving Krysty and the two men together.

She felt suddenly vulnerable without her familiar weapons and clothing, but quashed the feeling. Still, there was a hint of the unknown here that made her feel uneasy.

No one offered assistance without expecting some sort of payment.

"Who are you?" she asked.

"They call me the Admiral. My chosen name is Poseidon. You may address me as 'Admiral' or 'Sir.' I'm the senior officer here at Kings Point," the man said, smiling and enjoying the sounds of his rich bass voice. "Now, it's my turn. Who are you?"

"Krysty Wroth." There was no reason not to be honest.

He smiled when he heard the name. "You're a very lucky woman, Miss Wroth," Poseidon said. "If my submarine hadn't come along when it did, you would most certainly have drowned."

"Submarine?" Krysty had heard of such devices, but had never seen one.

"Aye, that's what I am truly, a submarine commander."

It seemed unreal for a man to be inside an underwater wag, and Krysty expressed the opinion verbally to Poseidon.

"Beneath the ocean at a certain depth, the activities of the surface world become meaningless," he replied. "We were passing by and then, the next thing I know, bodies were showing up on sonar."

"I owe you a life debt of thanks," she said. She still had a suspicious feeling about her self-proclaimed benefactor, but if what he said was true, then she was beholden to him.

"Not at all. Picking you up safely is part of my responsibilities as watchman of the sea."

Krysty took another sip of the lukewarm water. There was a question she had been dancing around, but she could no longer resist. She had to ask. She had to know.

"Where's Ryan?"

"Your companion? He's across the hall. Would you like to see him?"

Krysty felt twenty pounds of worry drop away from her body. She was still suspicious of how polite everyone was being, but she had no choice except to play along for now. Perhaps Ryan could help shed some light on what was going on in this place.

"Yes, I would. Please," she said, nodding.

Poseidon gestured, and the sec man standing behind him exited. He returned in less than sixty seconds with the person the Admiral knew only as her "companion."

When the pajama-clad Jak was presented to her, she tried hard to contain her disappointment. She was glad to see her friend, but had hoped that Ryan was the one they were talking about. Still, she knew the others—Doc, Mildred, J.B. and Dean, as well as Ryan—had to be around somewhere. Perhaps she and Jak had been the only two injured the night of the storm.

"Hey, Krysty," Jak said easily. Too easily. Krysty knew from past experience that he was sizing up everything and everybody in his field of vision.

"Hello, Jak."

"You okay?"

"Never better. Got a lump on the back of my head, that's all."

"Hair so big, helped protect you," Jak said, making a joke while continuing to take in the situation.

Krysty was waiting to see when the others would be presented. Apparently that wasn't going to happen.

"This is Jack? Jack Ryan?"

"No, no, just Jak. Jak Lauren."

"So his name isn't Ryan?" Poseidon said, gesturing at Jak.

"No. I'm sorry. I was thinking of one of my…other companions."

"Too bad. One of my favorite fictional characters is named Jack Ryan," Poseidon said. "Course, he's not the striking picture you are, son. No offense."

"Sure," Jak said, taking it very personally but not pressing the issue. There were no hidden throwing knives up the sleeves of the loose-fitting burgundy pajamas.

"Where are my other friends?" Krysty demanded.

"Other friends?" the Admiral pulled a perplexed expression onto his bearded face.

"In the boat, where I fell from." Again Krysty remembered the explosion, the sensation of falling and nothingness. The boat had either run into something in the storm, or a bomb or some kind of grenade had gone off in the hull.

Or they had been hit by something on purpose.

"I'm sorry, Miss Wroth. There were no other survivors," the Admiral said.

KRYSTY WASN'T BUYING the story Poseidon was selling. If Ryan was truly dead, she would know it. The bond they shared went way beyond physical—it was mental and spiritual and even had a bit of mysticism mixed in. Thanks to her mutant abilities and heightened awareness, both of which were returning to her faster and faster now that she was up and around, she just knew.

Other than the blow to the head she'd suffered, Krysty had experienced no other wounds, to either the body or the soul. That's how she knew Ryan wasn't dead. If he had died, the result of his passing would be like having a baseball-sized chunk of her own insides ripped out.

Still, the Admiral was in control of the situation.

For now, Krysty and Jak were going to have to play along. Both were feeling better now that their clothing had been returned to them. "Freshly laundered," Poseidon had announced. Krysty's long black fur coat was missing, but she really didn't mind for the time being. The weather outside was quite warm.

She was told her coat, along with her Smith & Wesson and other personal effects, was in storage, to be returned when she was ready to leave. Jak was in the same predicament. His prized .357 Magnum Colt Python and assorted blades, including the hidden leaf-bladed knives, were also being held.

"For safekeeping," Poseidon told them. "I wouldn't want you to be distracted from the tour."

A second sec man with an AK-47 had joined the first one as Poseidon led Jak and Krysty out of the base hospital. Krysty was surprised at how well everything was maintained—the walkways connecting the various buildings were clear, the grass—and there was plenty of it—was cut short. There were no broken windows or debris.

At least, in this part of the base. Within her line of vision, buildings could be seen in much worse repair. Poseidon pointed those out first.

"In time, those will be restored. It's a miracle this installation survived at all. There was an error somewhere that kept Kings Point from being pummeled with nuclear fire during the last dark days of the United States."

He stopped and saluted a brightly colored red, white and blue American flag that was snapping above them. The flag was tethered to a white metal flagpole. The two sec men also saluted, but not as crisply or as intently as Poseidon. Both men kept watchful eyes on their "tour group."

"We've got electric power for all of these sections," Poseidon bragged as he walked them over to a long, high-domed building on the edge of the coastline. "Armory, dormitory, briefing and tactical, hospital and, of course, the overlook arch for the submarine pens."

As the group passed other men, Krysty noticed only a few in proper naval attire similar to what Poseidon was wearing. Most were dressed in an amalgam of various styles of salvaged clothing similar to her own. She spotted leather, denim, cotton and flannel. The men in the civilian garb were also a striking mix of faces and nationalities, whereas the ones in uniforms were all clean-cut, square-jawed white men.

"Why some in fancy duds and others not?" Jak queried, echoing Krysty's thoughts.

"Only enlisted men can attain rank and position," the Admiral replied. "They are the elite who have the sanctioned right to wear the colors and insignia of the naval corps. The others you see are hired security."

"Grunts," Jak said. "Muscle."

"Precisely. They are well paid to do exactly as I tell them, with the promise of going higher if they exhibit the type of mind and character I am seeking for my navy. My followers grow in number each day as word spreads about the opportunity I offer here. I'm constantly amazed at how many men and women are just looking for the chance to improve themselves. There's not much in the field of career opportunities in this day and age.''

The group entered the long building. Poseidon led the way down a flight of metal steps to the wide, half-enclosed areas open for docking ships or submarines.

''This base was originally constructed in the old calendar year of 1979, during the declining years of the James Earl Carter administration. He worked up the base in grand style as a gift to his home state,'' Poseidon said. ''Small and attractive, and as you can see, durable.''

''Carter must've been one double-powerful baron,'' Krysty said.

''Not as strong as you think. He ruled for four years, then he was replaced with a new baron,'' Poseidon replied. ''His own people voted him out.''

''Voted?'' Jak asked.

''Um, threw him out. Fired him,'' Poseidon said.

''Sounds more like a leader of a ville to me,'' Krysty said. Jak nodded agreement.

''Don't use ignorance. This took place in the past, yet I still know it. History, you buffoons! Learn from the mistakes of others!'' Poseidon rumbled. ''I read this in a book in the base library. Most of the old texts were ruined, but one entire wall survived in readable condition, including a set of encyclopedias. Most illuminating.''

The Admiral gestured to a small, pale white submarine that had surfaced.

''We have a single working minisub, the *Moth,* that

comfortably holds a crew of eight but can accommodate twelve if needed. This is the same craft that rescued you and Jack Ryan, Miss Wroth.''

"Lauren," Jak protested.

"Whatever." Poseidon was playing the role of genial host to the best of his considerable ability, and Krysty had to credit the man's gift for gab. He was proud but not arrogant as he showed off his base, his men and his aquatic toys. Normally such a display would scream ego to her, since she'd been given the grand tour more than once by barons who quickly turned on her and her friends. Even the sec men were a familiar part of the routine.

But at the same time, Poseidon seemed genuinely interested in her opinions and comments. What did she think? Did she like this or that?

Jak wasn't as impressed. As he took in the white exterior tiles of the submarine, peering down over the rail at the tiny craft, he commented aloud, "Don't look like much."

Krysty was curious as to how Poseidon would respond to the insult.

The last thing she expected was laughter.

"You're right, Lauren!" Poseidon said in a tone of fellowship that made Krysty feel he'd used Jak's proper name as a reward for amusing him. "Looks like an oblong cake of lye soap floating in a cast-iron tub! No, the *Moth* is only for short-range use, a scientific-exploration craft. Not military issue at all. The real-deal submarine is in another berth, and trust me when I say I think you will find it to be more impressive."

As they stepped over to the sub he was discussing, both realized Poseidon had told the truth.

"This is the USS *Raleigh*," Poseidon announced. "One of the elite of the nuclear warships of the world before skydark. She is a Los Angeles-class boat, thirty-three feet in diameter for the highest speed capabilities—capable of passing thirty five knots when the reactor core is operating at full potential. She comes equipped with the BSY-1 combat system and the Mk 32 VLS system for vertical missile launch. Her hull is approximately three inches thick and composed of a vanadium and HY-80 high-tensile steel mix. She displaces an estimated 6,900 tons."

The group of five stepped out on the gangplank on top of the massive submarine for a closer look at the lookout station.

"Now are you impressed, Mr. Lauren?" Poseidon asked.

Jak didn't answer as he peered down the front of the deadly steel cigar.

"I'll take your silence as a yes," Poseidon said. "That ends the tour. I can't top the *Raleigh*."

"Don't we get to go inside?" Krysty asked.

"No, you do not. The interior of the boat is classified." Poseidon nodded to one of the accompanying sec men. "Take our guests back to the ward."

"I'd rather have something to eat," Krysty said. "I'm starved."

"And you shall. But in your rooms."

"Not in the cafeteria?" Krysty asked, trying to be as flirtatious as possible.

"I'm afraid not."

"Sounds like we're your prisoners," Jak said bluntly.

"No, but you are my guests, and I always take care of my guests."

Neither Jak nor Krysty particularly liked the sound of that.

Chapter Fourteen

After the two muties disappeared, Ryan feared the worse.

Perhaps he and the others were nothing more than a curiosity, five incredibly stupid outlanders baking and dying in the heat. How long could they last out there in the Lantic without food or drink? How long before they used their own weapons to ease the pain of the weaker ones?

Ryan knew land was close by. J.B. had used his minisextant and confirmed that the coast of Georgia was within their grasp...with the boost of an outboard engine or a sail or even paddles for the bastard raft they were currently calling home. The storm couldn't have taken them that far off course.

Suddenly the raft shifted and began to lurch forward.

"I take back every bad thought I've been thinking about the fish man and his wife," Mildred announced, sliding to the right, then to the left as the raft shifted again. "I think we're getting a lift."

"Those muties must be strong as horses if they're going to try and push us all the way in to shore," J.B. noted. "If that's what they're attempting to do."

"What else could it be?" Mildred retorted. "This isn't the easiest way to go about trying to sink us."

"We heading in the right direction, J.B.?" Ryan asked, shielding his eye and trying to scan the horizon.

"I believe so. I'd have to do another reading to be sure, but land should be straight ahead."

"What if they tear a hole in the raft?" Dean asked, shifting again as the raft surged forward a few more feet.

"He's got a point," J.B. said. "Be easier to pull us with a rope."

The Armorer took the coil he'd used back during the sinking of the *Patch* to secure Ryan in his frantic and futile search for Krysty and Jak. The lean man lashed one end of the line to a hard plastic ring at the nose of the raft and dangled the other end down into the ocean.

"Think they'll find it?" Dean asked.

The answer came quickly as the rope went taut in J.B.'s callused hands.

The jerking stopped, and they began to make smoother progress.

Time passed. About every half hour or so, the rope would slacken and the raft would slow and come to a stop. Then, in less than ten minutes, after the muties had gotten their wind back, the trip would resume once more.

All told, the journey took approximately three hours.

THE FIRST THING Ryan and the others saw as they approached dry land was a windmill, rotating slowly from a perch high atop a meshlike latticing of scavenged wood and metal. The fan blades of the windmill were painted a serene deep blue, much darker than the azure of the afternoon sky.

As they came closer to the shore, more windmills were revealed to their line of sight, smaller ones joining the first, all shapes and sizes. There were dozens of the rickety-looking support structures, each one with a bladed wheel on top, each wheel turning easily in the stiff breeze coming in from the sea. Some of the contraptions shared the same color of blue as the tallest one they had seen first; others were painted in warmer colors, such as red and yellow. Amusingly enough, a few were adorned with a shocking coat of pink.

A shambling maze of wooden steps led down into the mass of windmills from a dock located at the water's edge. Ryan saw no other boats or seaworthy crafts. In fact, there was no transportation to be seen at all.

They were now close enough to hear the creaking of the windmills as their blades turned in the breeze.

"Bless my befuddled soul, but we are in Holland," Doc muttered as he got his first real look at the community of windmills. The old man was still in a semi-state of delirium. "Wooden shoes for everybody, I insist! Tulips of all hues for the taking. Once, tulips were as valuable as precious metals and fine gemstones. An entire economy built on the bulb of a flower, now lost, now common."

"That isn't Holland, Doc," Mildred said. "You're off by a few miles."

"Woman, I am off more than a mere few miles," Doc retorted huffily. "I am a full-blown mental mess. My mental state is off by distances that can only be measured between the stars."

"I'm glad you said it and I didn't," Mildred said. "I'd give anything for a tape recorder right now."

The steady forward momentum the two amphibian mutants had created as they pulled the raft along suddenly ceased, and the rope stretching into the water went slack for a final time.

"Looks like the free ride's over," J.B. observed.

"Guess they didn't want a personal thank-you," Mildred added lightly, giving her man a quick one-armed hug around the waist.

"Think we'll have to swim the rest of the way in, Dad?" Dean asked.

Ryan didn't answer. He was peering at the dock and the windmills.

"No," he said finally. "We're still on a direct course with the dock. See the ladder?"

He pointed at the lower front section of the dock.

"Tide'll take us right to it, I hope."

The one-eyed man was proved right. The yellow raft uncannily drifted into the proper position. Ryan and the Armorer both reached out and grabbed the lower rung.

"Like this balloon was remote controlled or something," Dean observed excitedly. "Slid in just like a hot pipe."

Now that the raft was stable and they had a place to go, J.B. scanned the area as best he could before actually exiting into the unknown. "What's the drill?" he asked. "Our friends seem to have pulled a vanishing act."

"Not much choice in the matter, J.B. We go ashore and see who's been building windmills," Ryan replied. "Mildred, see if you can get Doc to snap out of it long enough to use his hands and his feet. We're going to have to climb out of here and get on dry land."

"I'm not sure how much walking he's going to be able to do once he's on the dock," Mildred warned, lifting one of Doc's rubbery arms and dropping it back down with a wet slap as it hit the bottom of the life raft. "I'm not sure how much more I'm going to be able to take myself. We're all as weak as newborns."

"Not me! I feel great! Hungry as a two-headed mutie tiger, but I feel good," Dean said. "I'm ready to do some exploring."

"Sure, Dean, I'm feeling the adrenaline surge, too," Ryan told his son. "We've found a safe harbor, but once we get up on that dock, I doubt we're going to be able to do much of anything beyond a measured crawl."

The one-eyed warrior reached out, taking a rung of the wooden ladder and pulling himself upright. He was the first man out of the raft, his blaster in hand.

"Come on, Doc," Mildred said. "Rise and shine."

"Are we there yet?" Doc asked weakly.

DEAN SPOTTED A TRENCH with running water as soon as they stepped off the dock and onto the grassy beach lands where the windmills were standing.

"Hot damn! Water!"

"Hold up before you go drinking, Dean," Ryan warned. "Odds are these windmills are pumping some kind of seawater."

J.B. cupped a handful to his nostrils and sniffed. "Yeah, this is salty. Least, it smells salty. Course, everything smells salty to me after being out in that raft as long as we were."

"Looks like a settlement over there," Mildred said, pointing toward a group of tents and other structures in the near distance. No one there had noticed the visitors yet, or if they had, they weren't too excited about it.

The architecture of the settlement was nonexistent. Most of the shelters that came into view as Ryan and the others warily approached were indeed nothing more than old tents. There was a handful of recycled travel trailers and a broken-down motor home that was more rust than metal. A large circus tent with a high ceiling and faded strips of red and yellow stood near the center of the misshapen community. Picnic tables of wood were scattered in front of the tent and by a natural well, which appeared to serve as the source for fresh drinking water and bathing since three old white porcelain bathtubs with the plugs permanently adhered into their drains were behind a portable curtain.

Most of the people seemed to be dressed in similar loose-fitting jumpsuits.

"What kind of ville is this?" Dean asked, cocking his head in a quizzical fashion.

"Not a ville. It's a commune," a woman retorted. "What you see is what you get, so don't go shooting off those blasters or trying to push people around. Mind your business like everyone else is doing, you're welcome to stay."

"A commune, you say? So, where are the flowers in your hair, madam?" Doc asked.

"Haven't worn flowers in years, but it's a nice sentiment. I'm Shauna Watson. I run the place, such as it is."

"Ryan Cawdor," Ryan replied. "This here's my boy, Dean. The older man is Doc Tanner. J. B. Dix is on his right. The lady's Dr. Mildred Wyeth."

Shauna Watson looked to be about forty years old. Her thick black hair was cut painfully short to the scalp. Blue eyes, the same color as the blades of the windmill the companions had first seen, were set in a tanned face. Freckles dotted the bridge of her pug nose. She'd been cute, once—that much could be seen. Now, approaching middle age had taken a new spin, giving her an elfin, gamine quality she'd carry to her grave.

Like the others in her commune, she was wearing a one-piece khaki jumpsuit with a zipper running down the length of the front from throat to crotch.

The zipper was open down to the navel, leaving little to the imagination regarding her small yet still firm breasts. The sleeves of the functional attire were rolled up high on her upper arms, revealing veined biceps. Shauna wasn't a woman used to sitting back and letting others do the work. Knee-high boots with a flat heel and a wide utility-type work belt completed the ensemble.

"Two doctors?" Shauna said, looking at Doc and Mildred. "We could use a physician."

"Only one to choose from, I'm afraid," Doc interjected, having returned to his usual demeanor once more. "I am a doctor of letters. My colleague is the general practitioner."

"Got a little girl broke her arm just yesterday. I've tried to set up a temporary splint, but I'm no medic. Would you mind?"

"Not at all, but I've got to get some kind of nourishment in my stomach," Mildred said. "The shape I'm in right now, I wouldn't be much help to anybody."

"Fair enough. We can get together some food while your party washes up." Her gaze fell to the holster of Ryan's SIG-Sauer, as well as the other hardware the group was carrying.

"What *is* the story behind the blasters? You and your group are packing enough heat to burn down my entire place here without even emptying the clips."

"Protection," Ryan said. "The only man without a blaster these days is a dead one."

"You free-lancing for Poseidon? Doing merc work?"

"No. We don't even know who Poseidon is," Ryan said.

"One of the men when we first obtained our vessel mentioned a Lord Poseidon," Doc said. "They mockingly called themselves disciples."

Shauna snorted. "Calling himself a lord now, is he? Guess it's a good a title as any. Yeah, Lord Poseidon is a real piece of work, showing up here all the time and bleeding us dry. Bastard. No naval vessels can enter this part of the coast without his say-so."

"We did—" Mildred began to say, and stopped.

"Yeah, and then you found out the hard way about his paranoid little piece of the world," Shauna added. "The Admiral doesn't like surprises. He's the one who blew your boat out from under you."

Ryan's eye narrowed. "He's the one who caused the accident?"

"Unless you had a chart with the locations of the mines."

Ryan felt like he'd just been knifed in the stomach and gutted up to his chin. The sensation was a mix of pleasure and pain. The mine that had wrecked the *Patch* had a source, and the source's name was Poseidon. His hand shot out and grabbed Shauna by the upper arm, pulling her close to him.

"I have a debt to settle with your Admiral," he grated.

"Don't we all?" a new voice said from the nearby

tent. The group turned and saw not a person, but the twin barrels of a shotgun sticking out of a window flap. "Let the lady go, One-eye, and we'll give you all the dope you need to know about Poseidon. Believe me, we don't exactly care for the son of a bitch, either."

"How did you know about our boat?" Ryan asked the woman.

"Mike told me. Mike and Ida," she replied.

"Mike and Ida?" Dean retorted. "What kind of stupe names are those?"

"Mike and Ida are what we call the two Dwellers who saved your ass, boy," Shauna said. "You've seen them, so you know they're muties. Far as I can tell, Mike must've heard the explosion, mebbe he was even out that way when it happened. He's the one who found you, came back and discussed it with his people. They sent him to me, and we were all in agreement to bring you in."

Ryan tamped down his rage and released his grip on Shauna's arm.

She rubbed her upper arm vigorously to return the circulation. Ryan's fingers had clamped down like steel bands.

"Now," she said, "I'm letting all of you keep your blasters, just to show we can trust one another. Here at the commune, our day-to-day survival depends on our word."

"My word's good," Ryan said. "You'll have no trouble from us."

"You speak for the ones with you?" came the voice behind the shotgun.

"I do."

"I'm coming out, then."

A tall lean man with long blond hair and brown eyes stepped from hiding. For a change, he wasn't wearing one of the jumpsuits. He wasn't wearing much of anything at all but a pair of oft-repaired, cutoff blue jeans and a worn pair of sandals. Besides staying cool in the heat, the reason for his lack of clothing was undoubtedly to maintain a rich brown tan, and to show off the ornate tattooing that covered his entire body.

The shotgun was still leveled at the group.

"Name's Alan Carter," the man finally said, lowering the weapon. "I heard who you are. I'm sec man for the commune."

"**Real** trusting for a sec man, aren't you?" J.B. asked.

"Not really. But you said the magic word when you mentioned Poseidon," Carter responded. "I, for one, would like to see him dead, and any enemy of his is a friend of mine."

Ryan took in the pattern of tattoos that wrapped around Carter's chest, back, neck, arms and legs. The canvas his body had provided was a work of skin art. The subject seemed to be a mix of demons and machinery: skeletons with blazing skulls atop roaring motorcycles; green-faced monsters with pop-eyes and fangs, their tongues lolling out long and wet behind them as they shifted gears with floor-clutch rigs as big as their freakish heads; even horned devils atop rocket ships, waving their pitchforks as they blasted off into the great beyond.

"Nightmarish," Doc said, also gazing upon the tattoos. "How do you sleep at night?"

"By closing my eyes."

"About the accident...were there any casualties?" Shauna asked.

"Two," Ryan replied, his voice nearly catching in his throat. "A man and a woman, Jak Lauren and Krysty Wroth. I don't suppose your Mike found any more survivors?"

"No, he didn't."

"They'd be pretty hard to miss. Jak's a full albino and Krysty's got the reddest hair this side of a sunset."

"Sorry, Cawdor, but no. You and your buds are it."

"Mebbe another one of his mutie friends?"

"No bodies, no trace. Nothing," Carter said.

"Take a moment to wash up," Shauna said, gesturing toward the community baths. "I'll get supper going earlier than usual in your honor. After you're done, come inside the big tent here. Obviously we need to talk."

Chapter Fifteen

"Funny, I still feel wrong speaking of them in the past tense. I can't think of them as being dead. Not yet." Ryan stood on those words and began to pace along the earthen floor of the large central commune tent. The rest of his friends minus Mildred, who was checking the injured child, and Alan Carter and Shauna Watson were seated at various places along the numerous tables inside the tent. Normally this was the community dining room, but it also served as a place for meetings.

A meal was being prepared at the back of the tent while they talked.

"Before, Krysty's death seemed to be fate spitting down on my head again," Ryan continued. "Now I've got a face and a name to put on who took her from me."

"Poseidon's been responsible for a lot of deaths, Cawdor," Shauna said. "How far you intending to take this?"

"As far as it goes," Ryan replied.

Shauna nodded back. "Good."

"Why were you here?" Carter asked. "We don't get many sea travelers."

"We were looking to head up the coast. Head for

the Carolinas, Virginia mebbe. Too damned hot down here," Ryan said. "No real agenda."

"I'd like to know more about these mutants," Mildred said as she entered, overhearing the end of the conversation and casually trying to change the subject from Ryan's lust for revenge on Poseidon. "Have they always been here?"

"As long as I can remember, Dr. Wyeth, but we don't know where the poor bastards were originally spawned," Shauna said. "There are old stories about a colony of test subjects housed on an old oil rig located far offshore. Scientists were living there while trying to create a new race of mutie. The Dwellers seem to be the result."

"So, how many of them are there?"

"About a dozen adults," Carter said. "A few kids. Most of their young are stillborn. Because of the high death rate, they treasure their children above all else. We never actually get to see the children. Except for me and a few others in the commune here, the Dwellers tend to shun contact with landers."

"Can't blame them for that."

"We have a trade deal with them similar to the one we have to maintain with Poseidon—except the mutants are much more fair and humane. No surprise there."

"They do talk, then? Ryan said he heard one speak to him," Mildred said.

"Right," Ryan added, but he really wasn't listening. Shauna's mention of a trade deal had him distracted. He was beginning to have the glimmer of an idea.

"Speech isn't very comfortable for them, especially English. The only reason Mike can talk as well as he does is because it's a carryover from his former humanity. They prefer to communicate in wordless ways. Their eyes, facial expressions—you know, body language."

"Tell me the pattern," Ryan said. "What's the usual way you go about trading?"

"Once a day, at sunset, we go and trade," Shauna replied. "What we have to offer is minuscule compared to the amount of seafood they bring us, but I think they like having us as neighbors, so they never complain."

"No, no, not the muties," Ryan said impatiently. "I'm talking about Poseidon."

"Once a week now that it's getting warmer," Carter said. "He should be sending a wag in to pick up his 'tribute' in the next day or two. Why?"

"Might have an idea. Let you know when," Ryan replied.

"Actually, before he got his navy fetish, Poseidon was rumored to be involved with the project that created the Dwellers," Shauna said. "Course, he couldn't have been more than a kid. I doubt he was the one actually doing the genetic engineering. Probably his old man or another relative."

"We have a lot in common with the muties," Carter added. "We all want to be left alone to live our own lives, simple as that. For them, Poseidon and his fleet aren't much of a threat, but for us, as long as he continues to show up demanding tribute for his so-called protection of our waterways, we can never hope to be safe.''

Doc cleared his throat from across the tent's interior. "The truth lies in the name."

"Dammit, Doc, you need to be resting." Mildred crossed the room and reached down to take Doc's pulse.

"I am resting, my good woman. I cannot remember a time in recent memory when I was more at ease," Doc retorted. "There's dry land beneath my boot heels, the sky is sunny and warm without a hint of rain. I am dry and relatively clean. Life, for the immediate moment, is good."

He was telling the truth. His pulse was steady and true, and the ashen color his face had taken on was starting to fade back to its usual healthier sallow pallor—the natural skin tone the old man wore when up to full fighting strength.

"Go ahead, Doc. I recognize the look in your eye. You've got something to tell us," Mildred said. "But try and keep it short. None of us are in the mood to be lectured at."

"Very well, Dr. Wyeth. As I was saying, the truth behind our unseen foe lies in the name he has chosen for himself. For one who has his origins in the sea, and continues to attempt to dominate his own little kingdom, the name of Poseidon is an inspired selection."

"How so?" Ryan asked, his own interest now spurred by Doc's comments.

"Greek mythology, sir," Doc said, propping himself up on an elbow as best he could without falling out of the flimsy folding cot, "the timeless tales of the ancient gods and the human heroes who tried vainly to live up to the examples set by their masters. Unfortunately for all of humanity, the gods, too, were as flawed as their human creations."

"Always wondered why everything was so screwed up," J.B. said.

"Poseidon was lord of the sea, and friend enough to man to present him with the first equine."

"First what?" Shauna said, frowning.

"First horse," Mildred translated. "Try and keep the florid speech patterns down to a level where we can all understand it, okay, Doc?"

"Of course, of course. Now where was I? Oh, yes. Poseidon was also brother to the mighty Zeus, the supreme ruler of all, and second only to him in eminence. Zeus was the storm bringer, ruler of the sky and master of the terrible thunderbolt. Poseidon's domain was nearly as great. His domain was the sea, and when he was not inhabiting the halls of grand Olympus with his brothers, Poseidon could be found below the waves in a magnificent palace of his own design."

"Sounds like the Admiral. He's always on or near or under the water somehow."

"Like Zeus, Poseidon was also a master of the storm, but only those at sea."

The memory of the storm and the subsequent accident was fresh in all of their minds.

Doc continued. "He carried a mighty trident, a three-pronged spear, with which he would shake and shatter whatever he pleased. In fact, Poseidon was commonly called 'Earth-Shaker.'"

"Lesson's over," Carter said. "The way they're waving in back, the food's ready."

A dinner bell was rung soon after, summoning all to dinner. The other members of the commune, which seemed to consist of less than one hundred total, were mostly women with a small mix of children ranging from eight to about Dean's age. A few elderly folk were also in the count Ryan silently made. He noted the lack of men of any age. All of them were starting to mill about and take seats at the wooden picnic tables in the tent.

"We'll all eat, and you can enjoy tonight's entertainment. We'll talk more tomorrow," Shauna said. "For now, you are our guests."

The meal that was being laid out before them was the first real solid nutrition any of the travelers had eaten since the visit to Tuckey's.

The feast began with the placement of a single tall plastic tumbler on the table at the hand of each diner. After the glasses were down, two women in the familiar jumpsuits walked down either side of the aisles with carts that bore large clear pitchers filled with an icy-cold brown liquid. The cold was a given since drops of condensation were beading the pitchers' exteriors.

Each cup was filled to the top with the liquid, and the remainder of the pitcher left at the table.

Mildred and Doc, recognizing the beverage, both responded by grabbing the plastic glasses and taking generous gulps.

"By the Three Kennedys—" Doc began.

"Ice tea!" Mildred finished.

The rest of Ryan's party followed suit, drinking greedily from the glasses.

"We believe in maintaining some of the old Southern traditions down here," Shauna said.

"Where'd you get the ice?" Dean asked. "You got a generator for a freezer?"

"Of a sort. We harvest wind power for irrigation and electricity. We have a shed with electric lights, and some outlets to run refrigerators and freezers for storage."

As the tea was being consumed, simple fresh salads came around. In the huge bowls plopped down at each table were lettuce, chopped celery, sliced radishes, onions, tomato wedges, strips of green pepper and a few bits of cucumber. An oil-and-vinegar dressing was also presented in small glass bottles. Dean was the only holdout who passed on filling his plate from the bowl, but everyone else happily partook of the chance for real, fresh vegetables instead of something dried or in a can.

After the salads, ceramic bowls of a pasty cornmeal soup with chicken broth were given to the diners. The soup was a filling and tasty appetizer that everyone lapped up. After the soup was gone, the table was presented with a platter of white fish in tomato sauce, with finely chopped onion, garlic, parsley and sea kelp. The many natural additives gave the fish a spicy flavor that Mildred commented on as reminding her of a favored aunt's cooking.

Shauna told the doctor all of the food was grown on the commune, and the spice she was tasting was undoubtedly coming from the fresh hot chili pepper that had been minced and added to the sauce for an extra kick, along with a smidgen of oregano.

"You speak with authority, madam. Sounds as though you know your way around a kitchen," Doc told his hostess.

"This is my recipe," Shauna replied. "And we have a few here who fancy themselves as chefs."

"You may present them with my highest compliments," Doc said. "I have paid ample tender in the past for food from restaurants that claimed to be eateries that were not even close to the flavor of this repast."

"That means he likes it," J.B. translated.

The fish beneath the sauce was boneless, fine and flaky, and the many pounds brought out quickly disappeared. The leftover tomato sauce was scooped up with chunks of coarse corn bread torn in hunks from round loaves. The bread tasted gritty, with hints of honey and molasses, and washed down easily with more of the sweetened ice tea.

For dessert, metal trays of steaming peach cobbler were brought out and dished up. Extra helpings would have been taken without hesitation, but the cobbler was such a hit there was barely enough to go around.

"Most scrumptious," Doc said.

No one could have put it better.

WHEN THE TABLES WERE cleared, as promised, there was entertainment.

Ryan begged off, citing lack of sleep and exhaustion, when all those close to him knew it was because he was still grieving for Krysty. They shared his grief while respecting his privacy. Ryan would socialize more with their benefactors—as well as his comrades—when ready.

Grateful to their rescuers, the rest of the group accepted the invitation and soon joined dozens of other members of the commune on blankets around a central elevated platform. The platform had a half roof for protection and used the natural amphitheater provided by an upthrust mass of rock.

The companions were expecting live talent, perhaps a singer, or a band with simple string instruments, or even some sort of theatrical play with actors reciting poetry or scripted words while treading the boards of a makeshift stage. From what they had seen, the commune seemed to be as low tech as one might expect, with oil lamps and torches for light and open fires for cooking.

"I hope it's not a storyteller," J.B. moaned sleepily. "I hate those long-winded stupes."

"Oral traditions have been a part of mankind since he first learned to stand upright, John Barrymore,"

Doc admonished. "Before the advent of written language, the telling of stories was the only way of preserving culture from generation to generation."

"Sounds more like tall tales and heaping mounds of crap to me," J.B. said, stifling a yawn. "Truth tends to get distorted in the telling."

"True enough, but hopefully they become entertaining, as well."

"Well, I'll be damned. An honest to God boom box!" Mildred said, her voice tinged with delight.

"Looks like a comm device to me. A big one," J.B. replied.

"It's a radio, all right, John, but only a receiver. No two-way communication. You can't use it to broadcast, only to pick up open signals sent out across the airwaves."

"I know what a radio is, Millie," J.B. said, sounding offended. "I just never saw one like that before."

Shauna had brought out a rectangular black monstrosity that was approximately four feet long and three feet high. Most of the "radio" was taken up by speaker capacity, with two large grid-covered sections on either end, and two smaller speakers in the upper corners. The front was slotted for the playing and recording of cassette tapes, while on top of the device was a concave indentation with a flip-top door where compact discs could be inserted. Various silver buttons lined the radio's front center section beneath the door for the cassette player.

On one end was a huge black knob and on the other, a knob of equal size but colored white. The device was topped off with a slender silver antenna, which she pulled up to full extension.

Carter stepped up next to her, holding an old automotive battery with a mess of retrofitting and rigging along the top terminals. A single wire with a female receiving plug head at the end came from the mass of wiring. He plugged this into a three-prong male plug coming from the back of the box, glanced at Shauna and nodded affirmative as the lights and dials on the front of the radio lit up in a faint mix of amber and green.

"You can say what you want about our neighbor, but Poseidon has great taste in music," Carter said with a grin to the audience, who all laughed in reply as he turned up the volume control.

First there was static. Carter turned the largest dial, and the sound got clearer and less distorted.

Then, there was a rich voice that resonated with loss, pain, hope and redemption all at the same time, a lyrical voice.

The unearthly wail of Roy Orbison came out of both speakers, crying for the lonely ones. And after Roy, there was the rhythmic beat of Buddy Holly telling them all that would be the day, and then the eerie mix of the twin voices of the Everly Brothers proclaiming their eternal innocence. The Big Bopper bopped once more from the grave. James Brown called out and his backing band, the Famous Flames, responded to his every vocal nuance. Four men from Liverpool, England, wanted to hold your hand. The king of rock and roll cried in the chapel, and then told you to lay off of his blue suede shoes.

One after another, the songs of the past played without stop, echoing out over the pocket of humanity clinging to life among the ruins of the dead earth.

Mildred, dwelling on her lost world and her lost friends, shuddered, then sighed, fighting to hold back the tears.

"What's wrong, Millie?" J.B. asked.

"No chatter. No advertising. Nothing but music," Mildred said in a mocking voice, echoing the tones of the radio DJs of her own youth. "It took us until the millennium and the end of the world to get rid of Madison Avenue, but by God, it might have been a fair trade. One civilization in exchange for some peace and quiet."

She paused, and added bitterly, "If only we'd been able to keep from blowing up most of the planet in the process."

The group of friends sat quietly after that, listening to the music play long into the night.

Chapter Sixteen

Morning brought yet another vibrant sunny day.

Dean awakened alone. Stretching, he got up from the mattress and walked outside. He spotted an older Hispanic woman from the night before and waved. She waved back, then gestured for Dean to approach.

"Morning," she said. "Did you enjoy the entertainment?"

"Sure did! I even liked the slow songs."

"Good, good. I have a boy about your age. I'll introduce you to him later after he has done his chores."

"Okay. Um, any idea where my dad is?" Dean asked.

"Probably having breakfast," she replied. "Of course, it is getting late."

"Thanks, I could use some breakfast myself," Dean said. "But I think I'll wash my face first."

The young man stepped over to the communal well and brought up a bucket of clear cold water, pouring it into a free-standing scavenged sink near the tubs. Dean poured a ladleful over his head and then slicked his hair back with a small black pocket comb. Looking at himself in a broken scrap of mirror hanging on the pole where the sink was mounted, Dean decided he looked presentable enough, and headed for the main tent.

Then he saw the inhuman shadow loom up from behind him.

Turning with a sharp cry of surprise, Dean dropped into a fighter's stance, ready to do battle.

Standing before him, at seven feet tall and with a quizzical expression, was a Dweller. Dean could tell from the shape of the face and the eyes this wasn't the same mutie that had assisted the companions yesterday.

Boy and mutie stared at each other.

Then the Hispanic woman passed by and called out, "Morning, Carl."

The Dweller slowly raised a hand in greeting to the woman.

"He won't hurt you, Dean," she said, continuing back on her way.

"You're welcome to the sink. I was just finishing up," the boy said, stepping away from the well and the small bathing area.

Dean didn't look back as he walked fast into the large communal tent with the picnic tables where he'd dined the evening before. There were a few of the commune members inside. At a rear table by himself with a platter of leftover white fish, fried potatoes and scrambled eggs was Doc.

"The sun always rises, and so does youth—eventually," Doc said.

"How's it hanging, Doc?" Dean snorted back as he sat down across from the old man.

"By a thread, dear boy. I fear it may soon drop off altogether."

"Where is everybody?"

"Out on a scouting mission. Your father wishes to learn more about Admiral Poseidon. I believe he intends to challenge him over the unfortunate deaths of Krysty and Jak," Doc said after chewing up a mouthful of meat and eggs.

"Damned straight."

"Beware the enticement of revenge, Dean."

"Eye for an eye, Doc. This Poseidon has it coming."

"Perhaps."

"Why didn't he take me?"

"It was decided to let you sleep in. I promised to tell you what was going on when you awakened. Frankly I did not feel much like getting up myself," Doc said conspiratorially. "My mind is back, but my body is still lacking."

Dean got up and walked over to a stack of wooden plates and utensils. He returned with one and a glass of water.

"Mind sharing?" he asked, gesturing toward the repast Doc was filling his own plate from.

"Not at all. Dig in."

Dean did. "I got to tell you, Doc. I like eating fish better than talking to them."

"Oh, you have met Carl," Doc replied. "He is quite the conversationalist."

"No, but he makes up for it in odor. Those Dweller guys stink!" Dean said.

"They are part fish, young Cawdor, what do you expect?" Doc replied, keeping his attention on his third helping of food. "Their scent was like pure ambrosia when they showed up at our raft."

"There's a man with a well-trained nose," interjected Shauna, who had stepped under the protective awning and into the tent in time to hear the end of the conversation. "You two didn't want to go with the others?"

"I did, but they wouldn't let me," Dean grumbled.

"And I," Doc added with a slight burp, "I am still weary from our sea voyage. Let the others scheme and plot this morning. I shall sup from this bountiful breakfast until I have had my fill, and then I plan to return to my deep slumber."

"That's fine," the woman said, turning to step back outside. She held off, then swung her sleekly muscled body back to face Dean.

"By the way, Ryan Jr.—" she began.

"Name's Dean."

"I'd watch my words around here when commenting on the Dwellers. They're a mite sensitive about having their mutie traits so baldly pointed out, especially from a runt like you. They can't help being what they are. Now, you might be—"

Dean interrupted her for a second time. "I call them as I see them. Or smell 'em."

Shauna's right hand shot up like it was spring propelled from where she'd been resting it lightly on the edge of the wooden camp table. Her steely fingers grabbed Dean by the earlobe and squeezed. He bucked in his chair and cried out, more in surprise than pain.

"Interrupt me again, and I'll toss you off the nearest dock myself," she said. "Didn't your daddy teach you anything about manners?"

"Lady, if you don't let go of me, my dad will slice you into so many pieces, your fishy friends won't be able to find enough left to use as cut bait," Dean said, but much of the bravado had leaked out of his voice like air from a burst balloon.

"He'll have to chill me first, Junior, and you'll still be dead."

"As I recall, madam," came Doc's calm tones from his end of the table, "the boy's father was discussing that very same subject a few weeks back." Doc paused to chew another mouthful of the cooked fish he'd been forking into his mouth while placidly observing the altercation between Dean and Shauna.

"What? About being chilled?" Shauna twisted Dean's ear again to emphasize her point. The boy involuntarily raised himself from his seat, attempting to keep the pain under control.

"No. About manners. Dean is young, a mere slip of a man just on the cusp of his teenage years. I assure you he means no disrespect to you, our host, or to the unfortunate Dwellers. The boy has lost a woman he loved as a mother and a longtime friend in the span of one stormy night. Any words out of his mouth right now are to be viewed as suspect. I suggest he's transposing his own anger at their perishing, and his emotional anguish, into aggression at yourself."

Doc's blue eyes misted up when speaking of Krysty and Jak. He took out his swallow's-eye kerchief and dabbed at his forehead and cheeks. "Emotional anguish that each of us you rescued is still trying to cope with in our own private ways."

Shauna pondered that, still keeping a white-knuckled grip on Dean's aching ear.

"You make good sense, Tanner. You said you were a doctor, but not a med guy. What, you a head-shrinker or something?"

"I?" Doc boomed, sounding offended. "My degree is in philosophy, my dear, and in philosophy, men have found answers to the questions that plague them for thousands of years. My wisdom comes from the words and teachings of the ancients, along with a healthy dose of education I've been exposed to while traversing these so quaintly—and so accurately—named Deathlands."

Shauna chuckled at that, and released her grip on Dean's earlobe. The boy slumped in his chair sullenly, rubbing the sore spot where her fingers had twisted the sensitive cartilage. His skinny arms crossed in over his chest in an unconscious protective position.

"Okay, Dr. Tanner, we'll let this one go. I haven't had to deal personally with a boy child in a long time, and I've forgotten how mouthy they can be. I'm still hoping we can convince your group to hang with us. We need warriors if we're ever going to get out from under Admiral Poseidon's thumb. I won't speak of it to Cawdor if you won't."

"My lips are sealed. As for Dean's..." Doc trailed off, leaving the boy an opening.

Dean stared up at Shauna. "Doc says nothing happened, I say nothing happened."

"Damn, but you are your father's son," she commented, and left the way she came.

"Thanks for the assist, Doc," Dean said. "My ear feels like she twisted it plumb off my skull."

"There was never any reason for you to fear, young Cawdor," Doc said, and suddenly, like a razor-edged jack-in-the-box, the cutting blade hidden within his walking stick sprang out from a secure and hidden place beneath the table. "Had she continued to press the issue, I would have been forced to sever her offending appendage at the wrist."

Doc returned the blade to its proper place and dropped his swordstick back into his lap.

"Now, be a good boy and please pass that bowl of potatoes. I must address my starch deficiency."

RYAN LOOKED DOWN at the colors of the coastline below him, the vibrant hues of the ocean and the dusky tones of the land, dotted with sporadic growth of forest and upheavals of rock, and knew in the bottom of his soul that any other time, he would have allowed himself to enjoy the sight. This part of Georgia seemed to have escaped the utter devastation other sections of the United States had endured. Krysty would have liked it. She liked any natural spot that was unblemished.

At his side were J.B. and Mildred, along with their

long-haired guide, Alan Carter. They all stood at the top of a one-hundred-foot observation tower built of wood and metal.

"There's two ways they can come," Carter said, pointing as he spoke. "One by land, one by sea. If they cruise up in one of his yachts, we know Poseidon himself is aboard. Supposedly he rarely steps onto dry land. Prefers the feel of the ocean beneath his feet. We joke he's part Dweller."

"Mebbe he is," Ryan said.

Carter pressed on. "However, he hasn't done a personal appearance in a long time. Too busy, I guess. If there's no boats on the horizon and a land wag pulls in like the pattern for the last few months, we can totally discount the Admiral's presence. He's not as inclined to show off anymore. He just wants his men to pick up his offerings and bring them back to the base."

"Fifty-fifty odds," J.B. mused.

Ryan grunted in reply. "Either way, we can take the bastard out. One method just takes a little longer, that's all. Doesn't matter much to me. I've got all the time in the world now."

As the two old friends talked, Mildred glanced around, trying not to betray any sign of nervousness. While she had never been frightened of heights before, the openness of the tower was beginning to get to her peace of mind. The sensations of falling were only increased tenfold when the wooden tower creaked and swayed in the stiff sea breeze that flowed in from the nearby ocean.

"Got a plan?" J.B. asked.

"Yeah," Ryan responded tersely, but didn't elaborate.

J.B. wasn't convinced, but the Armorer took the intonation of Ryan's voice and the loss he'd endured into consideration. What kind of plan was needed, really, beyond the healing power of playing avenger? He thought about asking Ryan to elaborate on the plan, then thought the better of it. His friend would explain what scheme he had in mind when ready.

"So, we know where they'll be coming from now," Mildred said. "How about we discuss our next move down on the ground, where it's safer?"

"Don't you worry none, Dr. Wyeth," Carter said. "This tower might seem shaky, but she's here to stay. We check her out on a regular basis. Being so close to saltwater and all, we have to."

"When do they come? How often?" J.B. asked.

Carter squinted his eyes as he scanned the sky. "Usually midmorning, before noon," he said easily. "Comes once a month during winter months, but during summer and early fall, they show up once a week. Mebbe ten days. There's no real accurate way to predict it. Since heat tends to spoil meat faster, he'll be sending men out or coming himself within a hand of days, I'd say. The good Admiral prefers his seafood fresh. Likes it raw, from what I hear."

Mildred made a face of distaste. "Likes sushi, does he?"

Carter, not really comprehending the reference,

smiled and said, "I'm sure he does, Doctor. He seems to enjoy everything else."

"Can you keep a lookout up here during the day?" Ryan asked.

"Why?"

"I need to know exactly when this Poseidon is going to arrive. Even a warning of a few minutes is better than nothing."

"Shouldn't be a problem. I'll discuss it with Shauna."

"Nothing to discuss," Ryan told him bluntly. "Here's the plan. If Poseidon floats in by sea, we go on board his ship and take him out, face-to-face, no mercy. If he sends a gathering party in by land, we take them out and ride back in style to his base, where again, we meet him face-to-face and chill him. Either way, we win. Simple as that."

Ryan turned and started to climb back down the ladder to the ground. The others watched him go. Suddenly the air on high didn't feel nearly as good.

OVERHEAD, THE NIGHT SKY was crystal clear, revealing the facets of each and every star. Evidence of past storms and conflict had once again vanished in a space of days.

Ryan was sitting alone in a naturally created nook near the rocks and sand of the beach at the far edge of the primary encampment of the commune when Shauna approached him with a covered plate of hot food and a battered bottle of tea. His back was to her, so she tried stepping lightly to keep from startling him. No go. He heard her in time to whirl around with his blaster. He pointed the weapon directly on a sight between her eyes and wordlessly waggled the barrel of the SIG-Sauer.

"Hello to you, too, Cawdor."

"Take the hint."

"Missed you at dinner," she said.

"Wasn't hungry."

"Bullshit. You're hurting and didn't feel up to conversation. I know the signs."

Ryan turned and stared at her. To her credit, she stared right back.

"You would make a hell of a great pirate, Cawdor. You already have the look."

"I don't get you."

Shauna pointed at his eye patch. "Required garb for any self-respecting pirate."

"Right. As I recall, pirates were also supposed to have hooks for hands and wooden pegs for legs and a talking bird on their shoulder," Ryan replied. "No wonder the poor gimps had to steal—they were crippled and half-blind."

Shauna laughed heartily at that. "Your friends said not to bother you."

"My friends were right."

"Well, I'm not having my key ally going to bed with his belly empty the night before a fight," Shauna said mildly. "I can hold my anger close just as well on a full stomach."

"I thought you said Poseidon may not show," Ryan said.

"He may not. Still, why take chances? Your plan is workable, and I've been wanting to bring down that bastard for a long time."

"Why do you stay here?" Ryan asked.

"Why not? Climate's good. Plenty to eat. People who care for me live here. I could do worse."

"What, with this Admiral you have to bow down and pay tribute to? That kind of extortion shit gets triple old fast."

"Sometimes..." Shauna's voice trailed off. "Sometimes, Cawdor, it's easier than trying to fight back. You have to remember, when the Admiral first approached us about trading, we were on a more equal footing. I had more men at the commune—good sec men. Couple of years pass, and then suddenly he's got the advantage. Some of our people go missing, or have accidents, or worse yet, join his outfit."

Ryan turned and looked at her profile in the moonlight. He knew from the pain etched in her face that the woman was telling the truth when she had told him she knew the signs of hurting.

"What did Poseidon do to you? Besides bleeding off your commune, I mean," Ryan asked.

"Not my commune. *Our* commune. Belongs to all of us, even you, if you want to stay." She placed a hand on his shoulder.

"You know what I mean."

Shauna sighed and sat down next to Ryan. "The good Admiral says he's a businessman. Once he gained the advantage, he came in here and started telling us how things were now going to be. My husband didn't agree. Poseidon invited him and a hand-picked squad to travel back to Kings Point for a summit meeting.''

She turned and looked Ryan right in the eye, her icy blue pupils locking with his own. "I never saw my husband alive after that."

"Fireblast," Ryan whispered. The epithet seemed woefully insignificant.

"I was ready to go after Eric and see Poseidon's head on a post, but I didn't have enough fighting men to support an assault. Poseidon made a point of not coming back around here in person after that. He might have been frightened or cautious or both. I don't know. I kept telling myself that Poseidon was a military sec type, not a fisherman or farmer. The folks here were more in tune with a band of underwater muties, peace and love and harmony with nature. Leave us alone, we leave you alone."

"The pain never left, did it?" Ryan said quietly.

"I'm as ready for vengeance now as I ever was."

She took Ryan's hand in her own. "I lost my man three years ago, Cawdor. He was a lot like you—stubborn and pigheaded. I heard the Admiral beat him to death with a whip in a public flogging, as a lesson, as a good old-fashioned example. I'm constantly amazed at how reverting back to the old ways for most seems to entail brutality."

"Human nature."

Shauna leaned over and kissed the one-eyed man gently on the lips. Ryan didn't refuse or encourage the gesture of intimacy.

"Been over three years for me, Ryan," she said.

"Shauna, I can't make love with you," Ryan replied. "Timing's all wrong, for now."

"I figured as much." Shauna pulled back and smiled. "I just thought you could use some company, that's all. You're a leader. I'm a leader. Leaders can't let themselves show weakness in front of their followers, no matter how close they are as friends or family. Part of the territory, right?"

"Part of the territory," Ryan agreed.

Chapter Seventeen

The wag rolled into Shauna's territory at approximately twenty minutes after twelve.

High noon, and the sky overhead was crisp and clear, so clear that objects as far away as a hundred feet still looked as sharp as if they were directly in front of your nose. The air was silent, precisely so, as if waiting in anticipation for the inevitable sudden sound or motion to appear in a rapid onrush to shatter the serenity.

The young lookout in the watchtower, flat on her stomach to avoid detection, had spotted the transport well in advance of its arrival. She had signaled the waiting group below with a prearranged motion that the convoy consisted of a single vehicle, just as had been predicted.

After the high sign had been given, there was nothing to do but wait. As they took their positions in the trench alongside the dirt-and-gravel roadway—a trench that had been widened and deepened to accommodate the lean and lethal attack force—Ryan had to wonder if such a simple plan of battle would work.

"Simple's sometimes the best way," J.B. said as he waited with Ryan in the ditch alongside the roadway. The Armorer's eyes wandered over enviously to the ordnance Shauna and Carter were carrying. Earlier Carter had led J.B. and Mildred to a secure place hidden away in a seaside cavern about a quarter mile from the cluster of shacks and tents that made up the commune.

From a grease-stained canvas bag, Carter had pulled out twin Calico M-955AS light submachine guns, complete with full shoulder butts and forward hand grips all molded in stark black metal and plastic. The Calico was a unique little weapon that was a cross between a machine pistol and a full-blown rifle.

"PDWs," J.B. had said in admiration, his voice echoing slightly in the cave. The cave was a natural formation fortified with large wooden beams jammed every few feet along the walls in a basic yet effective effort to prop up the ceiling and avoid the possibility of having the roof fall down around a visitor's ears.

"Pee Dee whats?" Carter responded.

"PDWs. Quick-speak for Personal Defense Weapons. They emerged in the predark days right before the nukecaust for nonsoldier types to use, you know; whitecoats, engineers, comm men, techies, drivers. Those guns you have there were made by Calico Incorporated of Bakersfield, U.S.A. First appeared in 1989, by the old calendar," J.B. rattled off with conviction.

Carter glanced at Mildred with a cocked eyebrow.

"One thing John knows is guns, Carter," she said. "He's probably the greatest weapons expert left alive in Deathlands."

"Do tell," Carter said. "I'm smart enough to know

these are good guns, but I didn't plan on being quizzed.''

"The Calico is a modular system, which allows a longer or a shorter weapon to be assembled from interchangeable components. You're got the full package there," J.B. said, pointing at the guns Carter was carrying. "Best of all is the Calico's amazing large magazine capacity. A small mag holds fifty rounds, the large one a hundred. You can always tell a Calico magazine by the shape of the mag."

"Really," Carter said. "And why is that?

"Calico is the only PDW to use a cylinder mag. Either the large or the small will clip down right on top of the gun, storing the cartridges in two helical layers. Ammo feed comes down from the top, while the spent cartridges eject underneath instead of out the side. Sweet little guns."

"Glad you approve. These are in good shape, but unfortunately what you pointed out about the ammo is true. We've got a 100-shot load and a 50-shot, and a backup fifty, and that's it. Most of the better stuff was lost the first time a group of us took Poseidon on.''

"What else you got?"

"In guns? Not much." Carter took another of the insulated sacks and revealed the remaining stockpile of hardware.

J.B. eyed the rest of the weapons dump. Carter wasn't understating the loss. A few 6-shot Colt revolvers, a rifle that looked as though it was an antique when Doc was still young and an astonishing lack of ammunition.

"Might as well toss these in the ocean," the Armorer said.

"Don't believe in that around here, Dix," Carter replied. "Guns don't belong in the sea."

"Anything else?" Mildred asked hopefully. "Some plastique? We're going to need it to go through with the plan."

"Doctor, I wouldn't have brought you all the way out here if I didn't have more," the tattooed man said. He flipped up a blanket revealing a green crate he'd been sitting on.

"Besides the Calicos, my private stash has one other distinct advantage going for it," Carter noted, pulling it out to the center of the cavern.

Hidden away inside the big rectangular metal storage container painted olive green was the "advantage." Thick white letters and numerals were stenciled on the sides of the container, which was roughly the size of a traditional footlocker. On the top of the box were smaller letters and numbers, all in a coded jumble beneath a torn red, white and blue decal of the American flag.

"These boxes are never the same twice. What's in it?" J.B. asked, recognizing the style of standard military-issue container from his many searches of redoubt supply rooms. The boxes could be used for anything from drab camouflage clothing to the near inedible delight of rations of self-heat cuisine. However, more often than not, the boxes were also dumps for ammunition, grenades or guns.

"You're so smart, you tell me," Carter replied easily as he lifted the box and placed it on a makeshift tabletop near the entrance of the cave.

"Could be nothing but an empty box, Carter. I've seen the package a thousand times before, but the present inside is usually long gone," J.B. remarked.

"Not this time, Dix," Carter said, working the combination of a moldy lock that kept the lid of the container shut down tight. "This time I've got party favors for everybody."

Carter lifted the lid with a proud flourish.

J.B. and Mildred both leaned over and peered down inside.

"Good Lord!" Mildred gasped.

"Dark night!" J.B. said.

Carter reached inside and removed a silver-and-red concussion grenade. He tossed it lightly in the air over to J.B, who calmly reached down his right hand and caught the lethal egg before it could hit the ground. Mildred involuntarily flinched.

"No need for worry, Dr. Wyeth," Carter said. "These things can't hurt anyone until they're armed."

"Old as those grens are, they could blow right in our faces!" Mildred retorted angrily. "I don't like taking chances!"

J.B. returned the explosive device to the metal and wire rack in the bottom of the steel container. "I count eight. Two burners, one concussion, one frag and four high-ex. Decent mix. Timers seem to be tight and clean. The outsides don't look too badly corroded, either. Last batch of grens we found, they were leaking like hell."

"I remember," Mildred said with a grin. "Dean knocked the box over and the entire lot nearly went off in our faces. Did a ten-second run to safety in nine seconds flat to outrun the timers."

"This time we're keeping the kid out of the grens," J.B. said.

Carter closed the container but left the lock unfastened. He then picked up both of the Calicos and slung them over his left shoulder. The extra magazine went into one of the numerous pockets of the blue jumpsuit he now wore.

"Grab one end of the box, Dix, and I'll carry the other. We'll divvy up the grens back at the commune. Shauna and Ryan will probably want to decide which ones we're going to use."

J.B. had already known that Ryan would say to take them all.

The rumble of the wag they had been warned about shook the Armorer from his memories. The hum of the internal eight-cylinder turbocharged engine was clean and uninterrupted, a muted throb that grew louder as the vehicle approached.

The wag was a familiar sight to both Ryan and J.B. From the flat-backed rear-access hatch to the bullet-shaped blunt nose and angled headlights, the vehicle was a near twin of the type they had recently liberated from a cache found inside an underground complex in Dulce, New Mexico. The primary difference was that the earlier wag had been factory new, with barely a hundred miles logged on the odometer. It had been fully loaded, too, with a barricade remover, a Watt-Olsen spotlight and a twin-speaker mounted public-address system.

There were no extras on the wag now approaching their hiding place, and the wag was in poor condition. The paint was nearly gone along the sides and front, revealing the thick armor plating that secured the passengers within safely. One side rack of headlights was shattered, a reminder of a past collision.

"Hotspur Hussar Armored Land Rover," J.B. breathed. His keen eyes quickly took in the superficial damages to the battered wag. "Seen better days. I'd say she's going about thirty miles per hour. Driver will have to slow up at the curve. I'd take the shot then."

Ryan nodded and raised the SIG-Sauer.

Originally Mildred had been the one chosen to make the shot, until Shauna had stressed the need for silence for her plan to work. Mildred's aim with the Czech target revolver was uncanny, but the blaster was explosively loud. Ryan had offered the SIG-Sauer to her, but she declined. It wasn't that complicated a shot, and Ryan's familiarity with his own blaster would make him the logical shooter.

The plan was indeed a simple one: take out one of the Land Rover's enormous rubber tires and make the men inside believe they were the unfortunate recipients of a blowout. With luck, they would all leave the wag to change the tire, eliminating the need for a firefight that would probably end up with casualties and a damaged, possibly inoperable wag.

Ryan wanted the wag intact. He wanted the way inside to Poseidon.

"Trojan horse," Doc had said when told of the plan. "A proved winner for centuries, Ryan. I see no reason why it should not work again."

As the wag rumbled past, Ryan took careful aim between the armored flanges protecting the rear right wheel well, and squeezed off a single silenced 9 mm shot. He was rewarded with a loud popping sound, not from the pistol, but from the rubber tire exploding as the bullet hit home.

"Hope they brought a spare," Shauna murmured.

"Hell of a good time to bring *that* up," Ryan whispered.

"Here they come," J.B. said. "Side door's sliding back."

The blown-out tire had achieved the desired effect. Two sec men, their rifles down, stepped out of the wag onto the packed dirt and gravel of the road. They were dressed in identical mirrored sunglasses, steel blue helmets and what appeared to be old-style bulky exterior bulletproof vests.

"What's with the uniforms?" J.B. asked.

"Sec teams that go off the base usually suit up," Carter whispered. "Intimidation and safety."

"No chest shots," Ryan said tightly. "Aim for the faces."

So far, the two sec men had no reason to suspect

an ambush. In their minds, at least for now, this was only an inconvenience, not the beginning of an assault.

"What do you think?" Carter whispered to Ryan. "Hit them now?"

"I think we should let them go about their business of changing the tire," the grim man replied.

"Sure you want to wait that long, Ryan?" Mildred asked. "What if they find the bullet?"

"They won't. Not unless they're looking and not until they have the wag jacked up. I figure might as well let them do the work for us." Ryan checked his gun. "Once the wag is off the ground, we'll introduce ourselves. No way they can get rolling again before they put on the spare."

"How many you think are inside?" Mildred asked.

"Don't know. Those Land Rovers are big bastards. They can hold eight men in the rear," J.B. mused.

"Not this one," Shauna countered. "That thing could seat twenty and it wouldn't matter. Poseidon keeps them lean. He's got to have ample room for the food he takes back."

"Like I said last night, my guess is four men. That was typical standard operations back when I ran with his men," Carter agreed. "It's also the same lineup as the last three times Poseidon's sent a transport out here by land. A driver and passenger up front, two others in the back. A pair to stay alert and watch for trouble, and a pair to use their backs to help load up the booty."

"So let's find out," Ryan said, watching as a third

man joined the duo in removing the blown tire. "But whatever you do, don't let them get back inside the wag."

As planned, Shauna left her weapon behind and made her way down to a far end of the ditch, far enough down to where it would appear she had merely been walking down the road and come upon the wag's unfortunate predicament, just an innocent encounter with a pedestrian.

Shauna stepped into the open and jauntily walked toward the downed Land Rover. "Need a hand?" she asked, granting them a dazzling smile. Mildred noted the woman had unzipped the front of her jumpsuit even more than usual.

"She's going to fall right out of that thing if she's not careful," Mildred whispered.

"So much the better," J.B. replied.

"Get ready," Ryan said.

Two of the men whirled toward Shauna with their AK-47s held ready when she spoke. The third man outside of the Land Rover was occupied with the jack.

The leader, a veteran sec man named Martin, relaxed when he recognized Shauna. He knew from experience she wasn't there to cause any trouble. Still, it was odd for the commune leader to be showing up so far down the road from the settlement, and why was she alone? Martin decided to let his partner handle the questioning. That way, he could let his eyes enjoy the view of Shauna's exposed breasts without having to play the heavy.

"What are you doing here, little lady?" the other armed man asked, voicing Martin's own concerns.

"Stealing your wag," Ryan's voice said from behind them.

To their credit, the sec men didn't surrender without a fight. However, Ryan and the others had the advantage of surprise. The firefight was succinct and to the point. All remembered Ryan's words about aiming for the heads, more specifically, for the faces.

Mildred's Czech target pistol fired once, and the large caliber bullet entered Martin's left eye, felling the man with a single shot. A red torrent spewed down his cheek as he fell forward, the bullet continuing to move through his skull and brain tissue, exiting the back of his head and finally stopping dead at the interior of the helmet he wore. Martin convulsed for a few seconds, his hands clawing in the dirt and gravel until he died.

In the same instant, twin pairs of mirrored sunglasses shattered like dropped china cups as the faces of the other two men dissolved from the auto fire of J.B. and Carter.

While his friends engaged the trio of sec men, Ryan had made his way around the back to the open side door of the wag and shoved his SIG-Sauer inside, aiming at the driver.

"Your pals are dead. You're next, unless you want to come out of that seat quietly."

The driver raised his hands.

"Good. I hate cleaning up brains off a windshield."

The spare was then placed on the wag without fanfare by the captured driver, under Ryan's close supervision. J.B. and Carter dragged the bodies into the former hiding place in the ditch while Ryan questioned the driver.

"What's your name?"

"Edgerton."

"You enlisted or merc?" Ryan asked, recalling that Carter had said enlisted men were the chosen elite in Poseidon's farcical attempt at a navy. Hired men were always more easily swayed. Bought loyalty was only worth as much as the highest bidder was willing to pay.

"Edgerton, Ray, sir! Enlisted man."

"Great," Ryan said.

A spare helmet and pair of sunglasses had been discovered in a storage drawer inside the wag. Ryan would wear the outfit and ride shotgun with the surviving member of the sec squad while J.B., Mildred and Carter hid in the back. Once they were on the base, the second part of the operation would be carried out with the grens and any other explosives they could scrounge up on-site.

Carter, Mildred and J.B. would play delivery boys. Ryan and Shauna were going in search of Poseidon.

But Ryan had one final stop to take care of first.

"I'M GOING WITH YOU, Dad."

"No, Dean, you're not." Ryan said.

"I'm not a kid anymore! You need me—"

"I need you right here," Ryan said firmly, cutting

the boy off in midprotest, "with Doc. He's still too weak to go off into a firefight. Somebody has to stay with him."

"Doc can take care of himself."

"Usually that's true. Not this time. Besides, he needs somebody to watch his back."

"But, Dad—"

"Enough, Dean!" Ryan's voice was as unyielding as an iron bar. When Dean heard that tone used, he knew enough to back off.

"One of Trader's rules was to never split your forces. 'If you've only got half your men, you've only got half your power,' he'd say. Course, the older I'm getting, the less inclined I am to always agree with everything Trader told me. We've already lost two people to this Poseidon. Jak was like a son to me in many ways, and Krysty was my soul mate." Ryan took a hand and mussed Dean's hair. "I'll be damned if I'll risk losing another loved one to that bastard."

"Jak was my friend, too," Dean said. "And I loved Krysty."

Ryan softened. "I know, son. Believe me, I understand. But I'm not asking you to stay here as a father. I'm telling you to stay as a leader. You don't want to be treated like a kid? Fine. Then act like a man and do what I tell you."

"Not fair," Dean said.

"Life seldom is."

Ryan stepped away and paused at the doorway of the tent.

"How long before you're back?" Dean asked.

"Not sure. No way of knowing. Half day there in the wag, according to Carter. Half day back if the wag's still running after we get inside the base. I'd say we'll be back here in a couple of days, unless something goes bad wrong." Ryan shrugged. "If the plan goes south on us, then I guess it doesn't matter."

"Two days, Dad. Two days, then I'm coming after you— even if I have to carry Doc on my shoulders."

Ryan nodded. "Should be long enough. Two days, then."

Dean was shocked into silence. He'd never imagined his father would agree to letting him come out in search of the advance party, even with a wait of forty-eight hours.

The one-eyed man held up a hand, gave a little wave to his son and walked out of the tent.

Before Dean could also exit, Ryan stepped back inside.

"Dean?"

"Yeah, Dad?"

"If you do end up carrying Doc around, remember that he's heavier than he looks." The attempt at humor was strained, but Dean still appreciated the effort.

"I won't forget."

What Dean didn't know was Ryan would have done exactly the same thing himself at Dean's age. He also knew the boy wouldn't be able to wait any longer than two days, which was fine.

In two days' time, Admiral Poseidon would be a dead man, and his so-called empire would be a ruin, even if Ryan had to die himself in the process.

Chapter Eighteen

"What?" Doc said in his most testy tone of voice. Looking every inch the academic he once had been, he peered down his long nose at the interruption.

"Been gone for two hours now," Dean replied flatly. The boy was standing at the entrance flap of the tent, his head cocked at an angle, one hand on his hip and the other holding open the flap. For a brief moment, Doc had thought Ryan himself had already returned from his journey to the lair of Poseidon. Dean had the same sharp, narrow face. The same deep-set dark eyes. The same curly black hair.

The same confidence some would see as insolence.

"I'm well aware of the passage of time," Doc replied, closing the crumbling paperback book he'd been reading.

"What's the book?" Dean asked.

"A collection of poetry by T. S. Eliot. The title of the collection is *The Waste Land and Other Poems*."

"Sounds like Deathlands," Dean observed.

"Yes, well, this is apt reading in our surroundings," Doc agreed.

"Where'd you get it?"

"They have a small library here. Mostly tripe. Blood-and-thunder adventure novels about men with action verbs for names and pink-and-lavender tinged bodice rippers of true historical romance," Doc said. "I noticed the bindings of the trashier books were the most worn, while this handsome gray-and-black thin little gem is still somewhat in one piece. Yes, a few worthy tomes were in the strongbox, and I couldn't resist reacquainting myself with Mr. Eliot's wonderfully written wisdom."

"Yeah, well, you ready?"

"For what?" Doc asked innocently.

"Ready to go. I been watching you, Doc. You're tougher than you look. You can walk."

"Thank you for the compliment, young man," Doc said. "Still, there's nothing we can do but wait…just as your father told you to do."

"Walking will do you some good," Dean continued. "We both know Dad's had enough time to get well ahead of us, Doc. He's probably already half there."

"Perhaps. Perhaps not. Voyages into the lion's den sometimes take longer than planned. Besides, I spoke with your father before his departure, and he said you had agreed to wait two days. A double hold, is how he put it to me."

"Actually he said a couple of days, Doc. Or mebbe he said a couple of hours. The way I look at it, a couple hours have long passed. Now, are you coming or do you want to stay here with the muties and the peace lovers?"

"You would do well to speak to your elders with a touch more respect, Dean," Doc said, a hint of flint sparking into his voice. He smiled tightly, showing off his perfect white teeth. "As evidenced yesterday with our hostess and now with me, you shall live much longer. I rather liked your flattery from a few moments ago. I would recommend you go back to the ploy of attempting to attract with sweet honey as opposed to vocal vinegar."

"No ploys. You coming or staying?"

"I'm trying to read." Doc sighed. "Readers are more educated, and as such, tend to be survivors."

"Yeah, well, we can't live forever, Doc. Even a time-traveling dog like you," Dean said, leaving Doc alone with his book.

Doc reopened the book and tried very hard to concentrate on the words of Eliot—one of the few poets from the twentieth century that Doc actually liked—but the poetry kept sliding off the page and out of his mind. Instead, he imagined Ryan's reaction if he found out Dean had been allowed to go off into the unknown alone.

"'I grow old...I grow old...I shall wear the bottoms of my trousers rolled,'" the old man read aloud as he stared down at the page. Doc pondered this for a full sixty seconds before he stood.

"I shall not!" he announced, looking at the cover of the book. "And yes, Mr. Eliot, I, Dr. Theophilus Algernon Tanner, do indeed dare to eat a peach!"

When Doc walked outside the tent, the Le Mat secure on his leg and the familiar black walking stick in one hand, Dean was waiting.

"Figured you might come around," Dean said.

"Have I become that predictable?" Doc lamented.

"No, but I was counting on you doing the right thing."

"The right thing is remaining here, safe and snug and fed," Doc replied. "But our friends have left us, and I suppose someone must play the role of cavalry."

"That's what I think."

"Let me return this book, and we shall be on our way," Doc said, stepping past the boy and heading for the storage tent where he had browsed through the small commune library.

"What changed your mind?" Dean asked, jogging to keep up with Doc's long strides.

"The mermaids, lad. The mermaids started singing to me."

Dean shook his head. There were times Doc didn't make a bit of sense.

"Why don't you keep the book, Doc? I doubt they'd ever miss it."

"Perhaps not. But who knows how many copies of this wonderful work survived the end of the civilized world?" Doc replied. "No, Mr. Eliot is much safer here with these good people than with me."

After Doc returned the copy of the book, he headed back toward the main road.

"Wrong way," Dean said.

"What are you talking about?"

"Come on, I'll show you." The boy headed for the northern side of the commune, where the small farm and gardens were maintained.

"Excuse me, young Dean, but I believe the road to our destination is that way," Doc said, pointing southward.

"Got something to pick up first. Found out about it last night from Chico."

"And who is Chico?"

The pair now approached a small fenced area. A young Mexican boy about Dean's age was standing at the gate.

"He's Chico," Dean said. "He lives here on the commune. I met him last night while you all were meeting. I had a feeling Dad was going to stick me here while he went after that bastard who killed Krysty and Jak, so I talked to Chico about my problem."

"What did he say?" Doc asked.

"He didn't. He brought me here and introduced me to Santos."

The two boys stepped through the gate. Doc followed.

Inside the ring was a massive gray Appaloosa with a thick neck and stocky body.

"Meet Santos. Chico is going to let me borrow him," Dean told Doc. "Santos belonged to Chico's dad, who was one of the people chilled here a few years back by Poseidon."

Doc eyed the horse. "A most magnificent—not to mention, massive—creature."

"He can hold us both with no problem, right, Chico?" Dean reached up and stroked the creature's neck.

"Right," the boy replied. "He's a good horse."

"If you intended to travel by horseback, why did you lead me to think we were going to be walking?" Doc asked peevishly.

"Wanted to know how serious you were. If you were going to walk, I knew you weren't going to try and talk me out of going."

"It is not my role to talk you out of anything," Doc said. "I am not your parent."

"Aces on the line, Doc. That's what I thought!"

Doc took Dean to one side away from the boy and the animal. "And how do you propose to return this animal, in case, well, you know...?"

"There's an old burned-out gas station on the way to the base," Dean said. "Chico's rode that far without his mom knowing. We're going to leave Santos there. If we haven't returned in a day or so, Chico will come out and get the horse back."

Doc scratched his head.

"You are a master schemer, Dean. I am not so sure expanding your education at the Brody school was such a good idea after all."

"WHAT CAN YOU TELL ME about this nuke sub Poseidon's got?" Ryan turned and asked the man who had identified himself as Edgerton.

Edgerton stayed silent, his body bouncing in the seat as the wag made its way back down the old two-lane blacktop toward Kings Point.

"Name, rank and serial number is all you're going

to get, Cawdor," Carter said. "That was the drill when I ran with Poseidon."

"You were a merc for him?" J.B. asked from the driver's seat.

"For about a year. Got tired of the pecking order. Besides, I hate taking orders. I'd heard about the commune upstate and decided that way of life sounded a lot more appealing."

"Did you ever get near the sub?" Ryan asked the tattooed man.

"No, I wasn't classified." Carter replied. "It's a big bastard, between five and six hundred yards long. Supposed to run off a pressurized water reactor. That's what's powered by the nuke generator."

Carter continued. "As I understand it, and he did give us a briefing one time in case things went to hell in a hurry, inside the reactor are fuel rods that produce the needed energy by nuclear fission. The water from the pressurizer is superheated in the reactor core and passed to a heat exchanger where it creates the steam to power the turbines."

"What happens if the nuke engine goes off-line?"

"Sub should have backup diesel engines in case the reactor fails. Trick there is fuel, but I know Poseidon must have an ample supply since he's been running these wags back and forth."

"You want us to try and take out the sub first or the buildings?" Mildred asked.

"Buildings," Carter replied. "Or any big wags you see like this one. The submarine pens will be closely watched, but other sections are left open since there's nothing worth stealing. Hit as many as you can and make damned sure the timers are synchronized.''

All in the wag but Edgerton checked their chronos.

"Midnight, and we're out of there and back to the wag. Even if all of the objectives aren't met.''

"They will be,'' Shauna said as the last remnants of the compassionate woman the group had first met slid away and were replaced with the mind-set of an assassin. "Ryan and I have our own assignment.''

"Sure you don't want to help us out, Edgerton?'' Ryan asked. "You've seen what these blasters can do. Three of your pals down and dead. Could go easier for you if you cooperate.''

"No, sir,'' the sweating enlisted man said.

"Fine. Keep your secrets.'' Ryan said. "I've never been a man for torture.''

"Hold up,'' J.B. said from the front of the wag. "Coming up on something that looks like it might be the place.''

Carter stepped forward for a look through one of the Land Rover's numerous ob slits, "Right, Dix. There's the rear gate. They should be expecting us with the fish fry.''

"Okay, J.B., you and Edgerton here are going to switch places. Here's the drill. If Edgerton gets cute or tries to warn the guard at the gate in the booth, I chill him.'' Ryan stared the younger man down. "Edgerton takes us in and parks the wag in the normal drop spot, we tie him up and he lives to drive another day.''

Ryan put on the mirrored sunglasses and helmet

and took the passenger seat, aiming the muzzle of the SIG-Sauer at Edgerton's right side, just out of the field of vision if the man on the gate got too curious.

J.B. joined Mildred, Carter and Shauna in the rear of the wag, hidden until the door was opened and they chose to reveal themselves.

"Take us in," Ryan said coldly.

Edgerton hesitated.

Ryan poked him in the ribs with the blaster.

"I said, take us in," he repeated.

Edgerton shifted gears and let the Land Rover roll forward.

"But if you want to live, you'll get us into the base without a firefight," Ryan growled. "If this gets fucked up, I'll chill you myself."

Four minutes later, everything that could've gone wrong...did, and they were captured.

Chapter Nineteen

The metal steps rang hollowly beneath their feet as a handcuffed Ryan and Shauna were led up to the top floor of the building. They were placed in front of an ornate oak door and made to wait while one of their captors went inside to announce their arrival. He returned and swung open the door, crooking a finger for them to enter.

"Welcome to Kings Point, Georgia. Home and berth to the USS *Raleigh*. My name is Poseidon. You may address me as 'Admiral.'"

Ryan stared contemptuously at the man who had identified himself as Poseidon.

The white-hot rage he always tried to keep strapped down within his soul came bubbling up freely, and he embraced it. He wanted his anger worn close, sharp and hot and piercing. Krysty and Jak were dead because of this egomaniac's paranoia, and no amount of discussion of motive or happenstance or fate was going to change that inescapable fact.

The woman at his side felt exactly the same way. Her intense hatred of Poseidon was radiating off her trim body in waves. Ryan could almost feel the heat of her dislike, like an overworked oven's door that had been left standing open.

"My, I really haven't made either of your hit parades, have I?" Poseidon murmured, steepling his fingers beneath his chin.

"Come a little closer and uncuff me, and I'll beat you to death with my fists," Shauna said. "Then you'll be on *my* hit parade."

Poseidon chuckled. "It's not that kind of parade, dear Shauna. Then again, I suppose music appreciation is well beyond both of your savage intellects. At times such as these, I know my tiny radio station here exists for my enjoyment and my enjoyment alone."

"Admiral?" said the sec man with the blaster who was standing behind Ryan and Shauna. "You want me to stay?"

"Yes. For now," Poseidon said. He looked at Ryan and Shauna. "Sit down, you two."

Neither moved. The sec man poked Ryan in the back with the nose of the weapon.

"Go on, sit. You heard the Admiral."

"Admiral, my ass," Ryan snorted, but he went ahead and eased into the plush chair. Beside him, a few feet away, Shauna did the same awkward movement since her hands were bound behind her back. Ryan rolled the word "Admiral" around in his head. He had always despised titles. Captains and kings, chiefs and colonels, bosses and barons…times changed, but the power-hungry types remained the same. Give a man enough money or power, and he always had the urge to elevate his station. Ranks didn't mean a thing when it came to living or dying, especially a self-imposed rank of authority in a long-dead military.

"I see you doubt my credentials, Mr. Ryan Cawdor," Poseidon said, and gave a loud booming laugh from within the cavity of his huge barrel chest. "Are you the jealous type? Does my position threaten your own sense of leadership?"

Ryan was surprised that the Admiral knew his name, but kept his acknowledgment of the revelation close to the vest. "Not at all. Call yourself emperor of all Deathlands if that's what stokes your engine. Way I see it, an asshole's an asshole—even in a fancy uniform."

Poseidon kept the wide smile, but a flinty spark of anger flared in his dark eyes. Ryan knew right then this was a man unused to being spoken to or challenged.

"Ah, the service could have done wonders with your aggression, Cawdor."

"I doubt it."

"No, no, becoming a member of the naval fleet would have molded you," Poseidon insisted. "The proper instruction and informed care could have made something more out of you than just a grubby lander with a blaster in his pocket."

"Well, I never was much of a follower," Ryan said. "Especially if the commanding officer was a regimented old fuck like you."

Poseidon's face was rectangular, with a wide, tall forehead topped off by a steel gray buzz cut. His eyebrows were a darker gray than the salt-and-pepper mix of his hair. Depending on how he held his head, the man's eyes seemed to be an asphalt shade of gray, but they shifted back and forth into a near blackness as Poseidon spoke, changing color with his mood.

The eyes were shining black now.

His cheeks appeared to be pitted with the sort of skin craters associated with chronic teenage acne, although the close-cut full beard he wore helped to cover any imperfections. Other than a nose that had been broken at least once in Poseidon's so-called naval career and a pair of ears too small in proportion to the rest of his massive body, the man was more than merely impressive—he was roguishly handsome.

Ryan wanted to pick up the nearest blunt object and begin to smash that very same handsome face into a mess of grue, but held back and instead estimated how quickly he could gut the big man from sternum to chin if given half a chance. He didn't want to shoot Poseidon. He wanted to kill him up close and personal, with his bare hands, soak the naval whites of the Admiral's uniform in bright red blood, but he curbed the impulse. Mildred, J.B. and Carter were still unaccounted for, and Ryan knew he'd have to play the game for now.

Men such as Poseidon seemed to be compelled to strut and show off their manhood whenever someone like Ryan stumbled into their camps. They weren't content to offer either a hand of friendship or the business end of a blaster. No, their joy came in preening.

The megalomaniacal always wanted to show off either their brilliance or their possessions.

The chairs Ryan and Shauna had finally sat in were made of mahogany, with black padded leather on the seat and arms. The immense desk across from them was made of the same wood and glowed with a sheen of polish. The room had a nautical feel: paintings of ancient whaling ships, a tapestry of an old Western-style paddle-boat steamer, ship instruments mounted on plaques. Elaborate models of submarines of the past lined the back windowed wall, beginning with one model identified as the squat *Turtle,* an early craft used in 1776 by the Continental army to attack the HMS *Eagle.*

"I see you've noticed my display of submarines," Poseidon purred.

"Hard to miss it," Ryan said.

"Right so, right so. Tell me, Mr. Cawdor, did you know that the roots of the modern submarine can be traced all the way back to the days of Alexander the Great?"

Ryan snorted. "I must've been absent that day from history class. Or asleep."

"Legend has it that Alexander descended into the ocean in the year 332 B.C. in a primitive diving bell," Poseidon said, sounding eerily like Doc did before the old man launched into a lengthy explanation Ryan had no desire to hear. "Such courage, to allow oneself to vanish beneath the waves during such an early and superstitious time of man. I'm sure even one as brave as he must have been questioning his own sanity once he was lowered."

"You might think about doing the same," Ryan said.

"Me?" Poseidon laughed. "I've spent more time under water than above."

"I think he meant the part about questioning your sanity," Shauna offered.

Poseidon chose to ignore the insult. "As time passed, others contributed, but it took a true military mind to seize the opportunities a submarine offered. A Dutch physicist, Cornelus Drebbel, actually built a working submersible with the design specifically created to destroy his opponents. But it took an American to actually make the concept workable."

"Yeah, the good ol' U.S. of A. has done right by me," Ryan said. "Done right by all of us. One hell of a legacy, purple mountains majesty and all."

"Don't bash America, Cawdor, especially if your opinion has no research to back it up."

"America—love it or leave it, right?" Ryan said, recalling Mildred's sarcastic take on being an American, and since she got to live the experience, he trusted her opinion a lot more than Poseidon's.

Poseidon laughed. "That's one way of looking at this great land of ours, yes. Now, where was I? Oh, right. In the eventful year of 1776, a Yale University student named David Bushnell designed the *Turtle*, a simple one-man submersible boat with the ability to sneak under a ship, plant a waterproof time bomb onto the bottom of the hull and escape before the explosion. Sheer genius."

"I'm sure it worked out fine," Ryan agreed, rolling his eye.

"Not exactly. The sub didn't function as planned in combat. Still, the germ of the idea was there, and American inventors continued to work toward creating a submarine that could actually sink an enemy vessel. Two world wars later, with the added bonus of the discovery of nuclear fuels and weapons, and the submarine became the most powerful part of any modern fleet."

"As I understand it, they also ushered in the nuke-caust," Ryan said.

"Quite right. In fact, your presence here has enabled me to accelerate my own timetable to test the capabilities of the *Raleigh*."

"You've got nukes?" Shauna breathed.

"A nuke. A single Tomahawk missile, but I'm negotiating for more. I'm hoping Mr. Cawdor will be able to assist in that quest."

"You go to hell," Ryan said as he got to his feet. "I don't know if anyone has bothered to point this out to you, Admiral, but the last war ended the need for submarines. I'm skipping out on the rest of the presentation about the good old days. You can save it for the starry-eyed recruits and sec men you've got running this dump."

"Sit down, Cawdor," Poseidon said, nodding to the guard behind Ryan. The guard lashed out with the butt of his blaster, catching the standing man above the kidneys. Ryan gasped from the blow, and reluctantly took the Admiral's advice as he shakily sat back in the chair.

"Sit down and tell me why you show such animosity for me. I admit, my reputation is marred with innuendo and lies—"

"I never even heard of you until I put in at Shauna's place," Ryan interrupted, shaking off the pain in his lower back.

Poseidon looked offended. "I find that hard to believe."

"Believe it," Ryan said. "Your rep must need some extra promoting. Hire yourself a storyteller, plop him into one of your wags and let him travel around Deathlands singing your praises."

"If you want to hold back even the barest whiff of a compliment, that's your business. I'm above such petty role playing," Poseidon said, still maintaining the air of civility.

"Bullshit. Role playing is what gets you off," Shauna said. "I'm sure you're waving a giant hard-on over having me tied to a chair. A helpless woman is the classic male power fantasy."

Poseidon approached the woman. Ryan noted as he got a better look at his opponent's build that the man was big but not fat. Poseidon had never been small, even as a child. Ryan knew the man would have been noticed in any ordinary group for his height and girth. He looked to be nearly six and a half feet tall, and the man's weight had to be around three hundred pounds of solid bulk.

"Tell me, Shauna, do you still harbor resentment

over your husband's death? Is that why you've brought this man here, to assist in assassinating me?''

Shauna was quiet.

"What has she told you, Cawdor? That I killed her husband? Took her authority? Hah! Saved her pathetic little community is more like it!''

"Yeah, I've heard about how well you've been keeping an eye on the seafood,'' Ryan retorted. "Not a flounder was overlooked.''

"Why are you here, anyway, Cawdor?'' Poseidon said. "I know Shauna doesn't have the necessary funds to hire you.''

Ryan kept silent. He almost said *To chill you* but curbed the impulse.

"Fate has placed you within my hands for a reason,'' Poseidon mused. "Yes, you might think you're here merely to take up some kind of cause against me, but I know better.''

"My boat ran up on a stinkin' mine out near the commune. It was during that storm that swept through here last week back. Mine blew my ride all to hell.''

"That was your boat, you say.'' Poseidon leaned on the wall, standing next to the sec man who was watching over the prisoners. "I wondered what had set off the charge.''

"Your mines killed my woman, Poseidon,'' Ryan finally said.

"Nonsense. I've killed no one close to you.''

"You destroyed the most valuable piece of my life over paranoia and greed,'' Ryan continued. "Now I'm here to destroy you.''

"So you say," Poseidon answered.

"There's no reason to be mining the Georgia coastline in the first place!" Shauna said. "Who do you think is going to attack? The Commies?"

"Actually it had crossed my mind, dear girl. However, the mines were planted there not so much to keep people out, but to keep your rabble on land."

"You're insane, Poseidon! You get more crazy every waking moment of your murderous life!" Shauna yelled out, her body shaking in anger, causing the chair to rock slightly.

"I knew it," Poseidon said tiredly. "You *are* still annoyed over the removal of your husband."

Shauna glared at the big man with a look of unholy hatred. "I swore I'd kill you. If there's any justice in heaven, I'll see the day pass where you're dead at my feet."

Poseidon shook his head and shrugged his massive shoulders. He looked at Ryan for agreement as he spoke. "Eric Watson challenged me. I fought back. He lost. End of transaction. Women take these things much too seriously. That's one reason I don't allow them on the base."

Ryan snickered. "I have my own theory about that, sailor boy."

"You're wrong, Cawdor. About a lot of things."

Shauna was so upset, her face was a bright blush of crimson. "He came to talk with you in peace and you killed him! Admit it!"

"I thought I already had," Poseidon said mildly, stepping closer to the bound woman. "Still, I don't need this mutie-loving slut making accusations or telling me what to do.''

Poseidon's hands snapped down and clasped Shauna around the neck. Her back was half turned to him, but his freakishly large hands were able to completely envelop her throat.

As she cried out, Poseidon stopped her voice with a squeeze so tight, his fingers began to whiten from the pressure being applied.

''Who's killing who now, Shauna, hmm?'' he said in a voice so calmly modulated, he might have been describing the weather.

Ryan reared to his feet like a surprised stallion, slamming his body toward Poseidon, but the butt of the sec man's rifle caught him once again, this time full across the back of the neck, blunting his frantic thrust. Ryan fell to his knees, his breath coming in gasps.

He watched as Poseidon's viselike hands tightened and lifted up the dying woman from the chair. Shauna barely had enough life force left to struggle. Her legs kicked once, twice, then hung limp.

''Too late, Cawdor. Much...too...late.''

Chapter Twenty

"Remove...that," Poseidon said, wiping his brow with an immaculate white handkerchief.

The Admiral was once again seated behind his majestic desk. He watched impassively as the sec man summoned two assistants, who arrived almost instantly and carried Shauna's lifeless body out of the office.

"Is that how you inspire loyalty in your little navy?" Ryan asked, still on his knees on the floor. "Killing anyone who gets in your way?"

"I do what it takes. My enjoyment of such actions is an occasional rare bonus. That bitch had been plotting against me for far too long," Poseidon said. "The female mind is unfathomable."

"Well, I'm always impressed when a guy strangles a helpless woman to death. That's three I owe you for, now."

"Three?"

"Three," Ryan said, but didn't elaborate.

Poseidon leaned back in his chair and cracked his knuckles. "As I was saying earlier, my reputation is marred with innuendo and lies, but so is your own."

"What do you mean?" Ryan said.

"I've heard of you and your little mercenary group."

"Don't believe everything you hear," Ryan said.

"Oh, I never do. Besides, as they used to say back in wartime, loose lips sink ships," Poseidon replied, miming the closing of a lock on his upper lip and throwing away the key. "Still, just between you and me—"

"And the tree trunk," Ryan added, glancing at the grim sec man who continued to hold position behind him.

"Never mind Jonesy. He hears what I tell him to, right, Jonesy?"

"Hear what, sir?" the sec man asked on cue.

"Good man," Poseidon said brightly, as if talking to a beloved pet. "Now, back to our discussion. There's change in the wind, Cawdor. Wild cards such as yourself are due to be eliminated. The more powerful of the barons are starting to communicate for the first time in decades. They speak on a regular basis by radio and through intermediaries via traveling caravans, and do you know why?"

"They were getting lonely?"

Poseidon looked at Ryan with a pitying expression. "Scuttle the sarcasm, Cawdor. You don't have the timing for it. No, they're starting to align themselves for protection from murderous thugs like you, self-serving renegades who roam Deathlands in packs, like mangy wolves, slinking into law-abiding villes and stealing food and supplies."

Ryan couldn't help it. Even if it meant another

blow from the rifle butt, he had to laugh aloud. "You're crazier than I thought."

"Don't mock civilization, Cawdor. It's what makes man rise above the animals."

"Civilization is also what destroyed the world. As I understand it, the barons in power back then didn't bother to ask anybody's permission when they wanted to do something, and it's still the same today. Once a baron gets some food in his stomach and some property and the jack to hire a sec squad, he stops listening to anyone but himself."

"But the ones in power will listen to their peers," Poseidon replied.

"I doubt it. Most of the villes I've been in have been hotbeds of hatred, closed-off parcels full of hatred and inbreeding. There's no way in hell there's going to be any sort of alliance."

"You're not thinking, Cawdor—that, or you're just being thick to annoy me. As many barons and villes as you and your merry band of outlaws have brought down, how could you expect otherwise? You aren't alone in spreading the seed of destruction, nor are you the first. There have always been the fringe elements who refuse to conform."

Ryan leaned back farther in the chair slowly, so as not to give any indication of an attack, then swung up one of his long legs, placing his boot heel on the top of Poseidon's desk. "Those arrogant bastards in charge of their pissant baronies and villes couldn't stop shouting and posing long enough to make a group decision on what kind of meat to serve at their first communal meal, much less come to any kind of agreement.''

''I shall be a part of a grand new alliance, where a council of baronies shall rule,'' Poseidon said confidently. ''I am at the forefront of the new wave to help reconnect the world.''

''How?''

Poseidon spread open his arms. ''The sea, Cawdor, the sea! No air travel! No safe and efficient way to crawl across the radiation pits scarring the landscape! What does that leave?''

''Let me guess. The sea.''

''Correct! From the day man crawled up from the muck and the slime onto dry land, the control of the seas from whence he sprang has meant dominance. All the great generals from all the great wars have been forced to take possession of the waters surrounding their territories, their lands. And once they lost the sea, they lost the war, and they lost their command.''

Poseidon paused. ''I have no intention of losing my power, Cawdor. Only increasing it.''

''With a bunch of hired mercs who would just as soon chill you as follow an order? I don't think so,'' Ryan said with a sneer. ''And I wouldn't count on any villes backing up your master plan, either. People always look out for number one, Poseidon. You're living proof of that.''

''Fear has a way of creating strange bunk mates,'' Poseidon replied. ''And I wonder how my standing in their eyes will increase once I present you for their entertainment.''

"Bring it on.''

"However, I indeed do tend to look out for myself, as you pointed out. That's why I collect reports—oral tales of a one-eyed man bringing retribution across the scarred lands of what's left of this great country of ours, and I have to dismiss much of it as fictions created beside a warm fire to amuse. Or do I?''

"You tell me,'' Ryan replied, not sure in what direction the Admiral was taking the conversation.

"The primary reason the reports are not to be believed is due to sheer logistics. You appear one day in West Virginia, and then a week later you're spotted in New Mexico. Reports have you in Maine, then you show up within days in Snakefish, California. And I think, How? How is this possible?'' Poseidon said, walking past Ryan's chair. "I think to myself, Could there be more than one man claiming to be Ryan Cawdor?''

"Looks like you caught me. I'm twins,'' Ryan said with as much hate and venom as he could muster up. "You can tell us apart by the eye patches. My brother wears his on the right eye. Says it's his best side—''

Poseidon's hand cracked out like it was spring-loaded, catching Ryan in his good eye. He grunted, but didn't move from the force of the blow, even as a multicolored explosion of pain blossomed in his right temple.

"You'll shut up, or I'll finish blinding you myself,'' the big man said, returning to his desk, where he composed himself and again steepled his large hands beneath his bearded chin.

"Then it occurs to me. Why not combine one tall tale with a second? There have been rumors of a futuristic method of traveling, a teleportation device ripped from the pages of old science-fiction novels. None of my contacts have ever seen or encountered anyone with firsthand knowledge, so all I have is theory, rumor, innuendo. Now I have someone with that firsthand knowledge."

"I'm afraid I'm going to be one colossal disappointment," Ryan said with a dry laugh.

"My plan to master the seas is one thing, but if I can control any who would challenge me with the forbidden secrets of instantaneous land travel, then I shall be master of the entire world, both surface and underwater."

"Good fucking luck."

"You're the luck I needed, Cawdor. You are the key to the gateways."

Ryan felt his bravado sink down into his boots. The son of a bitch knew.

"Take your best shot, Admiral. I have nothing to say to you."

"Then perhaps I have another way of convincing you," Poseidon said. He sat back down and pressed a button on a desk intercom. "Bring in our guest."

"Going to kill another woman to try and show me the error of my ways?" Ryan asked.

Poseidon ignored him. "There's an interesting fact

about the sea, Cawdor. Things can be thrown into the depths and never seen again, or things can be thrown into the depths only to be found by those who know what to look for. In fact, life in Deathlands is much like life at sea—you scavenge and try and live off the remains of the past, am I right?''

''If I say yes, will you spare me another lecture?'' Ryan asked bitterly.

There was a knock from outside the thick office door.

''Come.''

A man, also in a naval dress uniform, stepped into the room. He snapped off a quick salute to the Admiral, which was returned. ''Ah, Commander Brosnan. Glad you could join us. Mr. Cawdor isn't being cooperative. I need a persuader. Do you have it?''

''Outside, Admiral.''

''Then bring in the lady, please.''

The door opened, and as Ryan turned his face for a look, he discovered for once in his life he was struck totally speechless. A mix that was equal parts joy and anger swept across his soul as he stared in joyful disbelief at the woman standing between a pair of frowning, armed sec guards.

''I believe you know Miss Wroth,'' Poseidon murmured.

''We've...met,'' Ryan rasped, seeing the same expression on Krysty's face that he knew had to be on his own craggy visage.

''I thought you were dead,'' she said softly, tears welling in her luminous green eyes.

"I was," Ryan replied, fighting to keep himself seated and calm as he battled the urge to race over and take her in his arms. "Not now. Not anymore."

"Take her back to the brig—the secure cell. You may leave the albino where he is," Poseidon snapped. "See that she gets anything she wants. Food, drink, vids. Keep her happy and safe. However, double the watch, just in case Mr. Cawdor gets any foolish notions."

"Yes sir, Admiral." The commander gestured with a curled thumb, and the two armed escorts backed Krysty out of the room. Brosnan turned to close the door behind their departure, and the room fell silent.

"Yes, you never know what's going to turn up in the sea," Poseidon mused, getting up once more from his leather chair. The polished wood squeaked in protest as his enormous weight left the seat.

"You were there," Ryan said flatly, "the night the mine blew up our boat."

"Yes and no. I was there after the explosion, beneath the ocean and the storm in a minisub, a routine cruise interrupted by your stumbling into my domain."

"You're scum," Ryan snapped.

Poseidon smacked the top of Ryan's skull. "Don't go all sanctimonious on me! You're the one who rode in here, destroying my property and killing my men! That whore from upstate? No loss! Her husband? He's the one who came in here making demands of me! *Me!* So I keelhauled his whiny ass and gave him fifty lashes and he couldn't take it!"

The large man struggled to contain his anger. Ryan knew then and there he was peering at madness in human form. He was certainly familiar enough with it to know the signs.

"I saved her, Cawdor, along with that white freak," the Admiral said. "You owe me."

"I owe you dick."

"Then perhaps I'll take her back where I found her—half-drowned, unconscious and dying." Poseidon reached over and grabbed Ryan by the hair of the head, bending the one-eyed man's shoulder back over the top of the chair. "Don't try and bluff me, you snot-nosed punk. I'll break you like a glass bottle if you keep sassing me. That raspy voice and eye patch may frighten the ignorant and the stupid, but they hold no truck with me."

"Just what in the fuck do you want from me?" Ryan asked tightly.

"Information."

"Such as?"

Poseidon let Ryan's hair go and strode back to his desk, as calmly as if he'd never shown even the slightest glimpse of anger as opposed to the full-blown performance he'd given since killing Shauna. "Numerals. Symbols. The arcane scripture from the world when mankind was still in command of his manifest destiny."

"Could you be a little more specific?"

"Certainly. I want you to tell me everything, Cawdor," Poseidon said, his black eyes gleaming bright. "But first, what do you know about the access codes needed to get into a military redoubt?"

Chapter Twenty-One

Ryan was alive. Alive!

The thought wouldn't leave Krysty's brain.

He was alive, and Poseidon had lied. Krysty couldn't be sure if Ryan had just arrived or had previously been on the base. Her instincts told her the former; otherwise the Admiral wouldn't have brought her in to show off like a prize heifer. She was smart enough to know when she was being used as a bargaining chip.

The question was, why? What could he want or need from Ryan to use her as a hostage?

After allowing her and Ryan to glimpse each other, Poseidon had ordered her jailers to march her back, but not to the hospital psych ward where she'd been previously kept with Jak.

This time she was walked across the compound to a flat, ugly building made of the same off-white stone as the rest of the base. Apparently this had once been a mass of offices and tiny cloth-walled cubicles. Inert comp terminals were in each little half room. Some of the desks still held photographs in frames or other personal mementos that were very different from the ones she was used to seeing inside the utilitarian military redoubts.

Two cells had been assembled at the end of the largest central conference room.

Krysty had seen this type of setting before. Once, this was a building used for the conducting of military business. Now, a part of it had been remodeled as a brig for those who displeased Poseidon.

"Sit tight, bitch. We've got some smokin' plans for you once Cawdor shows the Admiral where the fireworks are hidden." The leering sec man gave her a shove, and she half fell, half stepped into the windowless room. The man who pushed her had answered part of her question. Krysty was being held to force Ryan to show Poseidon where something was hidden.

Krysty decided to play dumb. She didn't turn back or give off an angry retort to the sec man. If she kept quiet, perhaps he would stupidly say more. She merely went over and sat on the small mattress on the floor in the corner of the room. She attempted to wear her best beaten-down expression, the wilted flower, the helpless woman—whatever was most convincing.

Unfortunately for her plans, the sec man chose not to gloat any more, and blew her a kiss as he slammed the heavy door shut.

After the door closed, she waited. The sound of a lock being turned came from the steel frame. A dead bolt. This bit of information was filed in her brain, although she really wasn't dwelling on the immediacy of her surroundings at the moment. Krysty Wroth wasn't a passive type of woman. She was ready to go on the offensive. If she could escape, her value as a wedge would cease to exist, and Ryan would be free from his obligation to help Poseidon in exchange for her safety.

Her green eyes closed to slits. She wasn't seeing the outside world anymore; she was looking within. She drew her long legs beneath her in the lotus position and began to whisper in a soft, breathy voice a string of words, sentence fragments and prayers—a mantra she never relished in calling up from her unconscious because of the dangers to herself and to those around her.

But Krysty was alone now, and there was no one around her but her enemies.

"Earth Mother, help me. Aid me now, Gaia. Help me and give me the strength," she whispered.

She had been trained since childhood to hone this empathy by being in tune with the electromagnetic energies of the great Earth Mother, Gaia. By tapping into these hidden pools of energy, Krysty sacrificed her humanity to become a creature with the strength of a sheer force of nature, but only for a limited time, and the transformation took a terrific toll on her physical and mental well-being.

She hoped she would be strong enough to free herself now.

"Help me, Earth Mother, I need your embrace. Aid me now, Gaia. Help me and give me the strength," she chanted, faster now, her face simultaneously calm and urgent. "From the center of the world to souls of your children, give me the power...."

KRYSTY STEPPED UP to the door, a crooked smile of dark amusement on her face. She looked like a living embodiment of a dream, a walking human dream caught up in private songs and hidden thoughts. Her long fingers traced the frame of the reinforced cell door. Even in the near state of delirium that calling on the power of the Earth Mother always placed her mind in, she knew that one or both of the men who had brought her into the building would be outside guarding the door.

Two wouldn't be enough to stop her. Not even close.

The brutal ballet that was about to begin would be vicious and ugly, and luckily for the two walking dead men assigned to watch over her, blessedly brief.

One of the pair, a fortyish man named Murphy, heard a faint scratching noise come from behind the reinforced steel door.

"What's that?" Murphy asked, tilting his head and trying to pick out the source of the sound.

"What's what?" his younger partner, Fade, impatiently responded.

"I hear scratching," Murphy insisted.

"Probably rats. This building is crawling with the bastards. Screw 'em. Sit down and we'll play a hand of cards or something."

The older man had stepped up to the door of the cell now and placed his ear against it. "Sounds like they're inside with the girl," he observed.

"Lucky them," Fade retorted.

"Think they could hurt her?" Murphy asked.

"Naw. Not as long as she doesn't turn her back on them," Fade said. "Besides, what the hell difference does it make? Once the Admiral gives the order, we're going to pull a fuck train on that little morsel that'll cause her to be walking on her hands for months afterward."

"Oh, yeah?" Murphy was interested now. He felt the telltale sensations of an erection starting to grow in his denims. "I didn't know that. I haven't gotten laid in months."

"Hell, yeah! I heard that, bro. You know how Poseidon feels about women. Thinks they carry disease. Said we could do as we wished as long as we wore protection," Fade said with a chuckle. "Protection. She's gonna need it! I'm gonna ride that bitch so hard, she's liable to split in two. God damn, but I love the military!"

Fade stood up and walked over to Murphy. "Take a seat, Pops. Let me take a listen. If there are rats in there, I don't want them touching that girl 'fore I do."

The two men switched positions. Murphy sat at the small industrial green desk and picked up the deck of well-worn playing cards that Fade had been shuffling earlier. The middle drawer of the desk was crammed full with old porn mags that were near rags, and various other sedentary amusements to help pass the time when watching over a prisoner.

Meanwhile, Fade listened.

"Nothing," he announced.

"No, no, you gotta bend down. The sound is coming down lower. You think rats would be standing six feet high or what?'' Murphy said.

Fade shot his companion a glare, but went ahead and got down on his knees. He leaned into the door, and damned if the older guy wasn't right. He did hear some scratching sounds.

Suddenly the sounds abruptly ceased. He pressed his ear closer and waited for them to start a second time.

By doing so, Fade never saw what was coming as the door crashed hard into his skull and shoulder from the terrific two-handed push delivered from the inside, a push of such force the steel frame came free along with the locked door, dripping bits of metal, plaster and wood. The end result was the temporary immobilization of the sec man on the floor, and a jagged hole where the cell door had been.

Standing there, framed in the ruin and still wearing the beatific smile, was Krysty.

''Knock, knock,'' she said in an innocent whisper.

Her eyes shone with cold fire now, the pupils blazing as she took in the scene. The two men reacted as quickly as they humanly could, which didn't mean a thing to the voluptuous creature now in their midst. The parts of herself Krysty called human had been submerged, replaced with a red molten force. A lover of life and all it entailed, she was now the destroyer, no longer a creator, no longer a preserver.

In the killing state of mind Krysty had been forced to induce within herself, the sec men who had brought her here and locked her away were now moving in slow motion. Pathetic. The red mist of death swamped her mind. There would be no reasoning with her now.

No begging.

No mercy.

Fade was the first to die. He had managed to shift the broken door from his body and crawl away, scuttling on his hands and knees to a point where he could spin and pump a full clip of hot ammo into this crazy witch.

Krysty idly watched him as she might have observed an insect seeking refuge from being stepped on. The thought made her body temperature glow even hotter.

With ferocious velocity, Krysty's right boot shot out, catching Fade in the ear and jaw. Cartilage tore, and the eye socket of the man's skull shattered like a dropped eggshell. The upper part of his jawbone broke and tore away from the connecting tissue and muscle.

The end result was shocking. To Fade, and to the watching Murphy, she'd moved so fast the kick had barely registered, until the lower half of the man's face went from whole and solid to hanging like a wet burlap sack full of marbles. Unintelligible screams were coming from his throat and out of his ruined mouth and nose, a mix of snot and blood dripping from his nostrils.

Murphy looked at the scene, at his partner, and his mouth dropped open in disbelief. How hard had she kicked Fade anyway? What the fuck was in the toes of those boots? He'd never seen anything like this in all of his forty-four years of existence. Like some kind of adventure vid player set on fast forward, this woman, this *thing*, had broken a steel door in two, ripped out the frame and proceeded to kick the shit out of a man who in all likelihood would normally be able to pick her up one-handed without even breathing hard.

Murphy responded by pivoting in the padded swivel chair behind the desk, tossing aside the deck of cards, rising to his feet and running as fast as possible from the engine of destruction that had erupted in his midst.

Fade looked on in rage at the lower half of his own face sagging limply into his line of vision, then set his sights on the demon above him. He cursed her in a string of profanities that would have done any man proud.

But to Krysty, the bleating figure at her feet was merely a distraction. She watched, with a mix of bemusement and pity, as Fade managed to blindly shoot off a single round from the rifle he'd been carrying. In response, Krysty kicked out a second time, and a third, and a fourth, and a fifth—her movements a blur as each blow struck home, catching the join of Fade's chin and neck as if she were repeatedly punting a football.

Fade's features were destroyed beyond recognition, blood spraying up like the high-pressure contents of a burst water pipe. The lifeless head flew upward at a forty-five-degree angle, hitting one of the ringed silver ceiling lamps with a wet slapping sound. The screeching noise the man had been making before the final blow was replaced with a bellowslike wheeze from the wet hole between his shoulders.

All of this occurred within a span of mere seconds.

Murphy was up and running for his life. To Krysty, he was merely walking away at a leisurely pace. A casual follow-me jog.

The sec man was scared, as scared as he'd ever been in his mercenary life.

Fuck the navy and fuck Poseidon, too. No amount of jack was worth having to deal with this! Stickies and muties and bands of wandering marauders with killing on their mind was one thing, but this was beyond even the usual day-to-day madness of Deathlands.

"I'm sorry, I'm sorry, I'm sorry," came in a torrent from his mouth as he ran.

Behind him, Krysty stepped on Fade's still-thrashing body and began to make her move.

Murphy was babbling faster now, praying, begging, gasping as he ran. He didn't look back. He'd seen more than enough, the empty smiling expression on the woman's face coming up behind him was etched forever in his memory. He staggered, trying to keep his balance and hoping he wouldn't fall.

When he felt her iron fingers bite down on his shoulder and lift him bodily into the air, it was almost a blessing.

Chapter Twenty-Two

The world was concrete, stone hard and cool to the touch. The steps, the walls, even the low ceilings were all made of the same flat blue-gray concrete. Flickering fluorescent track lighting showed the path downward, along with helpful painted arrows on the walls. Poseidon, still in full dress uniform, led the way, followed by the tall, broad-shouldered sec man that had previously been keeping watch over Ryan.

Poseidon had called the man Jonesy.

Ryan, his hands cuffed behind his back, was third in line. The rear was brought up by a second merc with thick eyeglasses and blond hair who wore civilian garb. The man with the glasses hadn't volunteered a name, nor had Poseidon offered one. Ryan dubbed him Specs. The visually impaired J.B. wouldn't have been amused, but Ryan considered his being down an eye to the Armorer's two allowed him to say whatever he wished about anyone with glasses.

"More hired help," Ryan had said. "Couldn't get him to sign up for the draft, either, huh?"

"Mercenaries are a necessary evil, as is so much else these days," the Admiral answered. "I buy all of my men's loyalties in different ways, Cawdor. All leaders do. I'm sure you have ways of binding your own people to your allegiance.''

''My 'people' are my friends. There's a difference,'' Ryan corrected. ''But you wouldn't understand that.''

''And the woman? I can understand the need for physical companionship. She's one hell of a looker, so I know the sex must be good. But she's your Achilles' heel, Cawdor.''

''My what?'' Ryan asked.

''Your weakness.''

''Shows what you know. With her, I'm twice as strong as when I'm alone. Before her, I was a man with no direction. Now I know who I am and who I hope to become someday,'' Ryan said. ''I'm willing to risk having an Achilles' heel for that.''

''Then you're half the leader I've been told you were, and a fool.''

Poseidon fell silent, and their trek downward continued. If Doc had been with the four men, he wouldn't have been able to resist comparing the length of their descent into the mass of damp walled tunnels and dimly lit subbasements beneath the naval base to Dante's plunge into the inferno. The only difference was the temperature of the air.

Cool air. And while it wasn't exactly fresh, it was breathable, just like the air in the redoubts. Ryan glanced up at the join where the walls met the ceiling. Small metal slits were embedded in the concrete. Air ducts kept everything flowing.

''Nuke gen,'' Ryan muttered.

"Beg pardon?" Poseidon said from the front of the line.

"Nothing."

"No, Mr. Cawdor, I distinctly heard you mumble something in that monotone you call a speaking voice. 'Nuke gen' were your words, I believe. I just wanted to say your theory is correct. At least, as correct as I have been able to surmise without actual admittance into the hidden chambers below this base."

Ryan pondered the truth of Poseidon's statement. No wonder the Kings Point naval base had been able to survive as a working facility. Maintenance was much easier with electricity, and the nuclear generators that powered the mat-trans unit inside the gateways had plenty of energy to spare.

If Poseidon was to be believed, and *if* there was indeed a gateway chamber hidden down in the maze of subbasements they were currently in, then this would be one of the rare instances where a redoubt was housed in a logical locale, as opposed to a lonely facility stuck away in the middle of nowhere or inside a public place like the swamps of Greenglades.

And then, without fanfare, they arrived.

Ryan stood before the familiar shape of a redoubt entrance door and frowned. The door looked the same, and yet it was obviously a modification of the standard configuration, probably due to its location. He closed his good eye and reopened it slowly.

The door was still there, waiting.

Like Poseidon and his two sec men.

"Uncuff Mr. Cawdor, but take care," Poseidon warned. "He is supposed to be a master of hand-to-hand combat."

Specs unlocked the handcuffs. Ryan rubbed his sore wrists as he stared at the door.

"Your circulation should be fine," Poseidon said. "Open the door."

Ryan hesitated.

"Is there a problem?"

"Never seen one like this before," Ryan said. "Looks different."

Still, the vanadium-steel door recessed into the back wall of the subbasement was nearly identical to the other ones Ryan had opened before, except for the color, which was a bright stoplight green, and the shape, which was hexagonal. The controls looked the same—the same numeric keypad to punch in the entry code. Some of the numbers appeared to have been worn down from use.

"Don't delay, Cawdor. Open the door and let's be done with it. You have my word your woman isn't going to be harmed as long as you do as I say."

Mental pictures of Shauna Watson, dead in her chair, went through Ryan's mind.

The word of a madman.

"What's in here you want so badly?" Ryan said. "The mat-trans units don't even work right, and half the time, they're broken."

"Still, they are obtainable, and I want them," the Admiral replied. "Plus, I am aware of the massive stockpiles of weapons these redoubts may hold. I need nukes, Cawdor. My submarine needs nukes. Even as we speak, I have a crew on board the *Raleigh* awaiting my return. If I find what I seek within this hideaway, we shall depart on our test mission as scheduled.''

"What test?"

"Right now I have a single Tomahawk missile without a true nuclear warhead. I intend to test it farther up the coast on that miserable settlement of mutants and half-wits that Shauna called home. I'll miss their weekly tributes from the sea, but I'll soon be able to afford whatever cuisine I desire.''

"You'd chill them all as a bastard test?" Ryan asked, knowing that even without the nuclear payload the missile would still decimate the small commune.

"Well, it wouldn't be much of a test otherwise, now would it?''

"What if you don't find any nukes in here?" Ryan said, his mind working fast. The odds were slim missiles for a submarine were down here, but then again, this was the first time he'd found a redoubt at a military base. Any kind of stockpiles might be within.

"No nukes, no test," Poseidon replied. "I hardly intend to use my lone missile until I have more of them. Now, stop stalling and open the door before I have Jonesy start to break your fingers as an inducement.''

Ryan had no choice. He reached out and used his index finger to press the proper sequence of keys to open the door to the redoubt.

"Three-five-two," Poseidon whispered aloud, watching closely. "That's it?"

"That's it," Ryan said, and there was a rumbling noise from within the wall of the subbasement as the gears within meshed and bit. The door began to rise upward in a swift, steady motion.

"So simple," Poseidon mused. "Three-five-two, and the door opens. I had come down here before at night and wondered what the right combination might be. I tried an infinite number, each one randomly generated on a pocket comp so I wouldn't repeat myself."

The door was now completely open. All eyes but Ryan's were on the mysteries housed within.

"Now I learn my conjectures were always one number too many. The sec doors above ground throughout the base require a code of four numerals to all high-security sectors. Even if I had indeed stumbled onto the right pattern unknowingly, I would have always transmitted one number too many."

"Life's a bitch, ain't it?" Ryan said, then he fell forward, flat on his face as if he had tripped over a hidden wire or string. At the same time, he kicked out hard, smashing a boot heel into Spec's kneecap. A cry of pain and surprise burst out of the injured man's mouth at the same time as his leg went numb beneath him. The weapon he carried was forgotten and dropped to the floor as his hands clutched instinctively at his broken knee.

Ryan rolled to the left, managing to snag the carrying strap of the fallen AK-47 with his feet.

The clock was ticking; Ryan had been keeping an eye on his chron. Soon it would be midnight, then he would know if J.B, Mildred and Carter had been more successful in their mission than he and Shauna had been.

But first things first. The other sec man in front of Ryan, Jonesy, had spun the instant the commotion began, only to find Ryan was no longer standing behind him.

"Go ahead, kill the bastard," Poseidon bellowed. "We're in!"

The Admiral leaped into the doorway and got out of the way as Jonesy pulled the trigger of his automatic weapon and the lead began to fly, digging divots in the basement floor as Ryan rolled and dodged, trying to get his hands on the dropped weapon snared by his feet.

"No! Shit! Wait!" Specs cried before a series of red holes flew up his groin and stomach. Jonesy was keeping his trigger mashed down and aiming by instinct, trying to get a bead on the twisting Ryan.

When he took out the second sec man, Jonesy didn't even hesitate over the accidental killing—but he did when Ryan did a most unexpected thing.

Still unable to get his hands on the AK-47 tangled in his feet by the strap, Ryan instead hurled the rifle at Jonesy's face with all of the force his lower legs could muster. A desperate act, but an effective one. The heavy rifle flew into Jonesy's unprotected face butt first, knocking out three teeth and causing him to stumble backward falling flat on his backside directly with the door of the redoubt over his body. Momentarily stunned by the blow, the big sec man was dazed.

Ryan moved at a blur and from a kneeling position sent a roundhouse right into the man's already bleeding mouth.

Jonesy fell back flat, unconscious, his own rifle still in his hands.

Before Poseidon could step back out, Ryan snatched up the AK-47 and sent a burst of rounds through the door of the redoubt. The Admiral retreated inside, farther away from the door.

"Cawdor! What are you doing out there? Damn you!"

Ryan sprang to his feet and hit the keypad a second time, reversing the code to 2-5-3. The vanadium-steel door began to descend.

"You wanted in and now you've got it! Enjoy your stay, you cold-hearted son of a bitch!" Ryan roared, firing the rifle through the lowering door until the clip was empty. As the door slid down farther, the hapless Jonesy was caught on the floor at waist level. The door was relentless in its descent as it started to cut the unconscious man in two, his torso on the far side with Poseidon and his legs out in the basement.

Ryan debated pulling him away from certain death, then shook his head.

"I owe you for those shots to the kidneys," Ryan said as he turned away, not waiting to see the final bloody splash when the door hit home in the groove in the floor.

EVEN ON THE BEST OF DAYS and the easiest of missions, J. B. Dix wasn't the most patient of men. Mildred once told the man he was like a worm in hot ashes—always moving, always on the go.

Even J.B.'s sleep was restless, with constant movement of his leanly muscled arms and legs. Mildred was happy he didn't snore, but he made up for it by waking her up every hour on the hour with a stray limb whacking her in the nose or back or breast.

After the initial entry into Kings Point at approximately six o'clock, the captured Edgerton had decided to play hero and alert the guard. Before the sec man could press the panic button, J.B. had fired a burst at him through the ob slit in the Land Rover. At the sound of gunfire, Edgerton had hit the gas and taken the wag into a swerve, knocking down part of the guard booth in a crash of wood and glass and causing Ryan to shift in his position in the passenger seat.

Edgerton opened his driver's side door and jumped to the pavement, legs pumping as he sprinted for safety, screaming for someone to help.

Ryan cursed as he brought up the SIG-Sauer and fired, catching the fleeing man low in the left leg. As Edgerton fell on his side like a dropped rag doll, three more sec men came out from a second wag that had been parked in a motor pool off to one side of the guard shack.

The firefight was on.

Edgerton died in the middle of it, unprotected and alone.

Ryan and Shauna broke away, diverting the sec

men's fire and giving J.B., Mildred and Alan Carter a chance to escape, maybe salvage something from the mission.

What the trio couldn't know was that Ryan decided being captured alive wasn't so bad. What better way to see the leader up close and personal?

The other three, who remained free, had been forced to hide until nightfall.

Under the cover of darkness, it hadn't taken very long to plant their dozen grens, all preset to go off at midnight: a fuel-storage tower, the support beams over wheeled wags. There were many places to create chaos and diversion. Once things started to blow, everyone was to converge on where they had left the damaged wag, which was near the ruin of the gate and the guard shack.

Ryan and Shauna, if they weren't able to get close to Poseidon, were to abandon their objective and go home if they could. The rest of the squad wasn't to wait, but instead pull out for the commune.

Not that J.B. and Mildred were even considering that option.

They would all leave together, one way or the other.

"What do you think of this place, Millie?" J.B. whispered. "That far end is mighty nice, with the lights and construction and all. Wonder why he hasn't fixed up the rest of the base?"

"Too busy trying to rebuild that leaky piece-of-shit submarine," Carter replied.

"He's more vulnerable than I expected," Mildred

replied, her beaded plaits clicking softly as she turned her head to look down from the rooftop they were using for hiding and observation. "Lots of empty buildings and not enough men to properly police each one. This base might actually be a threat if Poseidon had the manpower to take care of it."

"Guess his plan to bring back the military isn't going as smoothly as he figured," Carter noted.

"I want to take a look inside the base hospital," Mildred said. "Men come in and go out on a regular basis. Must be a reason. They might have supplies we can take back, too."

"Sure," J.B. said. "We've still got about half an hour before the excitement starts."

"We can go in as we head back toward the wag," Carter added. "The hospital's right on the way."

"Wait, what's that?" J.B. asked, seeing movement on the roadway below.

THE WAN FIGURE with long red hair who had exited the squat building that housed the brig no longer even remotely resembled the killing machine that had run rampant only moments before. This woman looked ill, as if she wouldn't be able to stay on her feet long enough to make it across the paved roadway. She paused, hovering in the flickering light of a single working streetlight. The sky was dark now, and it would have taken a close inspection to see the traces of red on her silver-tipped cowboy boots and the drying ribbons of crimson on her clothing.

Her hands were nearly clean, since she'd found a

bathroom with water in a sink and a bar of ancient deodorant soap. She'd quickly washed the blood from her hands and fingers, half-sickened by her actions, necessary as they might have been.

Across the street, on the roof of another one of the flat, two-story buildings, the trio was watching the woman's progress, unsure of how to proceed. This was the first woman they had seen on the base. No one said anything as they waited, until the light revealed the color of her limp yet still luxurious hair.

Those in hiding knew the figure and the warning signs of fatigue she was now exhibiting. At least, two of the watchers did.

"Dark night," J.B. breathed.

"It's Krysty," Mildred stated.

"Who in creation is Krysty?" Carter asked.

"You'll find out soon enough," J.B. whispered. "She's heading this way."

Mildred turned and approached the roof-access door. "Come on, come on," she urged. "She won't be walking for long. I know she's called on Gaia, and we all know the toll that summons takes."

"Who's Gaia?" Carter asked peevishly, starting to grow annoyed.

"Later, Carter," J.B. said. "It's complicated, and we don't have time right now for another one of your lectures."

THE FRIENDS WERE ON the top floor of the two-story dormitory, and the room they were now in appeared to once have been a communal lounge for the enlisted men. Things were a bit messy perhaps, but still comfortable.

"Here, sit down," Mildred said, gesturing toward the most intact chair. Obediently the flame-haired beauty did as she was told. Once Krysty sat down, J.B. removed his leather jacket and draped it around her slumped shoulders. The collar of his worn jacket was made of silky black fur, similar to her own long coat, and she gratefully lay one cheek on the softness. She closed her eyes and immediately began a gentle snoring through her nose.

"She's zonked," Carter said, delivering his diagnosis. "They must've got her high on dreem or jolt or something."

"Shut up, Carter," Mildred said.

"Yeah, she's always like this when she summons up the, um…" J.B.'s voice trailed off. How exactly did one explain Krysty's mutie power? The sensing of danger, the reading of emotions, that was easy enough. Everyone had heard of doomies and their prophecies. The power of the Earth Mother was something else entirely.

"Summons up what?" Carter asked.

"I'll explain later," J.B. said. "It's complicated."

A strong, well-developed woman, Krysty always looked much smaller after a dance with the explosive force of the Earth Mother. J.B. was shorter than her unusual height, yet seemed to still tower over her now. Even her prehensile crimson hair was slack, limp and unmoving.

"Krysty," Mildred said, "Krysty, are you all right?"

The physician quickly checked her for any cuts, wounds or contusions. Apparently all of the blood on her clothing had come from other parties. Her skin was ice-cold, and Mildred knew she was in a form of shock that could only be treated with rest.

But there was no time for resting now.

"I know who this is. Cawdor's woman," Carter said. "She's not dead?"

"Apparently not," Mildred retorted.

"And the blood all over her isn't her own?"

"Nope."

"You mean she killed whoever with her bare hands?"

"Uh-huh."

"Cawdor must like them rough," Carter said. "There anything more you can do for her?"

"In here? Not much."

"I—I'm all right. I think," Krysty said, her eyes still closed. She reached up and rubbed her forehead gingerly. "But I've got one hell of a headache."

"Sorry, but it's going to get worse before it gets better," J.B. said, checking his chrono. "Those gren timers should start popping in eight minutes, thirty-two seconds, give or take a second. The timers aren't exactly new."

"We've got to find Ryan," Krysty said, standing and leaning on Mildred's offered shoulder for support. "Poseidon has him."

"Dark night! Any idea where?"

"Yes, I can take you there," Krysty said. "Jak's here, too, in the hospital."

"Let's get Jak first. We might need the extra hand," J.B. said.

"Hot damn, but is this a night for resurrections, or what?" Mildred asked excitedly. "We might just make it through this yet."

Chapter Twenty-Three

Ryan fought his way back from the subbasement hidden away beneath the entrance to the massive submarine pen of Kings Point, chilling a half dozen of the hired sec men after reloading the AK-47 with a clip he'd taken from the dead man with the spectacles back at the doorway to the redoubt.

In the heat of the moment, Ryan regretted not going into the redoubt and chilling Poseidon personally, but now that he knew Krysty was alive he was less inclined to hang around this pesthole.

The best strategy was to wait for a diversion. The squad of mercs he'd encountered in the stairwells beneath the base had to have been backups, told to follow Poseidon at a distance. So far, it appeared as though the sound of gunfire hadn't escaped out into the aboveground chambers.

Ryan had taken a small comm unit from one of the newer sec men he'd chilled. The airwaves were silent. He looked at his chron and hoped that J.B. had been able to plant the grens to go off at midnight.

Twelve o'clock, the chron read.

Ryan waited.

One minute past twelve blinked on the digital read-out, and the explosions he'd been counting on began to rock the base.

Both enlisted and sec men alike at the submarine pens fled their posts, seeking the source of the attack. The little radio at Ryan's side crackled into a mass of voices all trying to communicate. He took a deep breath and sized up a pair of sec men near a gangplank leading up to the *Raleigh*. Apparently even the explosions rocking half the base weren't going to sway them from their duty.

There was no way for him to sneak past. He would have to take the offensive.

Besides, there was still the matter of Poseidon's plan to take the sub out to Shauna's place for his test of the Tomahawk. Even if the Admiral was stuck in the redoubt for the next one hundred years, his evil could live on past his mortal form if one of his lieutenants decided to carry out a final order. All Ryan had to do was pull some wires and sabotage the underwater crate.

ADMIRAL POSEIDON INPUT the doorway code and stepped out of the redoubt, avoiding the pool of blood and other internal fluids that surrounded the bisected Jonesy.

"You're not as smart as you think, Cawdor," he muttered as he began to run up the steps.

Poseidon paused to catch his breath and accessed a small terminal in a corner of a stairwell at the halfway point. The screen lit up. He toggled some keys to access a security net. He was rewarded with an overview of the submarine pens.

"What the devil?" he said, watching as the group started to flee en masse.

Poseidon hit the keys and found another exterior view. He saw the white fire of an explosion rock the men's dormitory.

"We're under attack," he said in disbelief. Could Cawdor have brought in reinforcements so soon? Impossible! Poseidon returned to a view of the submarine pens and tried for a closer view of the *Raleigh*. The sub seemed to be secure, until he saw Ryan appear on the sec-camera monitor, a tiny image running like a two-legged engine of flesh and muscle toward the gangplank.

The pair of sec men standing guard at the sub's access hatch never knew what hit them. One of the men spun and got off a rush of shots from the automatic weapon he carried, and one lucky burst ricocheted off their attacker's rifle. But Ryan was unstoppable at that point.

There was no audio, but Poseidon could imagine the dry snapping sound as the one-eyed man threw his useless rifle at the sec man, then lunged forward and broke the first man's neck with a forceful twist. No audio, but he could almost hear the crunch as Ryan swung back with an elbow and caught the second sec man, who had just stood there stupidly and never even fired his weapon, full in the nose.

Poseidon beat the keyboard of the computer with both fists, his angry cries guttural as the words clogged in his chest. He picked up the monitor screen and hurled it down the stairs.

"Not over. Not yet," he raged, and turned at an all-out run for the surface.

"WHERE'S CAWDOR?" Poseidon rasped. He'd run all the way back up to the submarine pen, and he was out of breath. It had been a long time since he had been forced to exert himself past a quick walk, and he was sweating beneath his prim uniform.

"Hiding," the groggy sec man said with a sniff. Red blood was already beginning to dry on the front of his uniform tunic. "He's below. In the sub."

"Is he, now?" Poseidon chuckled. "What a wonderful idea. If Ryan wants a tour of the *Raleigh,* he'll receive a working man's look. But he'll not leave our submarine alive, I'll guarantee you that much. And after I've slung our Tomahawk at that commune and those mutie bastards, I'll blast his stubborn ass through a torpedo tube."

Poseidon glanced back. "What's your name, sailor?"

"Coleman, sir. Robert Coleman."

"Coleman, I don't recognize you as part of the regular detail assigned to the *Raleigh.*"

"No, sir. First time here, sir."

"You lost your weapon, Coleman, to the enemy who entered the same submarine you were supposed to watch. Those are serious offenses, Coleman. Court-martial offenses."

Coleman swallowed hard. "Sir?"

"Bugger it all, man, I'll save some time and take care of this myself."

And with that statement, Poseidon pulled his side arm and shot Coleman in the stomach.

Poseidon turned and dropped down the main sub hatch in a show of disgust, his wide waist and shoulders constricted by the narrow access way. He stopped and pulled the hatch cover overhead as tightly as he could to make sure the automechanism locked properly, then did the same for the secondary hatch, spinning the locking wheel with more force than necessary and being rewarded with a dull clunk as the bolts shot true.

No one was coming in or going out now, by God, without going through him first.

"Brosnan?" he called out.

"Aye, sir," the second in command replied from the control room. "What's happening above, Admiral? We're getting all kinds of conflicting reports."

"Never mind that now. Have you seen Ryan Cawdor in here lurking about?"

"No, sir."

"What is our status?"

"All primary systems green and checked. We are ready to dive when you give the order."

The Admiral went into the control room and glanced at the various panels of mech, electrical and hydraulic controls. One bank was dark and two others a mix of reds and greens. So what if the *Raleigh* wasn't armed with the standard complement of twenty-two Tomahawk nuclear missiles? He still had the one and it was ready to launch.

"Take us down, Commander," Poseidon said. "But take us down slowly. Easy."

"Yes, sir." Brosnan nodded to a waiting tech man. "Flood main ballast tanks."

The sub's hull sang with the sound of rushing air as the vents at the top of the ballast tanks flipped open. A rush of seawater entered from the bottom of the great boat and forced the air up and out in a mass of white bubbles.

Poseidon paced back and forth behind the periscope pedestal in the center of the control room. He was doubly excited; the maiden voyage of the *Raleigh* was under way at last. Once he'd found Cawdor, he'd let the one-eyed man watch as he fired on the commune.

That would show the bastard.

Brosnan's head was darting back and forth in a nervous birdlike fashion, his prominent Adam's apple quite visible above the collar of his uniform. His mouth was set in a downward curve as he observed the men under his watch. All of them jumped each time various clanging noises rang out in increasing fashion from the sub's cylindrical hull. Brosnan couldn't blame them. The very walls of the *Raleigh* seemed to vibrate with each metallic creak.

"What was that, sir?" asked one man, looking at Poseidon for reassurance.

Brosnan cut his eyes at the Admiral. The superior officer wasn't even listening. He was in his own en-

vironment now, away from the interior of the sub or
even the sea itself.

"It's the sound of the hull adjusting to the pressure
of the surrounding sea," Brosnan explained. "As the
Raleigh dives, it'll keep going until we reach a holding level. Old as this sub is, it was to be expected.
From what I've read, even new subs did the same
thing until they were broken in."

The explanation seemed to calm the nervous enlisted man. Brosnan hoped the logic was right. The
minisub they had been using was nothing like this
dank monster. He would never admit it aloud, but the
Raleigh made him nervous. Too unpredictable, even
if the voyage had been meticulously planned.

Not to mention Cawdor was somewhere on board,
hiding and waiting—but for what?

The submarine was far away from the pens of
Kings Point now.

"Engines, all stop." Poseidon's tone was flat as he
gave the order.

"All stop," Brosnan directed.

The Admiral himself stepped forward and peered
over the pilot's shoulder as the man dialed the an-
nunciator to a full-stop position.

Outside the submarine, the great propeller slowed,
then stopped.

"Commander Brosnan?" Poseidon's deep bass
voice rumbled even more impressively inside the confines of the control room.

"Aye, sir?" Brosnan glanced over at Poseidon.
One of the auxiliary pumps alongside was in the red,

and the last thing he wanted or needed was another red light glowing on the control board.

"Are you familiar with the child's game of hide-and-seek?"

It was a strange question, but Brosnan was used to that from his superior officer. "Yes, Admiral."

"Did you play it?"

Brosnan frowned, trying to free-associate and come up with Poseidon's line of logic. However, he answered quickly. "Yes, sir, I did."

"So did I, and I was damned good at the game," the Admiral replied. No surprise there. According to Poseidon, everything he had ever attempted had been a rousing success. Still, Brosnan knew from observation and evidence that most of the bluster was true. Especially when it came to games—from war games to board games to games of chance.

"You're good at games, sir," Brosnan offered lamely. He hated it when Poseidon went into this mode. It made him feel like the worse kind of ass kisser. Which, to a large degree, he was, but he didn't like having it trotted out so blatantly. Once, the blandly handsome Brosnan had dreams of his own. He was a scholar, a historian. He spent all of his days as a young man in search of information about the past, and his passion had been the military.

When he met the man who called himself Poseidon for the first time, it was like they were two pieces of a larger puzzle that had been joined at last.

But whereas Brosnan had no real taste for becoming a leader, Poseidon did. He made a deal with his friend, telling him in confidence of the still intact base at Kings Point. Poseidon had known of the place since he was a boy, and he had been living on the Georgia coast all of his life.

With Brosnan's knowledge and talents, and Poseidon's drive and ambition, they decided to rebuild the base from the ground up. A decade had passed, and Brosnan had watched as the older man's desire for power started to turn him in the direction of cruelty and dominance. But what could he do? Poseidon was the undisputed leader, and Brosnan was a man of books in a world of violence.

At Kings Point, Brosnan had his place. From time to time, he might have to assist in a bit of unpleasantness, but that was the cost for his position—along with the loss of his once close friendship with Poseidon. Oh, Brosnan was still the Admiral's confidant. Poseidon trusted no one more. However, now he shut the younger man out of his schemes until they were ready to unfold. Poseidon's dark plans were his own.

Brosnan found that suited him fine.

"I love games! I love to win! Nobody wanted me to be 'it,' because I was always able to track down each and every one of my friends," Poseidon continued.

"Really?" Brosnan said, tuning back in on the conversation.

Poseidon paused for effect. "Track them one by one."

"Track?" Brosnan laughed. "Strong words for a child's game."

"Even then I played to win, Commander. My childhood wasn't easy. There were only a few of us in that spacious enclave. Two girls, three boys. I was the youngest. I grew up behind glass with my father and mother observing me as intently as they might have looked at one of their own freakish experiments." Poseidon paused, lost in memory. "At times," he said softly, "I wonder if that was the only reason my dear mother consented to becoming pregnant in the first place."

Brosnan tried to shield his expression. Rarely had Poseidon offered a tidbit like this from his past even when they were at their closest, and to open up in front of the enlisted men was even more unusual.

"You are surprised at my candor?"

"Aye, sir. Yes."

"In war, men act differently, Mr. Brosnan. Make no mistake about it. At this moment, we are at war. When we left, the base was in flames. Under attack. We may have to run silent and deep for a long time before returning home."

Brosnan didn't answer.

"This is what being a submariner entails. The complete and utter mastery of a child's pastime. Hide and seek, seek and hide. You keep your vessel hidden while trying to find theirs. It's all laid out in the manuals. I've done my research and so have you. The finest manuscripts that I've been able to buy or steal. Many of them captured on discs of shining gold, and I was lucky enough to possess the computer hardware needed to access their information. I own the finest in fiction and nonfiction, including all of the known works of the master statistician, the great Clancy himself.''

"I know, sir. I've read them.'' Brosnan paused for a second. "All of them.''

"Not all, Commander. I also have two of his first editions, one inscribed in the author's own hand,'' Poseidon said. "A man has to keep some secrets, Commander. You read second editions, but his words of cursive were for me alone.''

"Aye, sir.'' Brosnan was starting to become worried. Poseidon was talking of trivial matters at a time when the fate of the *Raleigh* was at stake.

"You may restart the engines now. Maintain course, Mr. Brosnan. I have an errand.''

"Where are you headed, Admiral?''

"To rid ourselves of a barnacle,'' Poseidon murmured. "A particularly insistent one.''

"Cawdor?''

"Aye.''

"We could go ahead and start a search. He can't hide for long.''

Poseidon glanced around the control room. The two men at various stations weren't expendable. Neither was Brosnan. His knowledge of the operations of the submarine was only second to that of Poseidon himself, and if the Admiral intended to go gunning personally for Ryan Cawdor, then one of them had to remain behind.

"I can handle this alone. Don't look so resigned,

Brosnan,'' Poseidon said as he stepped from the room. ''I'll be back. Stout fellow!''

RYAN STEPPED into the sub's reactor room. The compartment was big—in fact, the room was surprisingly large. This had to be the widest open space in the entire submarine. As Ryan glanced at the mammoth reactor pulsing within, he understood why. Oversize circle-shaped rad detectors were hanging in all of the corners of the room, both fore and aft.

Ryan wished he had his own small rad counter for reference, the same one that had been attached to his coat's lapel for many a year. Dozens of times he had taken a deep breath and gazed at the tiny device, hoping the color indicator wouldn't shift drastically from the cool end of the spectrum into the high end. If the glowing arrow veered erratically across the scale and wavered uncomfortably in the orange sector or near red, Ryan knew the area was ''hot.''

Here, all he had to go on was the submarine's own warning devices, and from the looks of the detectors, he had to wonder if they were functioning at any capacity. He stepped closer to the one nearest him when he heard a slight clatter. Ryan had quickly discovered the *Raleigh* was by no means a quiet ship. The ancient hull and interior had groaned and pinged since they had first left port.

But this noise was new, and his keen ears believed it to be the sound of a footstep on a loose metal step or plate.

Ryan crept away from the rad counter and chose a

cubby area to slink into. The space was off to one side of the reactor, half-hidden by a bank of dials and other gauges. He crouched and waited to see if his mystery man would make an appearance.

There had to be submariners on board, even if the sub was running with a skeleton crew. Ryan would think the reactor room would be the first place for engineers and the like. Twice, as he had made his way down deeper into the *Raleigh,* he'd confronted Poseidon's enlisted men. Apparently, as Alan Carter had said, the hired sec squads weren't allowed on the sub, yet another reason for the apparently small number of fully trained personnel.

Both times, the men Ryan had faced had turned tail and run. He'd slammed one over the head with the stolen AK-47, but the other had been too far away.

Now, here was a possible third.

Again there was a slight clattering noise.

Then Ryan knew that his foe wasn't on the deck, but was on top of the reactor itself. He risked a glance around the side of his hiding place and spotted what he was looking for: an aluminum ladder leading up to the top of the great machine. He had no desire to climb up and take a closer look.

He reached out and touched the side of the reactor, feeling it thrum beneath the palm of his hand. What Ryan knew about the actual upkeep and function of nuclear reactors was very little. His own experience— and the one-two punch of an experience the entire planet had endured—was that no matter how good any nuke might initially seem, eventually it chilled your sorry ass.

The sailor started to come back down the ladder, and he wasn't going slow. The man was dressed in dark blue trousers, light blue buttoned shirt and a white T-shirt. Various hand tools were hanging from a worn and cracked leather tool belt. He was carrying a small box that appeared to be some sort of hand comp. A wire was dangling from the device. At the other end of the line was a minuscule oblong-shaped gadget. Ryan wasn't sure, but he assumed the entire rig was some sort of rad detector. Apparently the sailor didn't fully trust the wall-mounted counters, either.

Ryan remained half-crouched at the far end of the reactor. His knees were bent as he squatted, and he suddenly realized just how tired he really was. Still, he couldn't give in to fatigue now. He'd chosen to climb into the sub as a quick retreat. He'd never imagined Poseidon would put the craft to sea with him hiding within.

The AK-47 was slung across his back, just in case he had to use it. He was gambling on staying one step ahead of Poseidon. The noise of the rifle would identify his exact location quicker than shooting off a volley of fireworks.

The submariner reached the end of the ladder and hopped down the last two feet to the deck, almost slipping in the water that had collected from one of a thousand tiny leaks. Catching his balance, he walked quickly but carefully in Ryan's direction. A few more steps, and there would be no way for the man to miss seeing the hidden addition to the room.

Still, Ryan remained absolutely motionless until the sailor spotted him.

"Hey—" came out of the man's mouth as Ryan sprung like a ravenous tiger leaping for its shocked prey. He had snapped the muscles of his legs taut and let his body spring hard and direct. He hit the man just at his knees, driving his feet out from under him, plowing him onto the wet deck.

The sailor was a fighter. He responded to the attack with a ferocity to match, beating on the one-eyed man's shoulders and back. The two of them locked together for a moment of sheer animal fury before the man broke free, kicking out with one of his feet. Ryan was able to roll to the left and dodge, his body and clothing making wet slapping sounds in the puddles beneath him.

Ryan scuttled backward, planning to rear up on his feet, when the younger, already erect sailor pulled a long screwdriver from his belt.

"Come on, you hump," the young man said with a grin. "Come on. I'm ready for you. I can dust your ass and still get out of here before I start glowing green."

"Is there a problem with your shiny new toy?"

"Look around you. The reactor's leaking radiation in two spots, and there's not a damn thing I can do about it. Won't be long before all systems start going off-line."

The sailor brandished the weapon, making sharp,

stabbing motions. The deadly-looking tool was just as good as a knife in close-quarters fighting like this, and while Ryan wasn't frightened of going up against someone with a blade, he wasn't exactly thrilled, either, since he was knifeless at the moment.

Ryan decided he wasn't in the mood for this. He damned sure didn't want to get sick from rad poisoning, and the fighting sailor man was starting to get on his nerves.

He slid the AK-47 off his back and into his capable hands.

"Say hello to the fishes," Ryan said, and pulled the trigger.

There was a soft click, followed by a triple click. Ryan and his screwdriver-wielding foe realized at the exact same time the blaster wasn't loaded.

Chapter Twenty-Four

Dean and Doc warily approached the ruin that was once a tidy wood-and-glass guard's shack on the far end of the Kings Point naval base. The boy and man had made good time, following the remarkably well preserved two-lane blacktop down the coastline. Their steed had done well and they left him behind at the gas station inside a long-stripped garage.

The base was still some distance away, but Doc had found yet another hidden reserve of inner strength, and had kept up with the boy, both of them walking as quickly as possible without any delays.

Doc had surprised himself. "Amazing what a few day's rest and relaxation will do for a man, even one as brittle as I," he said.

"Save your breath for walking, not talking, Doc," Dean replied, getting a slight lead on his older companion.

Doc almost gave back his own comment, but then decided the boy was right.

Ryan would have told Doc the same thing in this sort of situation.

They had increased their speed the moment the explosions began to occur on the other end of the base. Tendrils of red fire and plumes of smoke reached into the night sky, giving Kings Point a look of a hellpit on earth.

"Twelve o'clock," Doc said, checking his old pocket watch. "The witching hour is upon us."

Dean held his Browning Hi-Power ready as he stepped closer to the sec gate next to the shack. The gate, which once could be opened electronically from the wrecked shack, was normally used for allowing wheeled transportation such as the wags to exit and enter. Now the gate was hanging open, a meshing of metal shadows hanging in the dusky air.

Dean glanced at Doc and mouthed a single word of question. "Dad?" he said, cocking his head toward the bullet-riddled checkpoint.

"Undoubtedly," Doc replied. "If I had any doubts about our being in the right place, this path of battle has quelled them."

Dean stepped onto the slab of concrete used as flooring for the checkpoint and peeked inside the remains. Inside, the primary color on the standing walls was the rusty red of dried blood. A sec man with a silly-looking hat was crumpled inside, his body twisted in the distinctive and peculiar posture of the dead.

"One guy in here chilled," he told Doc.

"So it would appear the Trojan-horse ploy got them this far," Doc said, scanning the area in the fading evening light. "The gate is open, not forced. I can only surmise that their cover was pulled back before they were able to get inside the compound without bloodshed. I was told they took one of the men who initially came in the wag alive so they would have a reluctant ally to ride back with them. That way, their prisoner could assist with passwords or any hidden signals or procedures.''

Dean figured it out. "Guy tried to play hero, didn't he, Doc?"

"Correct!" Doc said. "The prisoner attempted to alert his comrade in the guard house, and there was no choice but to take matters up a notch."

"Looks like a wag over there," Dean said, pointing at the abandoned Land Rover. "Think it's the same one Dad came in with?"

The pair approached the vehicle carefully. Doc noticed the bullet-riddled tires and pointed them out with his swordstick. Dean nodded. No wonder the wag had been dumped.

"Dean! Doc!" Mildred cried out, spotting the two familiar figures running toward the damaged wag. "Over here!"

"Tell me, young Cawdor, am I once again a captive to the ghosts of my withered mind, or is that really our good Krysty Wroth and Jak Lauren there before us?"

"We've both gone loco if they ain't, Doc," Dean responded, his face breaking out in a wide grin.

"Aren't," Krysty corrected automatically.

"Oh, yeah, it's really them!" the boy said, reaching out and hugging Krysty tight.

"Ryan told you to wait," J.B. accused.

"I did. For about an hour," Dean retorted. "Didn't want to miss watching this shit heap blow sky high."

Everyone laughed as they clasped hands in firm handshakes and delivered slaps on the back. They were together again, and it felt good.

"Bless my soul, but I am delighted to see the lot of you," Doc said. "But I am perplexed at Krysty and Jak's appearance."

After Jak and Krysty quickly explained what had happened to them, Carter impatiently brought up the next order of business: "So what's left besides getting the hell out of here?"

"Ryan's left," Krysty replied.

"Shit, woman, Cawdor's long dead by now. You heard the sirens. That enlisted man we questioned told us Poseidon's taken out the submarine and left his base to rot. Shauna's dead. You told me you saw the body yourself. Nothing's going to bring her or your man back."

"Ryan's not dead," Krysty stated in a tone of chilling finality. "Not yet."

"We'll find him," Dean said. "He's got to be here somewhere."

"That's it. I've had enough," Carter told them. "Loyalty is one thing, but you people go beyond even family. Your leader is chilled, or soon will be, and the Admiral has swam away leaving us holding an empty net. I'm going back home. You do what you want."

"You can't walk out on us now!" J.B. protested.

"This entire operation was about revenge, Dix!" Carter replied, spittle flying from his lips as he talked. "Cawdor's revenge for a woman not even dead.

Shauna's revenge for a husband who never gave a damn about her in the first place. Hell, I didn't like Poseidon, either, but I never would've taken it this far if not for her.''

"You loved her, didn't you, Carter?" Mildred said bluntly.

"Does it matter now, Dr. Wyeth?"

"I guess not."

"She couldn't let it go," Carter said again. "Damn, but I wish I'd never heard of any of you."

With those parting words, the tattooed man walked away into the night.

"Hold up," Dean said, running after him. The boy talked to Carter for a second, then returned to the others.

"You think Ryan's somewhere hiding out, watching the explosions? Or is he a captive on the submarine?" Mildred ventured.

"Don't know," Jak said, pulling his recovered Colt Python out of its holster. "Why don't we find navy boys and ask?"

THE DYING MAN LYING on his back on the metal flooring of the submarine pen offered no resistance. His name was Coleman. He'd never been a proper merc anyway; he was a techie at heart, and had only been watching over the *Raleigh* when Ryan attacked him because of a debt he owed and he hadn't been able to come up with the proper payment in jack.

So, he took a double shift to watch over the decrepit old tub, and had been on the scene at the wrong time after Ryan's escape from the redoubt. Coleman's partner for the evening had been the one who pulled the hardware and fired at the one-eyed man, so the warrior had been faced with no choice but to chill him in his boots. Coleman, however, had been frozen with surprise, so Ryan merely punched him in the face and relieved him of his rifle.

The very same rifle that Ryan had later found to be unloaded.

Coleman didn't like blasters. They made him nervous. He kept his weapon empty.

So Ryan hadn't chilled him—that had fallen to Poseidon's rage when he discovered that his prey had slipped on board the *Raleigh.* All it took to send Coleman sliding toward death was one shot from a Glock pistol in the stomach.

"Gut shot," Jak said. "Die soon. Die in pain."

Mildred's examination didn't take long. She shook her head as she looked at the gaping wound. "I'm getting damned sick and tired of being the one to sign the death certificates around here," she said.

One thing she'd learned in a hurry about being a physician in Deathlands—you had a low rate of patient survival.

"Looking for Ryan Cawdor," J.B. said. "You see him get on the sub?"

"Don't know who that is," Coleman wheezed.

"Big guy with an eye patch. Curly hair. Has a long scar going down his cheek into his chin," J.B. described, running a finger down the right side of his own face to illustrate. "He was probably a prisoner in cuffs or ropes."

Coleman managed a weak snicker. "He didn't look like no prisoner when he kicked my ass," he said. "The Admiral was royally pissed. Shot me on sight, and took the sub and your man out for a swim."

"Come on," J.B. said, "let's go. We're going after them."

"Where?" Krysty asked. "How?"

"There's got to be a boat around here somewhere. Mebbe this time we won't hit any more mines."

DOWN IN THE NUKE ROOM of the USS *Raleigh*, Ryan pulled the trigger one more time, and the AK-47 still refused to fire.

"Aw, shit," Ryan said.

"Looks like you're empty," the sailor said, lunging with the screwdriver. Ryan swung back with the body of the rifle, using it to parry the man's thrust. The metal tip of the tool hit the softer wood of the stock and plunged down, leaving a long scratch.

"Should've been you."

Ryan dropped the rifle, as he needed both hands free. He was starting to tire physically. All of the punishment his body had taken in the past few hours was coming home to roost.

Still, the day he couldn't dust a stupe swinging a screwdriver was the day he'd put a bullet into his own head.

Ryan feinted back, and his foe again lunged for his midriff, trying to bury the weapon up to the handle in the one-eyed man's stomach. Seizing the opening, Ryan caught the sailor's arm and thrust it down over one of his uplifted knees, breaking the arm with a loud crack.

The screwdriver fell to the deck.

Ryan kept his hold on his adversary's arm, twisting as hard as he could while rotating it in the shoulder socket. The sailor fell to his knees, screaming, then slumped limply, his body shutting down from the pain. Ryan felt about the same as the enlisted man looked. He sat down against the wall himself, breathing heavily.

A bosun's whistle shrieked at the end of the corridor. Ryan stepped over and looked at the comm-system panel that was recessed in the wall near the lozenge-shaped doorway.

"Ryan Cawdor, this is Admiral Poseidon."

The way things were going, he wasn't surprised.

"Talk to me, Cawdor, before you do anything foolish."

Ryan reached out and slapped down the Transmit button.

"Like what?" he snarled at the comm grid. "Blow this nuke engine sky-high?"

"Sub's out to sea, Cawdor. We've submerged, and we're all continuing to go down," Poseidon said, his voice crisp from the tiny speaker. "Harm the *Raleigh*, and you harm yourself."

"We're all going down anyway, you stupe bastard! The decks are wet with seawater. This piece of rusty shit is leaking like a fucking sieve. You've got men dead and dying down here because the sub's nuke is leaking radiation right through the protective plating. We've got to get off before we're all chilled with rad sickness."

"Matter of opinion, Cawdor. I am the senior officer here, and I will decree when we disembark."

"I might have something to add to that," Ryan said. "We still headed for the commune?"

"We are. You think you are going to stop us?"

"No, I just wanted to make sure I packed the right clothes."

"I harbored all sorts of grandiose plans for the maiden voyage of the *Raleigh*, Cawdor. Once she was one hundred percent ready, there were continents to visit, feats to duplicate, lands to conquer. Now here we are, barely off the Georgia shore, and already we need to turn back."

"Fine by me," Ryan said.

"Well, we can't. Our mission, minus one detour to the mass of windmills and tents that has been laughingly called a commune, is to find a new home. A safe base. Your destination, on the other hand, is oblivion," Poseidon noted.

"Not if I send you there first," Ryan said, and slapped off the comm unit.

Chapter Twenty-Five

Ryan sighed deeply and took a hard look at the circular rad detector on the wall directly above the comm panel. Some of the sub's detectors had indeed malfunctioned, their colors dead with age. Others showed a color shift from green to red, confirming what his deductions had already told him.

The *Raleigh* was a death ship. The great reactor that served as her heart was damaged.

Ryan decided to help it along. For his own safety, he exited the large reactor room and went into the next compartment, which housed the turbines. If he could get them to stop working, the submarine would be unable to function properly on either the generator or on fuel supplies.

But before he could begin the sabotage, the deteriorating condition of the submarine did the job for him. Ryan's timing was perfect. A moment more, and he would have been standing unprotected within the reactor room when the elderly system blew out, flooding the area with radiation and making the back of the *Raleigh* list uncontrollably.

"Fireblast!" he hissed as the explosion rocked the submarine. He hadn't expected it to blow so quickly. The rear ballast tanks between the inner and outer hull were already filled with water from the dive, but now were cracked open to the inside of the submarine, releasing a torrent of seawater. The reactor and engine-control rooms began to flood as the mighty power train of the vessel ground to a halt.

The extrastrong steel alloys and elaborate welding techniques used in the sub's construction couldn't handle the age and wear, and this was the final insult.

All electrical power aboard the sub blinked out when the reactor died. Secondary systems and emergency power kicked in, but in a greatly diminished capacity, and as the *Raleigh* continued to sink, Ryan knew that if he didn't figure out a way to escape soon, he'd be trapped inside the sub on the ocean floor until the air ran out.

He exited the turbine room and glanced down the passageway.

"Turn and face me, Ryan Cawdor," a deep bass voice said from behind him.

Across the cramped aft compartment, in front of a thick watertight wall that had dropped down across the bulkhead to seal off the ruptured lower hull, stood Poseidon. His uniform was soaked dark with water, and his nautical cap with the tiny trident patch on the front above the brim was gone. There was grease on his face and hands. Part of his beard looked singed.

Ryan had to squint to see him clearly. The space was beginning to fill with wet, hot steam. The two men had ended up meeting in the auxiliary equipment room of the *Raleigh,* where the sub's heat exchanger was housed between the nuclear reactor and the main turbine.

Poseidon knew he was now held hostage behind the safety wall that was straining to keep the water out and the air inside the compartment. But the large man's posture remained ramrod straight, and his hair was slicked back neatly from his broad forehead.

The Admiral was holding the Glock, the same blaster he'd used to reprimand Coleman back at the docking pens.

The pistol was aimed right at Ryan's heart.

"I'm going to kill you," Poseidon grated.

"Wrong. That's my line," Ryan replied.

"I have the weapon."

"Sure, a bucket of slop like you always has to have a blaster to back himself up. Or a sec man," Ryan retorted. "Have you ever put yourself on the line, Admiral?"

"In my youth, always."

"Then face me now, man to man, like the so-called leader you claim to be," Ryan taunted. This was a calculated gamble. He didn't feel up to unscrewing the lid off a predark jar of peanut butter, but at least if Poseidon didn't chill him with the blaster, he still had a fighting chance. Maneuverability was one advantage the one-eyed man had over his larger opponent.

And unlike Poseidon, Ryan still had a life to go back to, a life to fight for.

Poseidon slid the ammo clip from the Glock and tossed blaster and bullets away.

They stood, facing each other, neither ready to make the first move.

Poseidon spoke first. "Our angle of descent keeps getting worse, Cawdor."

"I noticed."

"You've ruined everything."

"No, Admiral, this was your deal," Ryan retorted. "I don't go looking for confrontations, but if you get in my face, I bite right back at you."

"I know. That's what makes you a worthy adversary, Cawdor. Do you know how boring my life had become until you came along? In less than a day, you've made me feel alive again. Reinvigorated. I could have done without you wrecking my ship, though."

"I didn't have to. The reactor went without me ever touching it," Ryan shouted. "And I'm not here to be your fucking motivation, you pumped-up stupe bastard! I don't want to stand here in a debate! We're running out of time."

"Time? Don't speak to me of time, mister. I can deal with time. Aboard American subs, you adhere to a true Greenwich mean time. No matter what the hour is up there—" Poseidon gestured with a thumb at the hull overhead "—down here, we're on my time."

The *Raleigh* lurched, and a muffled explosion could be heard from behind the bulkhead as the entire inner hull vibrated.

Poseidon didn't hesitate. Like a maddened bull, the large man charged up the slightly inclined metal floor directly for Ryan, the slick steel grates underfoot shrieking in protest from every pounding step of his well-polished black shoes. Ryan braced himself, but still wasn't able to keep his footing when Poseidon bowled into his upper body with a single hardened shoulder.

The Admiral wasn't fat. What hit Ryan was solid muscle and bone, sending him skittering backward down the cramped access hall and into the steel of a bulkhead. He felt his upper left rib cage compress under the assault, and it became hard to breathe.

He threw a left and caught Poseidon in the jaw, but the blow didn't even seem to register. As the bearded face loomed before his own, Ryan head-butted his foe, breaking Poseidon's nose. Blood ran from the Admiral's nostrils and into his mustache and beard, but he still didn't stop as he wrapped his hands around his adversary's throat.

"I'll see you drown with me, Cawdor," Poseidon grated as he squeezed Ryan's neck even harder.

Ryan kept silent as he tried to ignore the black spots beginning to dot his vision, and instead made himself focus on the array of deep purple veins standing out across his foe's forehead. Poseidon seemed to have an obsession with the neck. That was how he'd killed Shauna, and now the submarine's master wanted to do the same to him.

"High blood pressure'll kill you, Admiral," Ryan gasped, pushing the heel of his hand under and against Poseidon's bearded chin.

"Killing you will be all the exercise I need for a

long, long time," his opponent said, ignoring Ryan's relentless pressure on his chin.

Ryan abandoned the chin and shoved both hands upward, inserting his thumbs into Poseidon's eye sockets and locking them down with all his strength. The effort paid off as the man fell back with a roar, grabbing at both of Ryan's wrists and succeeding in seizing only one. The one-eyed warrior had no choice but to follow Poseidon's lead as the Admiral pulled him back and over.

Poseidon used the momentum of their mutual fall to smash his adversary headfirst into the wheel lock of an open doorway. Ryan slid to the floor, momentarily knocked senseless. Flakes of rust dotted his dank black hair, adhering from where he had impacted with the metal. He shook his head, fighting to keep his thoughts and actions clear.

Then he saw the wrench.

The tool that had been left behind by a sloppy sailor and had slid under a mass of boxy equipment.

He reached for the weapon, ignoring the pain in his ribs as Poseidon lashed out with a hard kick. Ryan had seen the foot coming and dodged as best he could; otherwise he'd be experiencing the smothering sensation of a half a rack of broken ribs, but the blow still stung like a piledriver's kiss.

Ryan swung the wrench two-handed, catching the larger man in the solar plexus. *That* slowed the Admiral, and he fell to his knees spitting blood.

Ryan lifted the wrench over his own head and brought it down on top of Poseidon's unprotected skull. The Admiral fell on his face and was still. Ryan nearly stumbled into a bulkhead from the wrench's weight as he let it drop. He'd never been so tired in all his life, but he had to get off the *Raleigh*. Racking his mind, Ryan wished for a fleeting second that J.B. were here. The Armorer's near photographic memory would have instantly recorded all the information he'd passed when traversing the submarine earlier.

Ryan was already having some difficulty telling the difference between some passageways.

However, this one took no extra memory.

As he'd made his way down deeper into the body of the submarine earlier, Ryan had made mental notes, and he remembered the Admiral's quarters as being located forward to the galley, near the other officer accommodations. The walls in this section were painted in a faded blue, with white trim on the molding and pipes overhead.

Ryan stepped into Poseidon's room. A footlocker was still in front of the tidy bunk, although both had slid slightly back and were now flush with the bulkhead.

"If I was a man like Poseidon, I'd always have a contingency plan," Ryan whispered.

He delivered a series of kicks with the steel toe of his boot until the small lock on the hasp of the footlocker was knocked off. Ryan knelt and lifted the lid, revealing what he knew to be a tangle of scuba equipment inside. He had used such equipment once or twice in his youth, and as he pulled out a battered air tank, which was snugly wrapped in a mesh of nylon harnessing, he hoped that someone as precise as Poseidon had claimed to be would have regularly maintained the gear.

Ryan screwed the silver-and-black regulator to the valve on top of the tank and hoped the gods who had kept him alive this long were still keeping a watchful eye. He held his breath and turned the knob that opened the tank's air flow.

He was rewarded with a *thipp* as air rushed into the tiny regulator and air hose. Ryan raised the mouthpiece and placed it between his lips. He tried a sample intake of breath. The air was musty, but breathable, and that's all that mattered.

He pulled a heavy cloth-and-metal weight belt from the bottom of the chest and placed it around his waist, followed by two face masks, both yellowed with age. Ryan chose one, and pulled the elastic strap wide enough to strap the mask on his forehead, above his eye.

At the bottom of the locker was an object wrapped in an old towel. Ryan unfolded the cloth and revealed an ivory-handled knife with a four-inch blade. The handle of the weapon was an ornately carved head and torso of the mythical Lord Poseidon himself. He couldn't have cared less. The knife was a weapon, and he carried it in his right hand as such, honed edge out and ready.

He grabbed an underwater flashlight, then stood, the tank on his back heavy and cumbersome in the small passageway as he stepped from Poseidon's quarters into the hall. The sub was continuing to go down, now with the tail end plummeting first, since the blast came from the engine room. Ryan pulled the tank and harness tighter, checking the length of the straps and adjusting the buckles. The gear still felt looser than he would've liked, but he knew he was out of time.

Ryan clambered up, heading aft from the enlisted men's mess and searching for the way out. Torpedo tube? Waste-disposal chamber? Swim for the hull breech itself? What other ways could there be for a man to escape a sinking submarine? Ryan knew from the tiny digital gauge on top of the tank he could count on an hour of oxygen, but that was under normal circumstances, and there was nothing normal about what he was trying to do.

That's when he spotted Brosnan's frightened face peering out at him from the rounded corner of a bulkhead. Ryan almost didn't recognize the younger man—all he could see were Brosnan's eyes, looking back at his own, gazing from behind a clear three-inch slit in a protective hood that completely enveloped the man's head.

Brosnan glanced down at the blade clenched in Ryan's hand.

"Cawdor," he said in greeting, his voice muffled by the hood.

"Brosnan," Ryan replied levelly.

"I'm not armed," the hooded man said, raising up his open palms to show empty hands.

"I am," Ryan responded.

"I've no feud with you. There's still time for both of us to get out if we work together."

Brosnan was stripped down to a white T-shirt covered in grease. There were scorch marks on his clothing. Ryan could see evidence of a nasty burn beginning to fester on the man's left forearm. The blister was already quite large and red.

"What happened to you?"

"Fire in the control room. Everything up there went to hell when the reactor went out."

"Where's the rest of the crew?"

"We were on a skeleton watch. There were only three of us actually piloting the *Raleigh*. I was the only one who got out. There are more of the enlisted men scattered throughout the sub. Many of them are probably trapped in the lower half, where you were."

"If they weren't already chilled, they soon will be. I sealed the compartments as I came through," Ryan replied.

"So what do you say?" Brosnan asked. "You want to live?"

"I'm listening," Ryan said. "What's your idea?"

Brosnan took a deep breath. "The escape trunk. It's equipped with a two-man airlock and twin hatches, one high and one low. Either one is capable of withstanding as much pressure as the hull of the submarine. It would normally be used to load cargo and supplies, but in predark days, it was also a secret access for special-ops teams like Navy SEAL commando squads. Deep-dive teams could enter and exit without anyone becoming the wiser."

"I get you. In our case, we can go the emergency route."

"Right. What do you say?"

"I say lead the way," Ryan said, gesturing with the knife.

Brosnan squeezed past Ryan in the cramped passageway and made his way to a small access ladder. As the man climbed up, Ryan's curiosity got the better of him. He could see where the protective garb was strapped down tight to the front and back of the man's upper torso with a thick nylon belt.

"What's the deal with the hood? You expecting another fire?"

"It's a Steinke hood, a combination life jacket and breathing apparatus," Brosnan replied as he twisted open the first access hatch into the escape trunk. The wheel turned slowly, with a series of rusty squeaks. Brosnan raised his voice to be heard. "I can charge the air reservoir from an air port in the side of the escape trunk."

As the smaller man disappeared into the trunk, Ryan slid the blade into his belt. He would need both hands free to assist. The one-eyed man followed Brosnan up the ladder.

When Ryan pulled himself into the small room, he felt himself lose the slight stoop he'd been walking with since coming aboard the submarine. The escape trunk wasn't wide, but it was tall.

"There will be an air bubble created under the flanges in the corners where we can stand while the trunk floods," Brosnan said as he closed the hatch in the deck. "There should be extra hoods in the wall compartment over there if you want one, but with the rig you're wearing, I don't guess you'll need it."

Ryan eyed the hooded gear that Brosnan was hooking up to a valve in the wall.

"That thing can't hold much air."

"It's not supposed to. I'm not worried about running out of oxygen. My fear is getting one crippling case of the bends. These hoods are only good for four hundred feet. That's the maximum depth they can be used safely."

Ryan shot Brosnan a questioning look as he knelt to double-check the hatch the hooded man had closed.

"These babies are buoyant, see," Brosnan explained. "They'll jerk you up to the surface like you were tied to a string. Like a rocket to the sky."

"You said four hundred feet was the max. How far down are we?" Ryan asked.

"Last time I checked, before the systems started going out in the control room, roughly three hundred feet. I'd say with all of the fireworks, we've gone way past that now. I'm gambling that I don't go shooting out of here like a bullet from a gun only to have my head explode halfway there."

"Sounds triple dangerous to me."

"I'll take my chances. I don't want to die drowning in this metal coffin sitting on a Tomahawk missile."

"Makes two of us," Ryan agreed.

"We won't be able to talk once I've filled the hood," Brosnan said as he took out a package from a storage locker opposite Ryan. He handed the surprisingly heavy parcel to Ryan. "This will be your responsibility once I open the outer hatch."

Ryan glared at the package. "What's this?"

"Life raft. Once the pressure's stabilized, pull that cord and inflate it. Then we'll shove the raft through. It'll go straight up to the surface. Give us a place to rest once we're up there."

Both men were now wedged opposite from each other in the crowded confines of the trunk. Brosnan gave Ryan a thumbs-up signal, and flooded the compartment. Seawater poured in, fast and white, surrounding their bodies at a rapid rate.

Ryan put the mouthpiece of the scuba gear into his mouth and pulled down the face mask. Across from him, Brosnan's face was impassive from behind the hood as the water washed them with a wet chill. The commander nodded and unsealed the upper hatch. Ryan inflated the raft, and together they pushed it through, an underwater balloon floating upward.

Brosnan left first. Ryan noted his rapid exit, and remembered the man's hopes of being on the surface long before Ryan could make the journey by swimming with the air tank.

Best time's the right time, went through his mind. Dean said that sometimes.

His son. Ryan wondered if the boy would think this kind of operation was the "hot pipe" of excitement he was always searching for when they traveled.

Ryan exited the submarine into the watery unknown.

Chapter Twenty-Six

Now that Ryan was out of the submarine, the trick would be keeping himself from surfacing too quickly. He had no desire to give himself a crippling case of the bends. No, unlike Brosnan, he would have to go slow, and not outrun the stream of air bubbles coming from the mouthpiece he held in his teeth. There was no rushing this sort of thing, and he was resigned to the long swim to the surface.

Even though the temperature of the ocean surrounding him wasn't freezing, it was still cold enough to make him wish he had taken an extra moment to dress himself in the sleek black wet suit he'd found on top of the scuba gear in Poseidon's footlocker.

Outside the submarine, there was no light. He waited, paddling in place while keeping the darker hull of the sub in his line of vision. His eye had to adjust, but there was murk on top of murk. The depths of the ocean were as black as the womb. Ryan thumbed on the flashlight, but even the steady stream of light punching a path through the gloom couldn't truly provide what was needed, and that was a sense of direction.

No time to think about that. Ryan kicked his feet and began to push himself upward, struggling against the water pressure weighing down upon his head. There was a roaring in his ears as he left the sub's black shape behind.

Ryan's throat felt tight. He felt a rush of claustrophobia, which was strange for two reasons. First of all, he normally didn't suffer from the affliction. Secondly he'd been held within the confines of the sinking *Raleigh* with no problem.

Still, this sensation wasn't totally alien to him. It felt almost familiar somehow.

Then he remembered.

The dream. The vision. The nightmare he'd suffered days earlier during the jump into the Florida redoubt. Ryan grimly sucked dry air from the oxygen tank strapped to his back, and the taste grew more and more metallic, as if the tank were almost empty.

He extinguished the thought. Paranoia would induce panic. He'd checked the tank himself. The charge was true. Breath easy. Push up.

Ryan's chest echoed heavily with the dull thud of a waterlogged pump, each heartbeat a resounding contraction of muscle in his body. He watched the bubbles from his mouthpiece float upward, capturing them in the light of the flashlight. He used the beam to follow their path with his good right eye, tracking them until they faded into the gloom, and tried to focus on what might lie beyond them up there.

He knew what he would find. There was no sky overhead. No clouds, no stars...nothing but water. He squinted, and took in the sight of the infinite green of the ocean. No lake or man-made pool had ever offered up such a color of green, a green duskier than the blackest of any moonless night, and just as dark and infinite.

The green was everywhere, surrounding his entire body and being.

In the dream, Ryan had been warm. That part of the mat-trans-induced mental journey was a falsehood. He'd known the ocean depths would be as cold as ice, and now he found he was incredibly cold, for there was no sun. No sky.

Only water. Only death.

Ryan willed his legs to kick, his arms to push down to check his descent, push past the strange eellike creatures that were swimming past, their mouths yawning open as they sifted through the brine for microscopic bits of plankton.

Push past the sinking hull of the submarine.

A red haze was starting to lay itself over his field of vision from lack of oxygen. True or imagined? He couldn't be sure. Ryan was tired, so tired now. A coppery, bitter taste filled his mouth, mixing with the traces of salt water.

A man always has a choice, came the grizzled voice of the Trader, whispering in Ryan's ear. *He can either live...or he can die.*

As his lungs began to ache and his heartbeat grew even louder in his ears, Krysty's face shone like a beacon in Ryan's mind's eye. He thought of his son, Dean, and how he wanted to see the boy become a man. He thought of J.B., who was like a brother to him. He thought of Doc and his endless supply of quotes and stories; of Mildred's love of people and knowledge of how to heal; and of Jak's unwavering trust and willingness to follow him into anything.

He thought of them all.

Ryan decided to ante up the jack and buy the package. He knew from previous experiences he was psi-sensitive. If he'd been exposed to some kind of bizarre doomie prophecy back in the gateway, then he was going to see it through.

As he had during his nightmare, he willingly clung to the image of Krysty—her lips, her body, her hair undulating in reaction to her many moods. But this time, he also clung to the images of his entire family. His friends. Or, as Poseidon had contemptuously referred to Ryan's group back at Kings Point, "his people."

Ryan struggled to make his body work, willing his muscles to pull taut and assist his ascent. In a burst of movement, he was rewarded with his legs kicking out and his arms pushing down. How many feet down? Four hundred? He unbuckled the web belt and released one of the weights strapped around his waist. Four hundred feet? Not far to go.

Up and out. Focus. Focus.

Something brushed against his ankle, then grabbed down hard.

Ryan was so startled, he almost spit out his mouthpiece. As he turned back, valiantly striving to keep his sense of direction intact, he saw a humanoid shape near his feet. Fireblast! Had that son of a bitch Poseidon gotten up with half of his head stove in and managed to follow him out here, as well? Or was it Brosnan, his hood having not functioned as planned?

He swung down his torch and the sickly yellow flashlight beam revealed the face of a Dweller. Ryan felt a cautious rush of relief mixed with fear. Why was the mutie fish-man down here? And did the mutant know Ryan wasn't one of Poseidon's men?

Shit on a dinner plate, how could he even begin to explain it?

Then Ryan realized he knew this mutie.

This was the one Shauna had called Mike, the one who had saved them after Poseidon's mine had ripped into their boat during the storm.

Mike gestured, and Ryan followed with the flashlight, revealing a half dozen other Dwellers swimming at an angle above them. They were busy with Brosnan's body, tearing the former follower of Poseidon limb from limb, their incredible strength hitting home to Ryan for the first time.

One of Brosnan's arms drifted lazily by, trailing blood, dark black streamers extending off into the twilight depths. Ryan saw a flash of white bone, and he aimed the flashlight down farther. He hadn't particularly liked Brosnan, but the man had given Ryan a fair shake in revealing the escape trunk. Ryan had no desire to stare at pieces of his burst and dismembered corpse.

They'd both gotten a fighting chance, but Brosnan was unfortunately the first man out of the trunk, and he possessed no such hidden advantage as Ryan did in having previously met one of the aquatic mutations who wanted to kill him. Who knew how long they had been dwelling here for this opportunity, day and night, watching for an attack to approach from below to wipe out their homes and the homes of their friends on land?

Waiting to defend it the only way they knew how.

Ryan almost laughed, suddenly understanding now how the reactor had blown up without the radiation rippling out and chilling them all. The Dwellers had seen the massive sub coming toward that part of the coast, and they'd used one of Poseidon's own magnetic mines against him.

Mike was no longer holding Ryan's ankle in his misshapen flipper of a hand. Ryan wondered if this was how he would perish, alone in the darkness, flailing out at the muties who now called this part of the ocean their home. The muties who had abandoned their eager ripping at Brosnan were now slowly surrounding him, one by one.

Ryan took a deep breath. The air coming into the mouthpiece really did taste foul.

The muties had now circled him, and he moved the flash from one to another, their eyes glowing yellow in the feeble light.

He realized he wasn't afraid of them; he hadn't caused them harm.

Twenty-four hours ago, the world had been an entirely different place. Ryan hadn't particularly cared if he lived or died, but that was before he'd learned that Krysty was alive, deliciously alive and whole.

He wanted to feel her touch again.

IF ONE HAD BEEN PRESENT on the water above, he would have heard Ryan before seeing him.

Air bubbles from his tank erupted on the surface of the calm sea in a series of burbles and pops before Ryan's head broke free from the ocean. The first thing he saw was the brightly colored naval emergency raft floating in the moonlight. He had almost forgotten sending it up.

The Dwellers, their attention on both the sinking *Raleigh* and the escaped Brosnan, had allowed the raft Ryan had shoved out of the hatch to arrive safe and unharmed on the water's surface.

Ryan nearly hadn't made it back. The precious oxygen in the tank had gotten more and more metallic as he struggled upward, his arms and legs becoming increasingly leaden as he struggled to keep moving, keep swimming. Mike had pushed and prodded Ryan onward, even pulling him the last stretch of the journey.

Ryan had been completely lost. He had no idea at any given time how close he actually was to the surface, as the night sky above offered no comforting sunlight to those below.

The mutie had led Ryan up through the darkness of the ocean safely, and now the weary warrior stretched out as well as he could manage on the rubbery canvas floor of the raft. He mused he was almost getting used to the sensations of trying to be comfortable in a life raft when the queer face of the mutie that had saved his life appeared, staring at him.

"What, you want a thank-you or something?" Ryan gasped.

The Dweller nodded.

"Manners are manners," Ryan replied with a weak laugh. "Thanks."

Mike waved once, and like a dropped stone disappeared from sight.

Ryan gratefully swallowed down the fresh sea air while unfastening the weight belt, then the air tank. For a moment, he almost started to save the gear, until realizing he'd never have use for it again. He dropped both into the water next to him, where they promptly began the long journey back down to the ocean's floor.

"Good fucking riddance," Ryan muttered.

"SOMETHING OFF the starboard bow, John," Mildred said. "I saw movement. Looks like something's floating out there."

"'Starboard'?" J.B. repeated. "Since when did you become so conversant with the lingo?"

"When in Rome, I guess," Mildred replied. "I watched a lot of TV as a kid."

Krysty turned on a large spotlight that was mounted at the front of the cruiser's cabin and illuminated a round circle of the water in the direction Mildred had pointed, but she knew what she would find even before the raft was revealed.

"It's Ryan," the redhead breathed, then added with more authority, "Ryan's out there."

"Dad!" Dean cried joyfully, pointing at the bobbing life raft in the distance.

Ryan saw the approaching boat and waved the flashlight back.

"Could be anybody. Could be Admiral Poseidon. Could be another one of those scaly Dwellers. Who could tell from here?" J.B. muttered quietly but without conviction. If Krysty said it was Ryan, then the Armorer would take her word for it. He felt a stir of excitement as he steered the sleek craft toward the spot Dean had pointed out.

Krysty and Jak reached down and grabbed the neck of Ryan's tattered shirt to help steady him at the side of the boat as they pulled up and over.

"Welcome back, lover," Krysty said, her flushed cheeks and anxious green eyes belying her light tone. "Decide to go for a swim without me?"

"Uh-huh. Come on in," Ryan rasped back. "The water's fine."

She smiled down at him, tears starting to run down her cheeks. Ryan took her hand, smiling back in return. Then, exhausted beyond all limits of human endurance, he closed his eye in confidence, knowing she would watch over him and would still be there when he woke up.

Epilogue

Down in the watery depths, down farther than human eyes could see and human lungs could breathe, down farther still, deep on the hidden floor of the black ocean rests the wreckage of man.

Sunlight can penetrate a full half mile into the sea, feeble light that didn't even come close to where the crushed hull of the USS *Raleigh* rested. Paper-thin creatures drifted past, blind in the dark. No bubbles of air escaped the many fissures where the welds of the plating of the once mighty submarine had given way.

The *Raleigh* and her crew were dead.

A man trapped down there would implode, fold inward on himself from the pressure. No human could survive such a crushing defeat. Poseidon had been wrong. He was no lord of the sea. He was a man, and man, despite his inventions and scientific magic that allowed him to travel beneath the sea, belonged on the land, not down there in the deep.

But what about a man who took the name of a god and caressed the three-pronged trident of power and dared to emulate the most fearsome of Olympians and shake storms of radioactive dust from his own great beard, claiming the title of Admiral and the command of his followers that went with the title. What about him?

Listen close—there were no sounds here, yet still, there was a tapping.

Down there, where there was no air, one man drank deep of the ocean and still lived.

Down there, in the silence, one man raged on....

Not dead.

Not yet.

**Stony Man leads America's best
in the war on drugs**

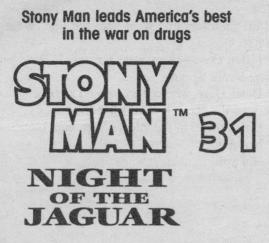

STONY MAN™ 31

NIGHT
OF THE
JAGUAR

A massive offensive on the drug front promises to turn
the tide in a losing battle. While the forces of the FBI, DEA
and CIA are harnessed in this united thrust, Stony Man's
deep-cover status earns front-line placement on the
hellgrounds of Bolivia. Mack Bolan leads a team into the
heart of cartel country—to face an enemy that may be
impossible to destroy.

Available in November 1997 at your favorite retail outlet.

Don't miss out on the action in these titles featuring THE EXECUTIONER®, STONY MAN™ and SUPERBOLAN®!

The Red Dragon Trilogy

#64210	FIRE LASH	$3.75 U.S.	☐
		$4.25 CAN.	☐
#64211	STEEL CLAWS	$3.75 U.S.	☐
		$4.25 CAN.	☐
#64212	RIDE THE BEAST	$3.75 U.S.	☐
		$4.25 CAN.	☐

Stony Man™

#61910	FLASHBACK	$5.50 U.S.	☐
		$6.50 CAN.	☐
#61911	ASIAN STORM	$5.50 U.S.	☐
		$6.50 CAN.	☐
#61912	BLOOD STAR	$5.50 U.S.	☐
		$6.50 CAN.	☐

SuperBolan®

#61452	DAY OF THE VULTURE	$5.50 U.S.	☐
		$6.50 CAN.	☐
#61453	FLAMES OF WRATH	$5.50 U.S.	☐
		$6.50 CAN.	☐
#61454	HIGH AGGRESSION	$5.50 U.S.	☐
		$6.50 CAN.	☐

(limited quantities available on certain titles)

TOTAL AMOUNT	$
POSTAGE & HANDLING	$
($1.00 for one book, 50¢ for each additional)	
APPLICABLE TAXES*	$ _____
TOTAL PAYABLE	$ _____
(check or money order—please do not send cash.)	

To order, complete this form and send it, along with a check or money order for the total above, payable to Gold Eagle Books, to: **In the U.S.:** 3010 Walden Avenue, P.O. Box 9077, Buffalo, NY 14269-9077; **In Canada:** P.O. Box 636, Fort Erie, Ontario, L2A 5X3.

Name:_____

Address:_____ City:_____

State/Prov.:_____ Zip/Postal Code:_____

*New York residents remit applicable sales taxes.
 Canadian residents remit applicable GST and provincial taxes.

GEBACK18

A deadly kind of immortality...

THE

Destroyer™

#110 Never Say Die

Created by
WARREN MURPHY
and RICHARD SAPIR

Forensic evidence in a number of assassinations reveals a curious link between the killers: Identical fingerprints and genetic code. The bizarre problem is turned over to Remo and Chiun, who follow the trail back to a literal dead end— the grave of an executed killer.

Look for it in January wherever Gold Eagle books are sold.

Don't miss out on the action in these titles!